I0782239

CYNTHIA HICKEY

The Threat

Cynthia Hickey

The Sheriff of Misty Hollow, Book 2

ISBN-13: 978-1-965352-37-3

Chapter One

Shea Callahan lifted the small box of personal items and carried them onto the porch of the small ranch house she'd recently purchased. A note tacked to her front door stopped her in her tracks.

Squelching the urge to read it, she pulled it free and dropped it into her box. Already running late with new deputies to meet since all the prior ones had left with the retirement of the former sheriff, she wanted to be at the office bright and early. Whatever someone needed so urgently as to leave a note could wait a few more minutes. "Come, Heidi." Her German shepherd bounded after her.

She climbed into the driver's seat of the Ford pickup she'd traded for her sedan and backed from the dirt drive to start her new life as the sheriff of Misty Hollow. It wouldn't be easy. She'd already heard rumblings in town about whether or not a woman could handle the job despite her taking down a ring of evil men a few months ago and helping bring the mayor down for his crimes a few weeks ago.

The morning mist clung to the rolling hills as she drove through town, past the old courthouse with its weathered stone facade and the diner where she'd noticed locals gathering for their morning coffee and gossip. The whispered conversations had stopped when she'd entered yesterday, all eyes tracking her movement to the counter. She'd ordered her coffee black and left without acknowledging their stares, but she'd felt their judgment burning into her back.

"Welcome, Sheriff." Doris Belwright, the station's receptionist, greeted her. "The new hires will be here by nine as you requested. Except for Deputy Sheriff Trevor Bolton who covered for us during the night. He's in the bullpen."

"Thank you." Shea passed through the bullpen. The desks were empty except for scattered reports and half-empty coffee cups that spoke of the overnight shift's activity. She set the box of her things on her desk and surveyed the small space. The office felt bigger than it had during her interview, the weight of responsibility settling on her shoulders like a heavy cloak.

"Coffee?"

She whipped around, reaching for the gun on her hip.

A handsome man with hair the color of dark chocolate and eyes like the Arkansas summer sun held a mug toward her. "Welcome, Sheriff." He smiled, revealing dimples in both cheeks. His gaze dropped to her hip. "Don't shoot me. I give up."

"Sorry." She took the cup and set it on her desk before thrusting her hand toward him. "Sheriff Callahan."

"Trevor Bolton." He gave her hand a firm shake. "I didn't know if you took cream or not."

"Black is fine." Her gaze flicked to the box on her desk, then back to him. Something about his easy manner put her on edge. In her experience, men who were this friendly usually wanted something.

"Well then, I'll let you get settled in." He gave a nod and backed out of her office.

Shea placed the mail on the desk in a pile to one side to go through after the morning meeting. She placed a photo of Heidi on the corner of her desk, her favorite coffee mug, and a pencil holder in the shape of a sheriff's badge that her best friend, Becky, had given her as a congratulations gift. That was it. All the personal effects of her office. The space still felt stark, impersonal, but it would have to do.

She plopped down in the leather chair behind the battered wooden desk, noting the scratches and water rings that spoke of years of use. "This is where we'll spend a lot of our time, girl."

With a soft woof, Heidi moved from under her desk and jumped onto one of the two chairs across from Shea reserved for visitors. She'd have to get the dog a bed for the office.

The note from her door caught her eye again. Unable to resist any longer, she unfolded it. The handwriting was shaky, uncertain: "Sheriff, my husband's been missing three days. Police in the next county won't help. Please call me. Martha Henderson." A phone number was scrawled beneath.

Shea's stomach knotted. A missing person case on her first day. She folded the note and slipped it into her pocket, making a mental note to call Martha after the meeting.

By the time she'd checked emails, replied to the ones she could, and organized the work she'd dole out at the meeting, nine a.m. arrived. She motioned for Heidi to stay, then headed for the conference room. Thanks to a tour from the former sheriff, Westbrook, she knew where everything was, though the layout still felt foreign.

"Good morning." Shea took up a position at the front of the room and eyed the five men staring at her. Their expressions ranged from curious to skeptical, with one—a man in his fifties with graying temples— looking openly hostile. "I've already met Deputy Bolton. I'm Sheriff Callahan. Please introduce yourselves." Since she'd gone through their files, she already knew their descriptions, ages, and their backgrounds, but having them tell her their names might break the ice before she gave them their orders.

"William Butler. Folks call me Bill," the older

man said, his tone clipped. He'd been passed over for the sheriff position twice in his career, according to his file. That probably explained the hostility.

"Richard Bombeck," said a man in his early forties with kind eyes and prematurely silver hair. He seemed more open than Butler, though still reserved.

"Lance Billings," offered a lanky deputy who couldn't have been older than thirty. His uniform was perfectly pressed, and he sat ramrod straight like he was still in the military.

"Mark Cutter," said the last man, also in his thirties, with calloused hands that suggested he'd worked construction or farming before joining law enforcement.

"Thank you. I've posted the schedule for everyone in the break room. We'll all take our turn at manning the office during night hours." She hoped her smile hid her nervousness. The silence stretched uncomfortably. "We've had a slow morning as far as complaints go. I've got Cutter and Butler on tonight's shift, so the two others are free until then. Is everyone okay with three nights on and four days?"

Heads nodded, devoid of smiles. She could practically feel their doubt radiating across the room like heat from a furnace.

Her own smile faded under their stern expressions. It would take a while for her to earn their trust. "I want open communication between us, Deputies. If you feel uncomfortable for any reason, I want you to come to me. If you have a gut feeling about one of the cases assigned to you, I want to know. We're all partners here."

Her gaze landed on Bolton, the only friendly face looking at her. As deputy sheriff, he was one rung under her, hired by the former sheriff. Hopefully, she could trust him to have her back. "Any questions?"

"Yeah." Butler crossed his arms, his weathered face set in hard lines. "You ready for this job after what happened up on the mountain?"

She frowned. "What do you mean?"

He shrugged, but his eyes never left hers. "Takes a lot out of a person being hunted and killing men in hand-to-hand combat." The words hung in the air like a challenge.

Out of a woman, he meant. Heat crawled up her neck, but she kept her voice level. "I wouldn't be here if I couldn't handle the job."

"She proved herself capable when she helped Westbrook bring down the former mayor." Bolton shot her a look, then locked gazes with Butler. The tension in the room ratcheted up another notch.

Butler's jaw worked like he was chewing on words he wanted to spit out. Finally, he stood. "If that's all, Sheriff, I've got paperwork to catch up on."

"That's all for now," Shea said, watching as the men filed out. Bombeck offered her a small nod of acknowledgment. Billings and Cutter remained expressionless. Only Bolton lingered.

"Don't let Butler get to you," he said quietly. "He's been doing this job longer than anyone, but that doesn't give him the right to be disrespectful."

"I can handle Deputy Butler," she replied, though she appreciated the support. "But thank you."

~

"Hold up, Bill." Trevor stopped the man before he left the building.

"Yeah?" He glanced back, irritation written across his features.

"You got problems with a woman sheriff?" Might as well get straight to the point.

"What makes you think I do?"

"Your attitude in the meeting."

"Dude." He smacked gum, the sound sharp in the quiet hallway. "I'd have reservations about anyone new. She might be one tough cookie, but she's never been a sheriff before. This ain't some big city where you've got backup every few blocks. Out here, when things go south, you're on your own."

"The town voted her in on Westbrook's word. That's good enough for me." Trevor crossed his arms. "It should be good enough for you."

"I didn't know Westbrook either." Bill shoved open the door and marched from the building, letting it slam shut behind him.

Trevor glanced at Doris, who'd been pretending not to listen while shuffling papers at her desk. "This kind of behavior is normal around here?"

"No, but the previous deputies all knew the man they worked for. Had for years." She reached for the ringing phone, then paused. "Everyone here is new now except for me. Change is hard for some folks." Before Trevor could return to his desk, she stopped him. "Accident on 105. You want it?"

"Sure." He stopped at the sheriff's office, where she was on the phone. He waited until she hung up.

"Problem?" she asked.

"I'm heading to an accident. Want to join me? Let the folks around here see a bit more of you?"

She nodded, grabbing her hat from the desk. "Come, Heidi."

The dog he hadn't noticed earlier jumped from a chair and padded after her, tail wagging. "She friendly?"

"Unless I order otherwise."

"Guess I'll be on my best behavior then." He grinned. "I'll drive."

From her stony expression, he guessed she preferred to drive, but she didn't argue with him. She opened the back door to the squad car and let her dog in, before climbing into the front passenger seat.

"That phone call—anything urgent?" he asked as they pulled out of the parking lot.

"Missing person case. Martha Henderson's husband hasn't been home in three days." She stared out the window at the passing scenery. "I told her I'd look into it personally."

"Good. Shows you care about the community."

They made the rest of the drive in silence. The accident wasn't what Trevor had expected. Instead of two automobiles, a tractor and a hay bailer awaited them on the narrow county road. Two men in denim coveralls stood toe-to-toe, arguing and waving their arms, their faces red with anger.

Callahan's widened eyes seemed to flick from blue to green as she surveyed the situation, and Trevor noticed her hand drift unconsciously toward her weapon before she caught herself.

"Didn't expect this." She shoved open her door and marched toward the two men, Trevor on her heels. "Gentlemen."

They turned as one, their argument momentarily forgotten. "Frank here ran right out of that field in front of me. Everyone but a fool knows I can't stop this tractor on a dime!" The older farmer's hands curled into fists. "He punctured one of my tires with that contraption of his."

"You were going too fast, Oscar. You should've seen me coming across that field. I had the right of way!"

Seemed to Trevor that they both should've seen each other, since the sides of the road had nothing but freshly plowed fields stretching to the horizon.

Callahan circled the scene, her shrewd gaze taking it all in before she stopped next to the hay baler. The machine had a bent attachment arm, and hydraulic fluid pooled beneath it. "Can you back this up?"

"Yes, ma'am, but Oscar should have to be the one to move. This is his fault."

"Sir, the tractor is sitting on three tires. Until the flat one is repaired or we can tow it, the tractor isn't going anywhere." She pulled out her citation book. "Deputy Bolton, will you direct traffic around this mess?"

"Yes, Sheriff." He took up position on the other side of the road and motioned cars through. A line of rubberneckers formed with every driver wanting to see what the commotion was about. Several rolled down their windows to get a better look at the new sheriff in action.

An hour later, after a tow truck had arrived and departed with the disabled tractor, the hay baler had returned to the field and traffic was flowing normally again. Sheriff Callahan told the men to take up who was responsible with a judge since there were no witnesses, but both were at fault in her opinion. She'd handed them both tickets for failure to yield and returned to the squad car.

"You handled that well." Trevor grinned as he slid into the car.

"You didn't think I would?" She arched a brow, her eyes flashing with that green fire he'd noticed earlier.

"Didn't say that." Wow, she had a chip on her shoulder the size of Texas. He turned the car around and headed toward town. "I thought you were fair under the circumstances. I'd have handled it the same way."

"Glad I have your approval." She leaned forward, peering out the window at something in the tall grass along the roadside. "Stop the car."

He pulled over to the shoulder. The sheriff slid down into the shallow ditch and returned with a tiny calico kitten cradled against her chest. The little thing couldn't have been more than six weeks old, its fur matted and eyes crusted with infection.

"Poor thing would have gotten run over." She glanced around the empty landscape, then settled the kitten more securely in her arms. "Hope you don't mind a friend, Heidi." She held the kitten so the dog could sniff her. Heidi gave a soft woof and then lay down on the backseat, seeming to understand she had a new charge to protect. Callahan smiled, and for the first time since he'd met her, her face softened completely. "The sheriff's department now has a mascot."

Grinning, Trevor shook his head. The new sheriff had a soft heart after all, hidden beneath all that armor she wore.

Back at the office, leaving the sheriff to get the kitten settled in a makeshift bed she'd fashioned from a cardboard box and an old towel, he returned to his desk and pulled up every article he could find on what had happened with Sheriff Shea Callahan on the other side of Misty Mountain.

When he finished reading, he sat back in his chair

and let out a low whistle. The beautiful raven-haired sheriff seemed as tough as nails except for the dog and kitten, but the news articles painted a picture of someone who'd been through hell and somehow emerged stronger. She'd been kidnapped, hunted through the wilderness, and forced to kill three men in self-defense. The way she'd reached for her gun when he'd startled her with the coffee told him she might be suffering from PTSD. Who wouldn't after what she'd gone through?

The question was…would that hinder her ability to do her job, or would it make her more determined to protect the people of Misty Hollow?

Only time would tell.

Chapter Two

Shea stared at the thick envelope on her desk. It hadn't been there when she'd left on the call with Deputy Bolton. Scrawled across the front in barely legible writing was the word, sheriff.

Her hand trembled as she reached for the letter opener in the shape of a dagger—a gift from her father when she'd graduated from the police academy. She opened the envelope and upended it. Photos fell onto her desk blotter like autumn leaves, scattered and ominous. Photos of her were taken without her knowledge. Moments when she thought she was alone: walking to her car after a long day of shopping for her new home, pacing her front porch while talking on the phone, staring over a scenic outlook on one of her hikes. The shots were taken at close range as if someone had hidden in the shadows to take them.

Her skin crawled at the violation. How long had someone been watching her? The photos spanned weeks, maybe months. One showed her in her pajamas, visible through her bedroom window. Another captured her at the grocery store, completely unaware of the lens trained on her. The realization that she'd been stalked this long without knowing caused bile to rise in her throat.

She peered into the envelope to see a small, folded piece of paper. Written on it was a message in the same shaky handwriting: "The town folks might think you a hero, but I know the truth. You'll pay for what you did on that mountain." She blew out a breath, trying to steady her racing heart. It was probably just someone who wanted to intimidate her. Or was it more than that? Her instincts, honed by months of therapy and hypervigilance, heightened. Someone wanted revenge for what she'd done.

The kitten she'd rescued earlier mewed from its makeshift bed in the corner, and Heidi lifted her head from her spot by the door. Even her dog sensed her distress.

Leaning back in her chair, she stared at the ceiling tiles, counting the water stains to calm herself. The leader of the human hunting ring, Darryl Hodges, sat behind bars. Or did he? She'd killed the man's brother, Bruce, during a fight that still haunted her nightmares. The feel of the knife in her hand, the look in Bruce's eyes as he realized he was dying—it all came flooding back. She returned her chair to four legs, then typed the men's names into the search engine of her computer with fingers that still shook slightly.

The search results painted a grim picture. Darryl

Hodges had almost died in prison fighting someone over extra food, but managed to survive. Multiple stab wounds had left him scarred but very much alive. Bruce was only mentioned once in his obituary—a brief, sanitized account that made no mention of his crimes. The third name, the only surviving sibling still free, Cletus, loomed in front of her on the screen. Was it this man who sent her the photos? If he were as warped as his brothers, he'd definitely come after her for the deaths of his siblings, despite her not being the one to kill Darryl.

She found an address for Cletus Hodges—a rural route outside town, the kind of place where screams wouldn't carry to neighbors. Her therapist's voice echoed in her mind: "Don't face your triggers alone, Shea. You have support now. Use it."

After a few minutes of battling whether she should go alone or not, she headed for the bullpen. Deputy Bolton stared at his computer screen, his brow furrowed in concentration. "Deputy, if you have some time, I'd like you to go with me to check out an address."

"Absolutely." He stood and flashed her the dimpled grin that sent her stomach turning somersaults. She really needed to stop thinking of him as a handsome man. He was a coworker after all, and she had more pressing concerns than her inexplicable attraction to the deputy sheriff.

To his credit, he didn't ask her why or where they were going. He simply went along, grabbing his hat and checking his weapon with the practiced ease of an experienced officer. Other than her group of college friends, she hadn't had someone trust her judgment so completely. The feeling was both comforting and terrifying.

Shea grabbed keys from behind the receptionist's desk. "I'll drive this time." She turned to Doris, who was filing reports with mechanical precision. "Who brought the envelope sitting on my desk? The big one."

"Some kid." The receptionist shrugged, not looking up from her work. "Scruffy little thing, maybe twelve or thirteen. Said someone paid him ten bucks to deliver the letter to the sheriff. Kid was gone before I could ask any questions."

"Did you see which direction he went?"

"Toward Main Street, but that was over an hour ago." Doris looked up then, noting Shea's pale complexion. "Everything alright, Sheriff?"

"Just following up on something. Thanks."

The questions started coming after a few miles of driving through a thick forest that seemed to close in around them like gnarled fingers. Ancient oaks and towering pines blocked most of the afternoon sun, casting long shadows across the narrow road.

"Looks like we're headed to the middle of nowhere," Trevor observed, his hand resting casually near his weapon.

She nodded, appreciating his alertness. "That's why I thought it best not to go alone."

"Go alone where?"

She shot him a quick glance, noting the way his jaw had tightened. "You're a smart man, so I'm guessing you've researched me and my time before stepping into Westbrook's role."

"Yes, ma'am."

"Shea." The use of her first name felt like extending an olive branch.

He smiled, and some of the tension left his shoulders. "Trevor." He sobered quickly. "I know you and your friends were targeted by a group of men who enjoyed hunting people. One of your friends died, and another was severely injured. You suffered injuries yourself and had to kill one of them."

"That about sums it up." She exhaled heavily, remembering Sarah's final moments, the way Jake had screamed when the arrow pierced his shoulder. "I…received some photos when we returned to the office. Pictures of me going about my daily life, and a note saying I'll pay for what happened on the mountain. We're headed to question the surviving Hodges brother."

His lips thinned, and she saw his knuckles whiten as he gripped the door handle. "You really think there's something to this threat?"

"I take every threat seriously." Especially after what she'd been through. She turned down a dirt road that was more ruts than pavement, the truck bouncing over potholes and loose stones.

A modest cabin came into view through the trees—weathered wood siding, a sagging front porch, and windows that needed washing. Chickens pecked in the yard, and an old hound dog lifted its head lazily from the front steps. A little boy around four years old spotted them and darted into the house, his bare feet slapping against the wooden porch.

Before Shea and Trevor exited the vehicle, a rail-thin woman stepped onto the porch, drying her hands on a faded dish towel. Her face was drawn, aged beyond her years, with the hollow look of someone who'd seen too much hardship.

"I'm Sheriff Callahan, and this is Deputy Bolton. We'd like to ask Cletus a few questions." Shea kept her voice calm, non-threatening.

"He ain't here. Ain't been home for three days." The woman's eyes darted between them nervously, and Shea noticed fresh bruises on her forearms.

"Do you know where he is?"

"Nope. Said he was going hunting." The words came out too quickly, rehearsed.

Hunting for Shea. The realization sent ice through her veins. "Are you aware of the type of hunting his brothers did?"

The woman paled and nodded, her grip tightening on the dish towel. "Not until Darryl's arrest. Are you saying my husband was part of all that?"

"That's what we're trying to determine, ma'am. Mind if we come in and look around?"

Mrs. Hodges stepped back and motioned them inside, though her movements were jerky and reluctant. "I'll be in the kitchen if you need me."

The interior was sparse but clean, with the kind of furniture bought secondhand and used until it fell apart. A toddler peered up at them from the confines of a playpen, thumb in mouth, watching with wide, solemn eyes that seemed too old for such a young face.

Shea and Trevor headed down a short hallway lined with family photos—wedding pictures, baby photos, and older shots that showed happier times. "I'll take the master bedroom," Shea said.

Trevor nodded and ducked into one of the other rooms, his footsteps muffled by the threadbare carpet.

How could anyone be married to a man who hunted people and not know? Shea wondered as she searched through the dresser drawers and the small closet. Darryl's wife was either a very good actress or really didn't know where her husband went when he said he had business. Bruce had been unmarried, living in a trailer that had yielded evidence of his crimes. Shea didn't buy the fact that the wives didn't know. They had to have had some inkling that things weren't right.

In a box on the top shelf of the closet, hidden behind old blankets, she found a tattered journal. The same handwriting as what she'd found on the envelope filled the pages in erratic, angry scrawls. One message said, "I'll be going after justice." Another, "She'll pay for what she did to my brothers." After seeing the photos, Shea could only surmise these scribblings were about her. Signs of a sick mind set on revenge, planning, and plotting in the darkness.

The entries grew more specific as she read: details about her daily routine, her new house, and even mentions of Heidi. He'd been watching her for months, learning her patterns, waiting for the right moment to strike.

~

Cletus watched from the protection of the woods around his house, crouched behind a thick stand of elderberry bushes that provided perfect cover. It didn't surprise him that the sheriff had discovered the third Hodges brother. All she had to do was ask around Misty Hollow, maybe run a simple computer search.

Now that she'd seen the photos and knew someone still hunted her, what would she do with his journal? He had no doubt she'd find the book. He'd left it there on purpose, wanting her to know just how much he knew about her life. The new sheriff was no dummy, but she was predictable.

His wife stepped onto the porch and hung a dish towel over the railing—their prearranged sign for him not to come to the house. No problem. His stomach rumbled with hunger, but he could wait until the sheriff and the deputy left. He'd learned patience from his brothers, learned to stalk prey until the perfect moment presented itself.

He had plenty of time to play a new game with the

sheriff. A game he had no intention of losing. This wouldn't be like his brothers' crude methods—chasing people through the woods like animals. No, this would be psychological warfare, breaking her down piece by piece until she begged for mercy. Grinning, he leaned against a tree and kept his gaze trained on the house. His wife wouldn't give him away. She knew the consequences of disobedience, just as Darryl's wife had. The Hodges men knew how to keep their wives in their place.

He cleaned his nails with his pocketknife, the blade sharp enough to shave with, stopping when he heard voices. The sheriff and the deputy stepped onto the porch, and he could see the tension in the sheriff's shoulders, the way she kept looking around as if she sensed his presence. Good. Fear was the first step.

The sheriff glanced around once more, her hand resting on her weapon, then headed toward the car with quick, purposeful strides. Cletus waited a few minutes before venturing from his hiding place and entering the house through the back door to get something to eat.

Tomorrow would be another fun day. Maybe he'd leave her another present.

~

"The journal clearly sounds like this man is out to get you," Trevor said once they returned to the car, his voice tight with concern.

"Do you believe the wife?" Shea asked, starting the engine with hands that had finally stopped shaking.

"About not having seen him?" Trevor shook his head. "I saw three plates sitting on the counter, and one had fresh food on it. I doubt one of them was for the baby."

"Yep. Not to mention the fear that flickered through the wife's eyes when talking to us." Shea glanced behind them as they drove away from the house, checking the rearview mirror compulsively. "Hodges was most likely watching us."

"I had the same feeling. The hair on the back of my neck was standing up the whole time." Trevor's admission made her feel less paranoid. "Want me to gather the rest of the deputies?"

"Yes. They all need to be on the lookout for this man." Her knuckles whitened on the steering wheel as she navigated the rough road. "I want his photo distributed to every business in town, every neighbor in a five-mile radius."

"You staying late at the office?"

She frowned, considering. "No. We know who is threatening me. There's no point in sticking around. If he contacts me again, the message will be waiting for me." The thought of going home alone to her isolated house made her stomach churn, but she wouldn't let fear control her life.

Trevor didn't plan on sticking around either. He could research Cletus Hodges from the house he rented in town, maybe reach out to some contacts in neighboring counties who might have dealt with the family before. The more they knew about the man, the easier he would be to stop.

"You've got secrets."

Shea's statement hit him like a two-by-four. "Like what?" He thought he'd managed to hide certain aspects of his past, had worked hard to bury those painful memories.

"Abused child. Serial killer brother locked up for life." She cut him a sideways glance, her tone matter-of-fact but not unkind. "I had to do some digging, but found what you wanted to stay buried."

His jaw clenched, old wounds reopening at her words. "My past will not affect my job any more than you say yours will." It had taken him a long time to get over the fact that his older brother had wanted to kill him, had nearly succeeded. A long time to get over the abuse and neglect he'd suffered as a child, the foster homes, the therapists who'd tried to help him make sense of the senseless. He refused to let his past define him. "My parents are dead, and my brother is locked up. That life is no more."

"I thought I'd put what happened on that mountain in the past, too, yet here we are." She pulled in front of the sheriff's station, the building's windows glowing warmly in the gathering dusk. "Sometimes, the past never goes away."

His past did, and he would not allow it to return. Realizing he was rubbing the stab wounds his brother had given him—scars that still ached when it rained—

he shoved open his door with more force than necessary.

"See you tomorrow." Shea whistled for Heidi when Trevor opened the front door to the building, then let the dog into her truck before driving away into the darkness.

Trevor stormed to his desk to shut his computer down for the night, his movements sharp and agitated.

"What's caught in your craw?" Bill asked from across the bullpen, looking up from a stack of paperwork. "Things not so rosy with the sheriff?"

"Things are fine." He grabbed his keys from the desk drawer, metal jangling against metal. "Keep an eye out for a man named Cletus Hodges. He's threatening the sheriff over what happened up on that mountain. If you see him, bring him in for questioning."

"Want me to tell the others?"

"Yes." Trevor marched to his truck and squealed tires from the parking lot, leaving rubber on the asphalt and Bill staring after him in surprise.

He shouldn't let the fact that the sheriff knew about his past rattle him, but so many people had looked on him with pity after the abuse he suffered. That's why he'd left Houston, why he'd changed his name and created a new identity. To start all over where no one knew about the scared little boy who'd been beaten within an inch of his life or the teenager who his own brother had stalked.

He'd calmed a bit by the time he arrived home,

changed out of his uniform into jeans and an old t-shirt, and planted himself in front of the television with a cold can of beer in his hand. The small rental house felt too quiet, too empty, and he found himself checking the locks twice before settling down.

Of course, Shea would dig into the lives of her deputies. A sheriff needed to know what kind of people they were and whether they could be trusted when things went bad. She'd known and still hired him, which told him she didn't pity him. Shea expected him to do his job and to do it well, which he would.

Work helped him to forget the nightmares, the flashbacks, the constant fear that had once consumed his life. He took a big gulp of his drink, letting the cold liquid soothe his throat. Work helped him cope with the memories that sometimes threatened to drag him under. Putting away the bad guys and helping the innocent gave him purpose, a reason to get up each morning and face the world. He'd managed to be as different from his parents and brother as someone could possibly be. It wasn't easy, and some days it still wasn't.

Should he be concerned that Shea Callahan knew about his past? No, he felt sure the sheriff would keep the news to herself. She had her own demons to wrestle with, her own secrets to keep.

He hoped. She had bigger things to worry about than what had once happened to him—like staying alive long enough to catch Cletus Hodges before he made good on his threats.

Chapter Three

The sheriff's office files didn't go back more than a few years due to a fire, so Shea headed to the local library the next morning before going to the office. She needed as much information on the Hodges family as possible in order to formulate a plan to stop the man before he came for her.

An eerie silence greeted her when she entered the library. The faint hum of old fluorescent lights and the soft rustle of paper as the librarian, a woman who looked to be in her mid-forties, turned pages in a book.

She glanced up at Shea with a smile. "May I help you?"

"I'm Sheriff Callahan. I'd like to look at old police reports and was told you kept copies here."

"Absolutely." She jumped to her feet, seemingly happy to have something to do. "Follow me." She led Shea to a small room with a table, computer, and a wall of filing cabinets. "Most police reports and newspaper articles have been downloaded, but not all of them. Everything here is public record. Let me know if I can be of any further assistance." She tarried as if waiting for Shea to ask for her help.

"Thank you, I will." After the librarian left, Shea closed the door and settled in front of the desktop computer. She typed Cletus Hodges into the search engine. Not only his name came up, but also those of his brothers. Still, Cletus, the older brother, had a police record worse than the other two combined, minus the terror on the mountain a few months prior.

Her stomach tightened as she read the summary of Darryl's offenses. Petty theft, bar fights, suspected drug trafficking, and an assault that resulted in the hospitalization of a man and almost caused his death.

Another article caused her breath to hitch. Cletus Hodges. Assault charges in multiple counties, an arson linked to a bitter dispute and…a murder that was never proven—that of a woman, Rebecca Holden, whose body had been found in the woods six years ago. Evidence had been circumstantial, but whispers had tied Cletus to her death.

Cletus looked to be far worse than his brother. He was a dangerous man indeed.

Further digging revealed connections between the Hodges brothers and Misty Hollow's shadowy underworld. She would never have thought a quaint city nestled in the Ozarks could have such a past. The peace of Misty Hollow, fragile as it was, could be shattered by

Cletus. It would be up to Shea to prevent that from happening. From all she read, this city had been through enough.

She rubbed her eyes as the fluorescent lights flickered. Exhaustion weighed on her. The dim lighting made the room oppressive. She quickly sent copies of the files to her work email, rushed from the room and past the librarian's desk, then pushed through the heavy front doors to the fresh air of Misty Hollow.

A glance at her watch let her know she would be late to the ten a.m. meeting. At the station, she bypassed her office and headed straight for the conference room. The other deputies glared at her when she entered. "Sorry. Got in the middle of something." She took her place at the front of the room.

"First off...anyone seen or heard anything on Cletus Hodges?"

Heads shook.

"Mean guy," Bill said. "Dangerous. Plays dirty. That's all common knowledge around these parts, and no one is talking. I doubt you'll find anyone who will tell you anything about the Hodges."

"His wife was pretty tight-lipped yesterday." She sat, folded her hands on the table, and explained in greater detail her interest in Cletus. "I'd like him brought in before I'm forced to face him."

"He won't be as easy to kill as his brother." Bill rolled his head on his shoulders. "I'd like to say you brought trouble to this hollow, but it arrived when the

Hodges did before my daddy moved here."

From what Shea has seen and heard, trouble came in many forms other than the Hodges. She dismissed the deputies to their duties and the night deputies to go home, then headed to her office where she printed out the files on Cletus and his brothers.

She spread the papers across her desk. The clock on the wall ticked off the minutes as she scanned the reports again. One detail she'd missed before stuck out. Cletus and Darryl had been arrested together at a bar fight in a neighboring town a couple of years ago. The arresting officer mentioned Darryl had seemed agitated, almost fearful, as if he'd been forced into participating. Had he been the weakest of the brothers?

It didn't make sense. Not after what she'd experienced on the mountain. Darryl hadn't been fearful in the least. More like bloodthirsty. What had changed?

~

Trevor knocked on the door of Shea's office. "It's way past time for lunch. You going to take a break?"

She shuffled the papers in front of her into a pile. "Haven't had time to think on it."

"You seemed off in the meeting. Is everything okay?"

Sighing, she leaned back in her chair. "Yes. Just busy."

He crossed his arms. "I know we just met, but I

can tell something is eating at you. You don't have to tell me, but don't pretend everything is fine. This department has each other's backs. I can help."

"It's nothing but town business." Her features hardened.

"Whatever it is, you don't have to do it alone." His tone softened.

Her jaw tightened, and her hands gripped the edge of her desk. For a fleeting moment, she looked as if she wanted to say something. Instead, she shook her head. "It's nothing more than paperwork."

"Please don't tell me you plan on going after Hodges alone." He frowned.

"Okay."

Ah, the new sheriff had a stubborn streak. "Let's go to lunch at the diner. The paperwork will wait."

"Fine." She set a heavy book on top of the stack of papers. "Afterward, I want to go by my place and pick up Heidi. I didn't think she'd be allowed in the library."

"Why'd you go to the library?" He asked as they headed for the car. "You can find out almost anything about anything on the computer."

She sighed. "I wanted the quiet."

The privacy, he figured she meant. He tossed her the keys. "I've learned you prefer to drive. In fact, you prefer to be in charge period."

"Guilty."

Did the woman ever smile? He slid into the

passenger seat.

A few minutes later, Shea parked in front of the diner, then turned to him. "If someone in this town would talk, who would it be?"

"I haven't been here much longer than you, but I bet the owner of the diner, Lucy, would know who we could talk to." He agreed Shea needed to prepare for a possible confrontation with Hodges, but he hoped it didn't become an obsession and interfere with the rest of her work.

They sat at a table near the window, Shea taking the seat where she could see the door. When the hostess handed them menus, Shea asked to speak to Lucy.

"She ain't here." The young girl popped her gum.

"Maybe you can help us." Trevor smiled. "We're looking for someone we can talk to about things that happened about six years ago. Would you know anyone?"

She smacked her gum harder, then nodded. "June Mayfield. She knows just about everything about everyone. Strange since she hardly leaves her house. She lives in the big Victorian on fourth."

After a lunch where they both ordered the special, cheesy potato soup with a thick slice of homemade bread, Shea drove to Fourth Avenue. A well-maintained, white Victorian sat among other houses in a variety of colors. An elderly woman leaning on a white cane with purple flowers stepped onto the porch as soon as they exited the car.

"I was hoping to meet the new sheriff." She smiled and ushered them inside. "I've chocolate chip cookies and sweet tea. Sit."

They sat at a small kitchen dinette set that looked as if it had come straight out of the fifties. "The idea of cookies and tea is a great idea," Trevor remarked.

"How can you think of eating anything else?" Shea whispered. "We're here on business, not for a social visit."

"We can have both." His grin widened. "Remember the old saying about drawing more bees with honey than vinegar."

She furrowed her brows. "I don't look at Ms. Mayfield as a bee. She's a resource."

"I've never been called that before." Ms. Mayfield set two glasses of tea on the table, then went back for the cookies. "But I have been asked questions about this town many times. I hope I can be of help."

Trevor reached for his glass of tea. Whoa. The woman added tea to her sugar. He fought not to make a face and set his glass down.

"I'd like to know what you can tell us about the death of Rebecca Holden six years ago," Shea said. "I've found the police report, but it doesn't say much other than there was no evidence to back up Cletus Hodges as being the murderer."

"There wouldn't be, Sheriff. Things happen to folks who speak out against the Hodges." She reached for a cookie.

"Does that mean you won't tell us anything?" Trevor asked.

"Not at all. I'm not afraid of much. Not at my age. I've lived a good, long life. If I can help put the bad people away, I will." Wrinkles spread across her cheeks as she smiled. "Ask your questions. As for Rebecca Holden…well, her body was found in the woods. All the authorities had to go on that it was one of the Hodges was the fact that she dated Cletus for a while, and a few folks witnessed an argument between them at the bar."

"Did he threaten to kill her?" Trevor bit into a cookie. Much better than the tea and still warm from the oven.

Ms. Mayfield shrugged. "I wasn't there, so all this is merely hearsay. Rumor has it that Cletus gave her a couple of slaps, then dragged her crying from the bar. The next morning, she was found dead." She frowned. "Why the sudden interest in poor Rebecca?"

Shea cleared her throat. "I've received a threat from whom I believe is Cletus. We're simply trying to gather as much information on him as we can."

The woman nodded. "The whole town knows about you killing his brother and locking the other one behind bars. Cletus was born bad. I'd watch your back if I were you, Sheriff."

"I plan to." Shea stood and thanked the woman for the tea and cookies.

Trevor did the same and followed Shea outside.

"What's the plan now?"

"I'm thinking I need to pay my old friend Darryl a visit."

Chapter Four

The next morning, after checking emails and assigning duties for the day, Shea left the office to pay Darryl Hodges a visit in prison. She'd come in early enough to manage to make the trip alone, she hoped. The drive would give her time to think, to prepare mentally for facing the man who'd tried to kill her.

The spray-painted words on her car jarred her to a complete stop. The letters, bold and jagged, were blazed in crimson across the driver's side door and hood. Justice for my brother. Evidence Cletus wanted revenge, wanted her to know he was watching, waiting.

The accusation felt alive, pulsing with malevolent energy. The man's rage lingered in the sharp edges of each word, in the deliberate way the paint had been applied with thick, angry strokes. Some of the paint had run in the morning dew, looking far too much like blood dripping down the white surface. Shea stood frozen, her breath catching in her throat. The metallic tang of spray paint mingled with the faint scent of pine carried on a slight breeze that rustled the leaves overhead.

Her fingers trembled as she traced the letters, not quite touching the still-tacky surface. Each stroke was a knife to her sense of security; a reminder of the nightmare she'd survived a few months ago on that godforsaken mountain. This wasn't an act of random vandalism. No, it was far more personal, deliberate, and loaded with meaning. Someone had stood here in the darkness, taking their time to craft this message of hate and retribution.

When had he done this? She'd left the truck here overnight, something she rarely did but had been too exhausted to drive home after the long day. The parking lot had security lighting, but apparently not enough to deter someone determined to send a message. The thought that he'd been here, so close to where she worked, made her skin crawl.

A sideways glance showed Trevor pulling into the lot in his own truck, earlier than his usual arrival time. He exited and marched toward the building with his typical purposeful stride, stopping abruptly when he spotted Shea standing motionless beside her vehicle. His eyes widened as he took in the painted message, and his hand instinctively moved toward his weapon before he forced himself to relax. He hurried over to her, his boots crunching on the gravel.

"Shea," he said, his voice low and controlled.

"That isn't just a warning. It's a challenge."

She didn't reply immediately. Fear, guilt, and anger clogged her throat like thick smoke. The memories of that terrible time on the mountain came flooding back—the terror, the desperation, the moment when she'd been forced to take a life to save her own. She cleared her throat roughly. "I know."

"Where are you going?" He tilted his head, studying her pale face in the morning light. "Under the circumstances, it isn't wise for you to go anywhere alone."

"I planned on visiting Darryl Hodges in prison." Her voice shook despite her efforts to control it. "Thought maybe I could get some information about Cletus, about how he thinks."

"Let's have a cup of coffee first. I'll go with you." His tone brooked no argument, and she found herself oddly relieved by his insistence.

She nodded and preceded him into the building, her legs feeling unsteady beneath her. She paused at the receptionist's desk long enough to ask Doris, who was just arriving with her own cup of coffee and a box of donuts, to have someone photograph the vandalism, then call the local auto body shop to see about removing the paint.

"My Lord," Doris breathed when she looked out the window. "That's just evil, Sheriff. Pure evil."

In her office, Shea plopped into her chair and waited for Trevor to bring her coffee. The familiar routine felt comforting somehow, a small anchor of normalcy in what was becoming an increasingly surreal situation. When he returned with two steaming mugs, she breathed deep of the aromatic steam, letting the warmth seep into her bones. The ceramic warmed her chilly hands, which she only now realized had been trembling.

Trevor sat across from her in one of the visitor chairs, his long legs stretched out in front of him. "Why were you planning to go alone?"

She shrugged, staring into the dark liquid in her mug. "The danger is escalating quickly. I don't want anyone else involved, don't want anyone else to get hurt because of my past."

"I'm already involved." His voice was firm, certain.

"How so?" She narrowed her eyes, looking up at him over the rim of her mug.

"Because I want to help you bring Hodges to justice. This isn't a lone ranger job, Sheriff. You have backup now, whether you want it or not."

Something in his tone made her chest tighten with an emotion she couldn't quite name. "Might as well call me Shea."

"Great. As I told you before—call me Trevor." He gave a quick smile that transformed his face, then sobered as the weight of the situation settled back over them. "You think Darryl will help you find Cletus?"

"No." She stared into the mug in front of her,

watching the steam rise and dissipate. "Maybe I'll learn something about his brother, something that will give me an idea where to look, how he operates."

"I doubt you'll have to look for him." Trevor's voice was grim. "He's coming for you. This vandalism proves it."

Before the girls' trip to the mountain, the threat wouldn't have bothered her much. Law enforcement received threats all the time—it came with the territory. But this one brought it all back with devastating clarity. She'd have to relive that time all over again, face the nightmares that had only recently begun to fade. The very thought frightened her to her core. What if she didn't survive this time? What if Cletus was smarter, more dangerous than his brothers?

When they'd finished their coffee and each grabbed a donut from the break room—Trevor insisting she needed to eat something—they climbed into a squad car. Shea kept her gaze carefully diverted from her defaced truck. She needed composure in order to speak to the man who had played a horrible game with her and her friends. A game that should've ended with her death and the deaths of everyone she cared about.

The drive to the state penitentiary took forty-five minutes through winding mountain roads that reminded her uncomfortably of that terrible time. Trevor filled the silence with small talk about the area, the weather, anything to keep her mind occupied. She appreciated the effort more than she could express.

When they arrived at the prison—a fortress-like structure of concrete and steel that seemed to squat malevolently against the mountainside—a bit of calm had soothed away the worst of the turmoil inside her. She would be able to face Darryl Hodges and keep her fear of the man from showing. She had to.

The security process was lengthy and thorough. They surrendered their weapons, passed through multiple checkpoints, and submitted to searches that left Shea feeling exposed and vulnerable. The guards were professional but cold, treating them with the same suspicious efficiency they showed all visitors.

The two of them were ushered into a small, windowless room with concrete walls painted an institutional green that had faded to an sickly yellow over the years. A metal table was bolted to the floor between two equally immovable chairs. Shea folded her hands on the table, trying to project calm she didn't feel. Despite wanting to come alone, she welcomed the strong, steady presence of Trevor beside her. He hadn't tried to talk her out of coming; he only insisted she not go alone. She might as well get used to him tagging along. He couldn't be dissuaded anyway, and honestly, she was beginning to appreciate his stubborn protectiveness.

Minutes later, the door opened with a harsh metallic clang that echoed in the small space. Darryl shuffled into the room, his orange jumpsuit hanging loose on his frame. He'd lost weight since their encounter on the mountain, and there were new lines around his eyes that spoke of sleepless nights and constant vigilance. His shackles were firmly bolted to the wall, keeping his hands secured but allowing limited movement. He glared across the table with eyes that burned with undiminished hatred.

"You've got some nerve showing up here," he growled, his voice rougher than she remembered. Prison had not been kind to him. "You killed my brother."

"In self-defense." She forced her voice not to tremble, drawing on every ounce of training and inner strength she possessed. "You killed someone whom I loved as a sister. What's the difference between what you did and what I did?"

The memory of Sarah's final moments flashed through her mind—her friend's terrified eyes, the sound of her scream cut short, the horrible silence that followed. Shea's hands clenched into fists beneath the table.

Darryl leaned forward as far as his restraints would allow, his chains rattling ominously against the metal anchor. "Doesn't matter, does it? Have you met Cletus yet?" He grinned without humor, the expression making his gaunt face look skeletal. "He'll make you pay. He's smarter than Bruce and me put together."

Shea shared a glance with Trevor, who was watching the exchange with sharp, alert eyes. She turned back to Darryl, keeping her voice level. "He's why we're here. Any idea where we can find him?"

"Why? So you can lock him up too?" Darryl's laugh was harsh, echoing off the concrete walls.

"Yes." Shea adopted a thin-lipped smile, seeing no use in lying. "Seems your brother wants to finish what you started."

"I hope he succeeds." Darryl laughed again, the sound more like a bark. "Let me give you some advice, Sheriff. Watch your back. Cletus won't stop until he's served his own brand of justice. He's patient, methodical. He'll wait for the perfect moment."

"Where would he go to ground?" Trevor interjected, his voice calm but insistent. "What places meant something to your family?"

Darryl's eyes shifted to Trevor, assessing this new threat. "Who's your boyfriend, Sheriff? Another victim for my brother to deal with?"

"Just answer the question," Shea said sharply.

"Why should I help you?" Darryl's smile turned cruel. "You destroyed my family. Now it's time for payback."

This meeting was going nowhere fast. Visiting the prison had been a waste of time, just as she'd feared. Darryl wasn't going to give them anything useful, and sitting here was only feeding his satisfaction at seeing her worried and afraid.

They endured another twenty minutes of Darryl's taunts and veiled threats before calling an end to the visit. By the time they returned to the station, the spray paint had been removed from Shea's truck, along with a significant portion of the original paint's top layer. While faint, ghostly outlines of the message could still be seen if you knew where to look. She'd need a complete new paint job to cover it up properly. With a heavy exhale, she marched to her office and called the local garage to schedule the work.

~

Did the sheriff think Darryl would betray his brother? Not even a woman could be that stupid. Cletus frowned as he passed the sheriff's station in a borrowed pickup truck, careful to keep his speed steady and his ball cap pulled low. He took pleasure from the fact that the sheriff's truck would need a new coat of paint. How did she like this new game? He thought it a real hoot.

The message had been just the beginning. He had so many more surprises planned for the good sheriff. Each one would be more personal, more terrifying than the last. He'd make her understand what it felt like to lose everything, to have your world torn apart by violence.

The deputy who followed the sheriff like a protective shadow might need to be dealt with. Or maybe her sidekick would add to the challenge, make the game more interesting. While the hunting parties on the mountain had been his brainchild originally, he'd rarely indulged in the sport himself. He had his own family to take care of, his own responsibilities. This time, he planned on enjoying every minute of the hunt.

His wife and kids would have to fend for themselves for a while. It was too dangerous for him to spend much time at home anymore. His wife wouldn't slip up and let someone know he came around—she knew better than that—but one of the children might innocently mention daddy's visits. He couldn't risk that happening, not when he was so close to getting his revenge.

The stakes were too high. Justice needed to be done, and he was the only one left to deliver it.

~

Trevor leaned on the door jamb of Shea's office, noting the way she rubbed her temples as she stared at her computer screen. "Want me to dig deeper on the Hodges family? Since they've been in these parts for generations, they're bound to own property somewhere we haven't found yet. A lot of these mountain families own hunting cabins, old homesteads. He might be holed up in one."

She glanced up from her screen, her eyes red-rimmed with fatigue. "I've been doing that since we got back, but with both of us searching, hopefully one of us will find something. Thanks."

"Not a problem. Bombeck and Cutter are out on calls, so that leaves me here with time on my hands. I might as well make myself useful." He turned and booted his computer to start the search, determined to find something that would give them an advantage.

By quitting time, he'd found little other than each

of the Hodges' main home properties and those of the other men who had terrorized Shea and her friends months ago. There had to be more. These mountain families typically had land scattered throughout the region, passed down through generations. He'd found old photos online of the brothers with deer they'd killed, always in front of rustic cabins or hunting stands. Not everyone owned a hunting cabin, but he'd be surprised if at least one of the Hodges didn't have access to remote property.

Not finding anything under their names, he began searching for their spouses, relatives, and even deceased family members whose property might still be accessible. At quitting time, he'd found a couple of promising possibilities. After printing them off, he headed back to Shea's office.

"I found a couple of places we could check out—both owned by relatives of the Hodges family."

She turned away from her computer and held out her hand for the papers, her movements betraying her exhaustion. "How far away are they?"

"One is very close to your place, maybe a fifteen-minute hike through the woods. The other is about a mile further up the mountain, more isolated. If Cletus isn't staying at one of those, he could be camped out in any number of abandoned cabins or hunting stands up there. That will make finding him much harder."

"At least we have a place to start." She stood and grabbed her jacket from the back of her chair. "Let's go.

We'll stop by my place and pick up Heidi. No one can sneak up on us with her around."

She grabbed the keys to her truck from her desk drawer. "Want to follow me home?"

"Sure. But Shea?" He waited until she looked at him. "We need to be careful up there. If Cletus is holed up in one of these places, we'll be walking into his territory. He'll have every advantage."

"I know." Her jaw set with determination. "But I can't just sit around waiting for him to make his next move. I need to take control of this situation."

Heidi met them as they pulled up to Shea's small ranch house, her tail wagging furiously and stirring up dust in the gravel drive. The German shepherd's obvious joy at seeing her master brought the first genuine smile Trevor had seen on Shea's face all day. She patted the dog's head affectionately, then gave the command to follow. "Lead the way, Trevor."

He glanced at the GPS on his phone, then at the rapidly darkening sky. "Says it'll take about thirty minutes on foot to reach the first location. I doubt there's much of a road, if there is one at all."

"Driving up will just alert Cletus if he's there and give him time to flee. I don't mind a hike." She checked her weapon and adjusted her utility belt. "Besides, I could use the exercise after sitting behind a desk all day."

"Okay." Trevor led the way past her property line and into the thick woods that covered the mountainside like a dark green blanket.

It would be full dark in little over an hour. He didn't relish being in unfamiliar woods after sunset, especially knowing that somewhere out there was a man who wanted to kill them both. Neither he nor Shea knew this area well, despite it being relatively close to her home. If Cletus was around and chose to make his move in the darkness, they'd be at a serious disadvantage.

The terrain was rougher than expected, with fallen logs and hidden ravines that made the going slow and treacherous. Heidi ranged ahead of them, her superior senses alert for any sign of danger. The forest was surprisingly quiet—no bird songs, no rustle of small animals in the underbrush. Even the insects seemed subdued.

After twenty-five minutes of steady climbing, Trevor stepped into a small, overgrown clearing. The "cabin" didn't look to be more than a large deer stand or hunting blind, elevated on stilts about eight feet off the ground. A set of wooden steps, gray with age and obviously handmade, led to a simple door that hung slightly askew on its hinges. With his hand resting on the butt of the gun at his hip, Trevor approached cautiously.

The steps wobbled ominously under his weight, and he could see where several boards had been replaced over the years. At the top, he knocked firmly on the door frame. When no answer came, he turned the knob and pushed the door open slowly, ready to draw his weapon at the first sign of trouble.

The interior was sparse but functional. A bucket for a toilet sat in a small alcove behind a hanging blanket that provided minimal privacy. The stand sported windows on three sides, offering excellent views of the surrounding forest—perfect for hunting, or for watching for unwanted visitors. A rolling chair that had seen better days sat in the corner next to a small propane heater. A heavy sleeping bag had been spread out against the back wall, and several empty beer bottles and tin cans showed someone had stayed there recently. The air smelled of stale cigarettes and unwashed clothing.

Could be Cletus. Could be any number of people who used these remote shelters. Trevor couldn't tell how long ago the place had been occupied, but the trash looked relatively fresh.

He rejoined Shea at the bottom of the steps, noting how she kept scanning the tree line while he'd been inside. "Someone's been here, but I can't tell when. Could be days, could be weeks."

"Should we stake out the place?" she asked, her voice barely above a whisper.

"If you're up to it." He grinned, trying to lighten the mood. "I have nothing going on tonight except laundry and a frozen dinner."

"Are you sure? You aren't on night duty. Don't be afraid to turn me down." But her expression said she hoped he wouldn't.

"Isn't often I get to spend time in the dark in the woods with a pretty girl." He waited for her to tell him he'd overstepped his bounds, that their relationship was strictly professional. When no rebuke came, he relaxed slightly. "We should be able to see the stand from over there and avoid detection." He led her to a thick cluster of bushes about fifty yards away that offered good concealment.

They hunkered down and prepared to wait, while Heidi settled between them with the patient alertness of a trained working dog. The temperature was dropping with the sun, and Trevor wished he'd thought to bring coffee or at least a thermos of something hot.

The sun set gradually, casting them into the deep darkness that only comes in wilderness areas far from city lights. Trevor's eyes adjusted slowly to the gloom. The only illumination came from a sliver of a moon and a brilliant display of stars that would have been beautiful under different circumstances.

Time passed slowly. An hour. Two hours. Trevor was beginning to think this was a waste of time when a twig snapped somewhere ahead of them. Heidi's ears perked up immediately, and the dog growled low in her throat, stopping only when Shea put a firm but gentle hand on her back.

The form of a man in a dark hoodie stepped into the clearing, moving with the careful stealth of someone trying not to be detected. He had what looked like a canvas duffel bag slung over his shoulder and carried himself with the wary alertness of someone who'd spent time living rough. The man clicked on a small flashlight and shined it briefly on the steps before heading up them, each footfall careful and measured.

Trevor and Shea rose from their hiding place simultaneously, weapons drawn. "Stop. Sheriff's department."

The man turned halfway up the stairs and immediately dropped his bag, raising his hands high in the universal gesture of surrender. "I have permission to stay here," he called out, his voice shaky with fear.

Trevor shined his flashlight on the man's face, noting the weathered skin and graying beard of someone who'd lived a hard life. Definitely not Cletus. "Who gave you permission?" He suspected the answer before the words left the man's mouth.

"Cletus Hodges. Said I could stay here until deer season starts up. He said he don't need it before then."

Shea stepped forward, her weapon still drawn but pointed downward. "When and where did you last see Cletus?"

"Three days ago at the supermarket in town. He saw me panhandling outside and offered me this place." The man's voice was humble, grateful. "It ain't much, but it's a whole lot better than sleeping under a bridge or in a cardboard box."

"What's your name, sir?" Trevor asked, holstering his weapon as it became clear this man posed no threat.

"Zeke Washington. I swear on my mother's grave I ain't done nothing wrong. Just trying to get by until I can get back on my feet."

"I can see that, Mr. Washington." Trevor pulled a business card from his pocket and held it out to the man. "If you see Cletus again, give us a call. We have some important questions for him."

"Yes, sir. I'll do that." Zeke took the card carefully, as if it were made of gold.

They made their way back through the darkened forest, flashlights cutting narrow paths through the black void around them. Trevor led the way, following the same route they'd taken up, while Heidi ranged ahead to scout for obstacles or dangers. All that work, all that hope, and it had turned out to be nothing but a dead end.

But at least now they knew Cletus was still in the area, still moving freely through the community. That was something, even if it wasn't the breakthrough they'd hoped for.

Chapter Five

Shea stared at the pile of messages depicting petty crime lying on the desk in front of her. Helplessness rolled over her in waves like a rising tide threatening to drown her. Too many. So many that she started to think they were nothing more than distractions from the larger threat looming over her like a storm cloud. Still, she needed to tend to them all. Each complaint represented a citizen who'd trusted her with their safety, and she couldn't let them down, even if it meant playing into Cletus's hands.

The messages ranged from bicycle thefts to vandalism, from scattered mail to broken windows. Each one meticulously reported, each one another thread in what was clearly a coordinated campaign designed to stretch her resources thin and keep her running in circles. She grabbed a handful, put them in order from farthest to closest to the station, then dispersed some to the other deputies who were equally overwhelmed, and headed for her car.

The morning air carried the crisp bite of early autumn, and the leaves on the trees around the station had begun their slow transformation from green to gold. Under normal circumstances, she would have found the scene peaceful, even beautiful. Instead, everything felt ominous, as if the very landscape was holding its breath in anticipation of whatever Cletus had planned next.

"Hold up." Trevor jogged to her side, his long stride easily catching up with her determined pace. "Nowhere alone, remember?"

"It's minor stuff, Deputy." She reached for the vehicle handle, her fingers already closing around the cool metal. "Petty theft, some vandalism. Nothing that requires—"

"Don't assume anything." He grinned and slid into the passenger side before she could finish her protest. "We'll get all this done faster if we work together, and two sets of eyes are always better than one."

With a roll of her eyes that held more affection than annoyance, she entered the car, handed Trevor her carefully organized list so he could navigate, and drove to the first complaint on her roster. The radio crackled with periodic updates from the other deputies, each one reporting similar patterns of minor crimes scattered throughout their assigned areas.

A small red-brick house on the outskirts of town sat nestled among mature oak trees whose branches formed a natural canopy over the modest yard. A frazzled woman with graying brown hair hanging loose from what had once been a neat bun met them on the front porch. Her hands twisted anxiously in her apron, and dark circles under her eyes suggested she'd lost sleep over the incident.

"We've never had anything stolen before in twenty-three years of living here." She pointed to a large magnolia tree whose white blooms had long since given way to dark green leaves. "My son Tommy always leaves his bike propped right there against that tree when he comes in for dinner. Same spot every night since he was old enough to ride."

"When did you first notice it was missing?" Shea asked, pulling out her notebook to document the details.

"This morning when Tommy went to leave for school. He came running back in, all upset, saying someone stole his bike." The woman's voice cracked slightly. "It was his birthday present just three months ago. We saved up for months to buy it."

"Did anyone see anything?" Shea glanced at the two houses across the narrow street, then at another house situated on the lot next door.

The woman nodded eagerly. "The old woman in that white house with the green shutters doesn't miss anything that happens on this street. Mrs. Patterson. She's lived there for forty years and knows everyone's business."

"We'll go talk to her." With Trevor at her side, Shea made her way across the street to the white house where an elderly woman sat in a wooden rocking chair on her covered porch, a lit cigarette dangling from her weathered fingers.

Mrs. Patterson looked to be in her seventies, with silver hair pulled back in a tight bun and sharp blue eyes that seemed to take in everything at once. She wore a faded housedress and well-worn slippers, and her porch was decorated with an assortment of potted plants and wind chimes that tinkled softly in the morning breeze.

"Sure, I saw it plain as day, except it was nighttime." She took a long drag from her cigarette and blew the smoke away from them. "I'd come out for my last smoke of the evening—doctor says I should quit, but at my age, what's the point?—and I saw a person in a dark hoodie ride away on that boy's bike. I yelled for him to stop, but since I was already in my pajamas and slippers, I couldn't do much more than that. He never looked my way, just kept pedaling down the street like the devil himself was chasing him."

Why was it always someone in a dark hoodie? Shea made a note in her pad. "Could you tell anything else about the person? Height, build, age?"

"Not too tall, moved like a young person. Could've been a teenager, hard to say in the dark." Mrs. Patterson flicked ash from her cigarette. "Happened around ten-thirty, maybe eleven. I always have my last smoke at the same time."

They knocked on the doors of the other neighbors,

but no one knew even as much as the observant Mrs. Patterson. Most had been inside watching television or already asleep, their windows closed against the cool night air.

"What's next?" Shea asked as they returned to the patrol car, Trevor consulting the list she'd given him.

"Mail tossed into a ditch." He looked up with a puzzled expression. "About two miles from here."

She frowned, starting the engine. "Seriously? Someone called in scattered mail?"

"Yep. The message says someone ripped open several pieces of mail and tossed them in a muddy ditch along Riverside Road." He turned the message slip so she could read the details. "The complainant is pretty upset about it."

"What a waste of time and resources." But even as she said it, Shea knew they had to respond. Every complaint mattered, no matter how trivial it seemed.

The next stop revealed a disgruntled elderly man in his eighties leaning heavily on a carved wooden cane. His white hair was disheveled, and his face was flushed with anger and embarrassment. Scattered around his feet were soggy pieces of mail, some torn open and others merely soaked from their time in the drainage ditch.

"I had important medical forms in those papers!" His voice shook with indignation. "Now, someone knows what's wrong with me, what medications I take, when my doctor appointments are. Is nothing sacred anymore? Can't a man get his mail without some hooligan pawing through it?"

"I understand your frustration, sir," Shea said gently, helping him gather the salvageable pieces. "We'll file a report and see if we can find any witnesses."

"Doesn't appear so, sir," Trevor agreed, scanning the empty rural road. "But we'll do everything we can to find who's responsible."

Returning to the truck, Shea swallowed back a sigh of frustration. At this rate, she'd be at the office late into the evening doing paperwork that led nowhere and solved nothing. "Do you get the feeling we're being sent on a senseless goose chase? Like something big is going to happen, and I'm supposed to be too distracted and exhausted to respond properly?"

"Sure. It's all part of the psychological game Cletus is playing with you, but we still have to play along for the sake of the citizens of Misty Hollow." Trevor's voice was matter-of-fact but understanding. "These people deserve protection, even if it's being used against us."

"I know that." She scowled, not liking the implication that she couldn't see the bigger picture. Her jaw tightened with frustration. "I'm not some rookie who doesn't understand tactics."

"Next stop is the diner." He tilted his head to peer at her face, noting the tension lines around her eyes. "No offense intended, Shea. I meant it when I said I have your back. We're in this together."

"Why?" The question came out sharper than she intended. "We just met a few days ago. You don't owe me anything."

"You're the sheriff. I'm your deputy. We're partners." He flashed that disarming smile, revealing those dimples that made her stomach flutter despite her best efforts to remain professional. "It's as simple as that. Besides, I don't like bullies, and Cletus Hodges is definitely a bully."

They arrived at the diner to find a scene that made Shea's heart sink. The words "Don't Look Away" were spray painted in stark black letters across the cheerful red brick wall, and the large front window lay in glittering fragments across the sidewalk. The owner, Lucy—a woman in her fifties with graying blonde hair and worried brown eyes—looked shaken as she swept up the glass with methodical, angry strokes.

"This happens to my diner more times than I want to think about," Lucy said, her voice tight with frustration and fear. She glared at Shea as if she'd personally committed the crime. "First time was maybe eight years ago, then it stopped for a while. Now it's starting up again. What's going on in this town, Sheriff?"

"It's just someone stirring up trouble," Shea replied, though the words felt hollow even to her. "Kids, maybe, or someone with a grudge."

"I think it's more than that." Lucy leaned on her

broom, her knuckles white from gripping the handle too tightly. "Folks are saying trouble followed you down off that mountain. That you brought this curse with you."

Shea stiffened, feeling the familiar burn of anger and guilt in her chest. "Rest assured, ma'am, that I will get to the bottom of these crimes and find whoever is responsible."

Her phone rang with its shrill electronic tone, and she pulled it from the holder on her belt. "Sheriff Callahan."

"This is Doris." The receptionist's voice sounded harried. "Farmer Ben's goats are loose on Main Street again. They're blocking traffic and causing quite a commotion. I tried getting a hold of Bill, but he's way down near Langley on that domestic dispute call. Richard's dealing with a fender-bender on the highway. No one else is answering their phones."

"Deputy Bolton and I are on our way." She turned back to Lucy, who was watching the conversation with obvious frustration. "I'm sorry for your trouble, and I promise we'll find who did this."

"You and the deputy come back at lunchtime," Lucy said, her tone softening slightly. "I'll fix you something on the house. Least I can do while you're trying to sort out this mess."

With the help of several good-natured citizens who seemed to treat the goat roundup as entertainment, Shea and Trevor managed to herd the animals into the trailer that Farmer Ben brought. The elderly farmer scratched his grizzled chin with confusion.

"My gate was wide open when I woke up this morning," he said, shaking his head. "Latched it tight last night like I always do. Never had that happen before in thirty years of keeping goats. We got ourselves a crime spree happening, Sheriff?"

"Looks that way, Ben." The answer felt inadequate, but what else could she say? That a psychopath was orchestrating a campaign of harassment designed to drive her to the breaking point? "But we'll get to the bottom of it."

Thankfully, most of the incidents seemed harmless at first glance, but Shea could feel something sinister lurking behind the apparent pettiness. Each crime was carefully calculated to cause maximum disruption with minimal risk, designed to keep her running in circles while wearing down her credibility with the townspeople.

They took Lucy up on her offer and settled into a booth near the front of the diner a little after noon. The replacement window wouldn't be installed until the next day, so a large piece of plywood covered the opening, making the usually bright interior feel dim and oppressive. It didn't take long for a line of concerned and increasingly agitated citizens to form.

Trevor stood when he saw what was happening. "Okay, folks. We know there's something unusual going on in this town, and the sheriff is doing everything she can to address it. How about giving her some peace for thirty minutes so she can eat something? Then, she'll be happy to listen to your concerns."

The crowd grumbled but reluctantly returned to their seats, though Shea could feel their eyes on her like physical weight. Conversations continued in hushed tones, and she caught fragments of worried discussions about property values, safety concerns, and speculation about what was causing the sudden surge in criminal activity.

Shea shook her head as she picked up her sandwich. "If Cletus is behind this and wants to turn the town against me, he's succeeding beyond his wildest dreams."

The server, a young woman with nervous energy and tired eyes, brought Shea's BLT with cream cheese instead of mayo, a generous portion of French fries, and a steaming cup of coffee. She set the plate down with apologetic efficiency. "Sorry about the chaos, Sheriff. Most folks appreciate what you're doing."

Shea had never felt more like a fish in a fishbowl than she did while the other diners watched her eat. Every bite felt scrutinized, every movement analyzed. She could hear whispered comments about her competence, her experience, her ability to handle the job. The sandwich, which should have been delicious, tasted like cardboard in her mouth.

Leaving half of her fries untouched, she shoved her

plate away. The line of people immediately reformed, their expressions ranging from worried to accusatory. She sighed deeply and turned to face the first person in line.

A man with a red face and flashing eyes posted his fists on their table, leaning forward aggressively. "What exactly are you doing about this crime wave, Sheriff? We elected you to protect us, and right now it feels like things are getting worse instead of better. Sheriff Westbrook vouched for you, said you were the right person for the job."

Others nodded in agreement, their murmurs of support for the angry man growing louder. Shea rose to her feet, preparing to address their concerns, when the bell over the diner door jingled. The former sheriff, his features set in grim but determined lines, stepped through the crowd to the front of the line.

"That is enough, folks." Westbrook's voice carried the authority of decades in law enforcement. "Sit down, Harvey, before you make a fool of yourself." He crossed his arms and fixed the crowd with a stern look that had probably intimidated countless criminals over the years. "You all know good and well the sheriff isn't responsible for these crimes. I had someone row a boat out to my favorite fishing spot to complain about this situation. That had better not happen again."

His gaze swept the crowd, making eye contact with several people who suddenly found their shoes very interesting. "Sheriff Callahan is very capable of getting to the bottom of what's happening in Misty Hollow. She's proven herself time and again. How about you all give her a chance to do her job and leave me to enjoy my retirement?"

Heads nodded again, though some people looked more convinced than others. A few folks had the decency to look embarrassed and returned to their seats without further comment.

Westbrook turned to Shea, his expression softening. "Don't let them get to you. I dealt with the same foolishness when I started here twenty-five years ago. People get scared, they want someone to blame." He smiled and shook both her and Trevor's hands with a firm grip. "Now, there's supposedly a catfish in Miller's Pond that's bigger than my boat, and I intend to catch him before winter sets in. Keep your chin up, Sheriff."

"Thanks, Westbrook. I will." Feeling as if she could face the rest of the day, Shea tossed money on the table next to Trevor's contribution and strode, head high, toward her patrol car.

More of the folks they visited throughout the afternoon mentioned spotting someone in a dark hoodie near the various crime scenes. Others reported seeing shadowy figures darting into the tree line when they investigated disturbances. Despite the numerous sightings, no one seemed to catch anyone on camera, and the descriptions were too vague to be of any use.

Night had fallen like a heavy curtain by the time

they finished working their way through the seemingly endless list. Text messages from the other deputies let her know they faced the same problems in their assigned areas. With every crime scene they investigated, another incident was reported somewhere else in the county.

She released a heavy exhale as she and Trevor approached an old mill that sat beside a creek on the outskirts of town. The building had been abandoned for decades, its weathered wooden walls and rusted metal roof creating deep shadows in the darkness. Shea shined her flashlight around the area, noting overturned trash cans and spray-painted graffiti on the mill's walls.

"Over here, Trevor." She directed his attention to some clear footprints in the soft earth leading away from the mill toward the woods. The tracks looked fresh, made within the last few hours.

Distant laughter drifted on the evening air, young voices echoing through the trees. Hand resting on her weapon, she led the way toward the sound, following a well-worn path that wound through dense undergrowth. After a few minutes of careful progress, they emerged into a small clearing where the acrid smell of wood smoke filled the air.

A fire still smoldered in a makeshift ring of stones, sending wisps of gray smoke toward the star-filled sky. Empty beer cans lay scattered around the clearing along with fast-food wrappers and cigarette butts, but whoever had been there was long gone. The ashes were still warm, suggesting they'd missed the gathering by maybe thirty minutes.

"I think Cletus has hired himself some young ruffians to cause havoc throughout the county," Shea said, kicking an empty beer can with frustration. "He wants me to know he can make me jump through hoops, keep me running around like a headless chicken while he plans whatever he has in mind."

"I agree completely." Trevor glanced at his phone screen, checking the time and their remaining calls. "One more call to make and we'll be done for the night. A break-in at Mrs. Lindell's place. She's a widow who lives alone over on Sixth Street."

At the woman's modest house, Shea paused in the doorway and stared at a living room that looked like a tornado had torn through it. Furniture was overturned, drawers had been pulled out and their contents scattered across the floor, and family photographs lay amid shards of broken glass. Things had definitely escalated compared to the minor vandalism they'd dealt with throughout the day.

The older woman's voice trembled with fear and shock. "I was out in the barn feeding Bessie—that's my cow—when I heard the front window shatter. Sounded like an explosion." She clutched the neckline of her worn terrycloth robe with shaking fingers. "I could hear things being thrown around, voices shouting, so I stayed hidden in the barn until the noise died down. Then I waited a few more minutes to make sure they were really gone before coming in and finding…this.”

“You were very wise to stay hidden, Mrs. Lindell,” Shea said gently, surveying the destruction. “Can you tell if anything specific was taken?”

“Not right offhand. They made such a mess.” She looked around helplessly at the chaos that had once been her tidy home. “My husband's war medals were in that drawer, and my grandmother's jewelry box…I can't tell what's missing and what's just buried under all this.”

“Do you have someone you can stay with tonight until we can get this cleaned up and make the house secure again?”

“No.” Her shoulders sagged with the weight of her loneliness. “It's just me after the death of my Duncan two years ago. All our children moved away for work.”

Shea's heart clenched at the raw sadness on the woman's weathered face. “We've been dealing with similar incidents all day, Mrs. Lindell. I'm confident this was random vandalism, not a targeted attack.”

“How can you be sure?” The woman's gaze locked with Shea's, searching for reassurance. “This was more than one person, Sheriff. I saw at least two people dart into the woods when I peered out the barn door. There might've been more.”

“Would you feel better if I arrange for a patrol car to check on you throughout the night?”

She nodded gratefully. “That would be such a relief. Thank you, Sheriff.”

Shea and Trevor stepped outside into the cool night air. "Let's take a look around before we go. I'll circle to the right, and you go left," she said. "Meet me back at the barn."

She clicked on her powerful flashlight and moved slowly around the perimeter of the house, scrutinizing the ground. Near the broken window, she found two distinctly different shoe prints in the soft dirt, but the evidence suggested at least three different shoe sizes. Teenagers hired by Cletus, most likely. She'd bet her favorite pair of boots on it.

Thinking back to the discarded beer cans at the mill, she surmised the kids had drunk enough liquid courage to escalate from simple mischief to genuine property destruction. Were they finished for the night, or would tomorrow bring a repeat of today's chaos?

"Shea?" Trevor approached from the direction of the barn, his flashlight beam dancing across the ground. "I found some more footprints back there, but nothing else useful."

"I found evidence of at least three different people." She shined her light on the clearest footprints. "Definitely teenagers, based on the shoe sizes."

"Busy little troublemakers."

"Hold the light, please." She took out her cell phone and snapped several photos of the evidence. "Let's document the damage inside the house, then call it a night. I'll arrange for someone to board up that window first thing in the morning."

Trevor insisted on driving back to the station, noting the exhaustion in Shea's movements. Inside the patrol car, he turned to face her. "You're working yourself into the ground, and it's only going to get worse if you don't pace yourself. How long do you stay up at night going over this case? Two hours? Three? The town needs you at your best, Shea, not running on fumes and caffeine. You should take tomorrow off. Spend some time with Heidi, get some real rest."

"It's tempting," she admitted, rubbing her tired eyes. "But there's too much to do right now, too many people counting on me. I appreciate your concern, Trevor, but I'll rest when Cletus is behind bars."

She had a job to do and intended to finish it, no matter what it cost her personally.

As Shea lay in bed that night, staring at the dark ceiling while her mind raced through the day's events, she absently rubbed Heidi's soft ears. The German shepherd had sensed her distress and pressed close against her side, offering what comfort she could.

Why the petty crimes, Cletus? How do these seemingly random acts play into your larger plan for revenge? What wickedness do you have planned for tomorrow? Rolling onto her side, she spooned against her dog's warm body, taking comfort from Heidi's steady breathing and loyal presence.

Darryl and Bruce had been upfront and aggressive about the deadly game they played, hunting their victims through the wilderness with guns and knives.

But Cletus preferred a sneakier, more psychological approach. He was breaking her down piece by piece, undermining her authority and credibility while keeping her too busy and exhausted to mount an effective defense.

Wherever his real attack came from, whenever he finally revealed his true intentions, it would come from out of nowhere like a coiled snake waiting to strike. And Shea had the sinking feeling that all of this—the vandalism, the petty theft, the orchestrated chaos—was just the opening move in a much more dangerous game.

Chapter Six

The morning passed with an eerie quiet that made Shea's skin crawl. The sudden silence felt more ominous than the chaos of the previous day. The rash of petty crimes had stopped as quickly as they had started, like someone had flipped a switch. She didn't receive one complaint about trespassing, vandalism, theft—nothing. Even the usual calls about barking dogs and neighbor disputes had ceased entirely.

She found herself checking her phone repeatedly, wondering if the system had malfunctioned. The quiet should have been a relief, but instead it felt like the calm before a storm. Cletus was planning something; she could feel it in her bones. The sudden cessation of harassment wasn't a sign that he'd given up—it was a sign that he was moving to the next phase of whatever twisted game he was playing.

"Wanna grab lunch?" Trevor peeked into her office, his tall frame filling the doorway. Behind him, she could see the empty bullpen where the other deputies sat at their desks, looking almost bored for the first time since she'd taken the job.

"You don't have anything going on?" She glanced up from the stack of cold case files she'd been reviewing, trying to stay productive during the lull.

"Nope. No one does. It's been a nice, quiet morning for once." He grinned, but she could see the wariness in his eyes that matched her own feelings. "Lucy doesn't mind dogs if we want to eat outside. Fresh air might do us both good."

Shea glanced at Heidi, who was sleeping peacefully in her usual spot by the window, one ear twitching occasionally as she dreamed. "She's fine here." She stood and grabbed her jacket from the back of her chair. Although she wasn't really hungry, eating would break up the monotony of the day and give them a chance to discuss their next moves. Not that she meant to complain about a quiet day—they were rare enough in law enforcement—but this particular silence felt loaded with potential danger.

"Is it some kind of hunting season?" she asked as they climbed into the patrol car. The October air carried the crisp scent of falling leaves and the promise of winter, and she noticed more trucks than usual parked around town with rifle racks in their rear windows.

"No, why?" Trevor started the engine and backed out of the parking space, automatically scanning the area for anything out of place.

She shrugged, settling into the passenger seat. "Thought that might be why Cletus has grown silent. Maybe he's gone off into the woods to hunt deer instead of people."

"More likely he's messing with your mind, trying to keep you on edge." Trevor's voice was matter-of-fact, but she heard the underlying concern. "The Hodges family has always been known for their psychological games."

True. From everything she'd learned about the family, they did like to play elaborate, cruel games with their victims. The hunting expeditions on the mountain had been just one example of their twisted entertainment.

Once they'd been seated at their usual table near the window—Shea automatically taking the chair that gave her the best view of both the door and the street—and both ordered the daily special of loaded potato soup with cornbread, Trevor slid a folded sheet of paper across the table. His expression was carefully neutral, but she could see the excitement in his eyes.

"Here's something productive we can do since we actually have time today."

She arched her brow and unfolded the paper to reveal a detailed topographical map of Misty Mountain with three red circles drawn on it in ballpoint pen. "What's this?"

"The top three places I think Cletus might be holed up." He leaned back and crossed his arms, a hint of satisfaction in his expression. "Each location is pretty secluded, accessible only by barely maintained dirt roads that lead to cabins that can generously be called habitable. I spent some time on the phone this morning calling around to some of the local old-timers, and they all said these three cabins hadn't been used in years. The original owners died, and their kids moved away, can't be bothered with maintaining remote mountain property."

"Good detective work." She studied the map more carefully, noting the elevation markers and the distance from main roads. All three locations were isolated enough that someone could hide there for weeks without being discovered. "This gives us something concrete to work with."

She tilted her head and looked at him with renewed curiosity. "Why'd you really leave Houston? And don't give me that line about wanting a slower-paced life. I can tell there's more to it."

He looked startled by the sudden change of subject, his spoon pausing halfway to his mouth. "I thought this town would be quieter, more peaceful. Guess I was wrong about that."

"Surprised?"

"A bit." He blew out a slow breath when their server brought steaming bowls of soup loaded with cheese, bacon bits, and green onions. The cornbread was still warm from the oven, and the butter melted instantly when he spread it on.

There was more to his leaving Texas than wanting a slower-paced life. She'd bet her badge on it. The way his jaw tightened when he mentioned Houston suggested painful memories. "No family left behind? No girlfriend waiting for you to come back?"

He shook his head, keeping his eyes focused on his soup. "I grew up mostly alone. Both my parents are dead—Dad from a drunk driving accident when I was twelve, Mom from cancer when I was in college. As far as siblings go, I have a brother in prison for multiple murders, but I'm sure you already know that from my personnel files. As for romance..." He shrugged. "Haven't had time for it. Hard to maintain relationships in this line of work."

His tone was carefully casual, but she could hear the pain underneath. "Why all the personal questions?"

"Just making conversation. We're partners now, might as well get to know each other."

"Fair enough." He set his spoon down with a deliberate clatter and fixed her with an appraising look. "What about you? Family? Romantic entanglements?"

"A handful of close friends from college, that's about it. My parents died in a car accident when I was twenty-two." The familiar ache of loss tightened her chest, but she pushed through it. "No siblings, no romantic complications."

"Right. The friends who were with you on the mountain?"

Tension took up residence between her shoulders

like an unwelcome visitor. She'd started the personal questions, so she'd have to see them through. "Like you said, it's hard to maintain relationships in law enforcement. When Westbrook told me about this position and that no one else was running for it, I applied. The town voted me in on his recommendation."

"Now you need to prove yourself worthy of their trust."

"Exactly." In addition to bringing down Cletus and his network of troublemakers, she had to prove to the citizens of Misty Hollow that she was capable of stepping into Westbrook's considerable shoes. If the current crime wave stayed away and normal life resumed, the town might gradually accept her leadership.

After they finished eating and split the bill—Trevor insisting on leaving a generous tip for their patient server—he drove her back to the office to pick up Heidi, then headed toward the first location marked on his hand-drawn map.

The drive took them deep into mountain territory where the roads became progressively narrower and more rutted. Ancient oak and pine trees crowded close to the path, their branches forming a canopy overhead that blocked out most of the afternoon sun. It was the kind of isolated area where someone could disappear completely from civilization.

The first cabin sat in a small clearing, its log walls

weathered to silver-gray, and its metal roof streaked with rust. No smoke rose from the stone chimney, and the windows were dark. The grass and weeds around the structure hadn't been flattened by recent foot traffic, and fallen leaves had accumulated undisturbed on the sagging front porch.

"If Cletus is using this place, he's being cautious about covering his tracks," Shea observed, studying the scene. "Maybe approaching from the back through the woods."

Side by side, their hands resting on the guns at their hips, and Heidi ranging ahead to scout for danger, they approached the cabin cautiously. The silence was broken only by the rustle of wind through the trees and the distant call of a crow.

On the porch, Shea reached out and pushed open the front door, which was barely hanging by one rusted hinge. The hinges creaked ominously as the door swung inward. Thick dust covered the plank floor inside, undisturbed except for small animal tracks that led from the cold stone fireplace to a broken window where wildlife had been entering and leaving.

"No one's been here in months, maybe years," Trevor said, peering out the back window. "Nothing outside to show anything other than raccoons and possums have been visiting this place."

"Let's head to the next location."

The second cabin was in slightly better repair, with a newer metal roof and intact windows, though several panes were cracked. When they arrived, Shea stood on the front porch and peered through a window into the dim interior.

"Someone's definitely been staying here, but I don't think it's Cletus." She pushed the unlocked door open, motioning for Heidi to stay outside and keep watch.

The interior told a story of transient occupation. Tattered sleeping bags were spread across the floor, along with chipped ceramic plates holding the melted remains of candles. Fast-food wrappers and empty bottles were scattered everywhere, and discarded hypodermic needles glinted in the dim light filtering through dirty windows.

She couldn't picture Cletus as a drug addict based on everything she'd learned about him. No, they'd stumbled onto a location where homeless addicts were squatting. The smell of unwashed bodies and stale cigarettes hung heavy in the air.

"We need to get someone up here to secure this place and get these people into treatment programs," she said, covering her nose with her sleeve against the stench.

Trevor nodded and stepped outside to try to get a cell phone signal. The mountains interfered with reception, and it took several minutes before he found a spot where he could connect. "I'll have to wait until we get back to the office to make the calls. No signal out here."

"That's fine." She headed through the debris toward the back of the cabin, stepping carefully around broken glass and other hazards. A bathroom with a clogged toilet added to the foul odor permeating the building. She pulled the neckline of her shirt over her nose and peered into what had once been a bedroom. More of the same chaos from the main room—sleeping bags, drug paraphernalia, and trash everywhere. It looked like at least five or six people had been living in the squalid conditions.

She didn't have a problem with homeless people finding shelter in abandoned places, especially during the harsh mountain winters. But she did have serious concerns about drug addicts creating dangerous conditions and potentially attracting criminal activity to the area.

Stepping outside for fresh air to clear the stench from her lungs, she noticed dark clouds gathering on the horizon. One more cabin to visit, one more chance to get a clue about where Cletus might be hiding.

She checked the weather app on her phone, frowning at what she saw. "Thunderstorm warning. Severe weather is moving in within the hour."

"We'll have to make this quick," Trevor said, studying the ominous sky. "I wouldn't want to be stuck up here during a mountain storm. These dirt roads turn into mudslides when it rains hard."

The drive to the final location was treacherous, the dirt road so full of bone-jarring potholes that Shea wondered if her dental work would survive the journey. The patrol car's suspension groaned with every impact, and she had to grip the door handle to keep from being thrown around the cabin.

The abandoned cabin seemed to loom against the backdrop of trees swaying in the wind from the approaching storm. Weather-beaten shingles on the roof curled like chocolate shavings, and thick vines had clawed their way up the weathered walls, weaving through gaps where boards had rotted away completely. The structure looked like it might collapse at any moment.

Shea stepped carefully over the threshold, leaving Trevor to search the outside perimeter with Heidi while she investigated the interior. The wooden floor beneath her feet sagged ominously with each step, and she could hear mice scurrying in the walls. She clicked on her powerful flashlight and slowly scanned the room.

A flicker of metallic silver in one corner caught her attention. She turned the beam toward it and froze, her blood running cold.

Fresh graffiti covered the wall in bold letters: SC. Shea Callahan? The spray paint looked recent, still glossy and untouched by the dust and grime that coated everything else in the room. Thick drips of red paint ran down the wall like tears...or blood. Scattered on the floor below were empty paint cans, their nozzles crusted with dried paint in multiple colors.

She glanced nervously out the window to see

Trevor and Heidi methodically searching the perimeter as the first fat raindrops began to fall. Thunder rumbled in the distance, and lightning flickered among the dark clouds.

Her eyes landed on another pile of debris in the opposite corner. Her pulse quickened as she recognized scraps of paper, some smudged with muddy boot prints. She crouched down carefully, brushing aside the scattered pieces with her flashlight beam. Her breath hitched when a photo of herself—a grainy image from the Misty Hollow Gazette announcing her appointment as sheriff—stared up at her with the headline "New Sheriff Takes Office."

Other pieces of paper showed fragments of articles about the mountain incident, printouts from social media, and even what looked like surveillance photos taken with a telephoto lens. Someone, almost certainly Cletus, had been gathering detailed information about her life, her background, her daily routines. But why leave such valuable intelligence materials here, where the elements could destroy them?

"Find anything interesting?" Trevor asked, shaking rain from his jacket as he entered the cabin.

"I'm not sure if it's Cletus himself or someone he's hired, but whoever was here has been collecting news articles and photographs of me." She fumbled for her phone with trembling fingers and began snapping pictures of the evidence. Lightning briefly illuminated the cabin through the broken windows, throwing stark shadows on the walls and making the graffiti seem to pulse with malevolent life.

Trevor moved to stand behind her, studying the collection of materials over her shoulder. "Nothing here that isn't common knowledge, though. All this stuff was published in the newspaper or posted online."

"That's what bothers me. I was meant to find this." She pushed against her thighs to straighten, her knees protesting from crouching on the hard floor. "Could you give me a list of the men who told you about these three possible hiding places?"

"You think it's a setup?" His voice was sharp with sudden understanding.

"Maybe. Too convenient that we'd find evidence pointing directly at me in the third location we checked." She holstered her weapon and moved toward the door. "This feels orchestrated."

A sharp crack sounded outside—the unmistakable sound of a heavy branch breaking under someone's weight. Both she and Trevor froze instantly, their eyes locking in silent communication. The sound was too loud and deliberate to be caused by wind or a small animal.

Her ears strained to catch any additional sounds over the increasing rainfall. There—the faint rustle of leaves and undergrowth as someone, or something, moved stealthily around the cabin's perimeter.

Heidi's low growl confirmed their suspicions. The dog's hackles were raised, and she was staring intently toward the back of the building. Shea placed a calming hand on her head and whispered, "Shh."

She swung her flashlight beam toward the broken window, but the dense blackness outside prevented her from seeing anything useful. Her fingers curled around the grip of her service weapon, and she drew it slowly, keeping the barrel pointed downward.

Putting a finger to his lips for silence, Trevor pressed his back against the wall beside the window and carefully peered outside, motioning for Shea to turn off her flashlight. She complied immediately, plunging them into complete darkness except for the occasional flicker of lightning.

A low creak sounded, but not from outside the window—it came from the direction of the front porch. She'd been in law enforcement long enough to distinguish between the normal sounds of an old building settling and the deliberate pressure of someone trying to move stealthily across wooden boards.

Someone was definitely outside, probably trying to determine if the cabin was occupied.

She inched toward the door, her weapon ready. Her boot caught the edge of a glass shard from a broken bottle, and the faint tink of metal against glass seemed deafeningly loud in the tense silence.

Heidi lost control of her training and bolted out the door, barking furiously as she charged into the storm. Her deep, aggressive barks echoed through the trees, growing fainter as she pursued whoever had been lurking outside.

A tremendous crack of thunder directly overhead made Shea jump, her nerves already stretched to the breaking point. The storm was moving in fast, and the rain was becoming a downpour that would wash away any tracks or evidence.

She released the breath she'd been holding and sagged against the door frame, adrenaline making her hands shake slightly. "It was definitely a trap."

"Appears that way." Trevor rolled his shoulders to release tension, his own weapon still drawn. "If Heidi hadn't been here to scare away whoever was watching us, we might have had some answers. Or we might have walked into an ambush."

"Are you blaming my dog for letting them get away?" Her voice carried a protective edge.

"Not at all." He holstered his weapon and held up his hands. "She might very well have saved our lives. I'm just frustrated that we were so close to a breakthrough."

"You're disappointed we didn't catch him."

He shrugged, his jaw tight with suppressed anger. "Not disappointed that we're both still breathing and unharmed, but yeah—we were close to finally getting some real answers."

"This whole thing feels wrong." She turned her flashlight back on and swept it around the room one more time. "We need to question Cletus's wife again. It's entirely possible she lied to us about not knowing his whereabouts. He could be staying at home during the nights and only hiding out during the day when he knows we might come looking."

She stepped onto the sagging porch and whistled sharply for her dog. The rain was coming down harder now, and she could hear Heidi crashing through the underbrush somewhere in the distance.

When the German shepherd finally emerged from the dark woods, her coat was covered in thorny burrs and wet leaves, but her tail was wagging with the satisfaction of having chased off an intruder. Shea spent several minutes pulling out what burrs she could reach, then opened the back door of the squad car for the dog.

"Want to head over to the Hodges place now?" she asked, settling into the passenger seat. "Mrs. Hodges won't be expecting us in this weather. If we approach quietly, we might catch Cletus there."

"Good plan." Trevor slid into the driver's seat and started the engine. "Though this rain is going to make the drive interesting."

The windshield wipers struggled to keep up with the downpour as they navigated the treacherous mountain roads back toward civilization. More than once, Trevor had to slow to a crawl when the headlights revealed washouts or fallen branches blocking their path.

When they finally reached the Hodges family cabin, Shea was surprised to see that it was lit up like a Christmas tree. Warm yellow light shone from every window, creating a deceptively welcoming scene against the stormy darkness.

Trevor parked well away from the house, hidden behind a stand of pine trees. "We're going to get soaked."

"Neither one of us will melt." Shea shoved open her door, immediately feeling the cold rain soak through her jacket. "Let's move fast."

They approached the house as quietly as possible, but a dog chained to the front porch started barking frantically as soon as it caught their scent. Shea stifled a groan of frustration. If Cletus was inside, he'd just received advance warning of their arrival.

She rushed toward the front window, pressing herself against the wall beside it. Through the rain-streaked glass, her gaze met the startled eyes of Cletus Hodges as he sat at the kitchen table eating dinner with his family. The man looked exactly like his brothers—same cruel eyes, same aggressive jawline, same aura of barely contained violence.

Cletus bolted to his feet so fast his chair toppled backward, and he sprinted toward the back door of the cabin. "He's headed out back!" Shea shouted, drawing her weapon as she raced around the corner of the house with Trevor close behind.

They arrived just in time to see Cletus leap onto the saddle of a saddled horse that had been waiting behind the house. He kicked the animal's flanks, and they galloped into the trees, quickly disappearing into the storm and darkness.

They'd lost him again, but at least now they knew for certain that Mrs. Hodges had been lying about her husband's whereabouts.

Furious and dripping wet, Shea strode to the front door and pounded on it with her fist. "Sheriff's department. Open the door."

A clearly worried Mrs. Hodges opened the door slowly, her face pale and frightened. Two small children peered out from behind her skirts, their eyes wide with fear and confusion.

"I'm sorry, Sheriff," the woman said, her voice barely above a whisper. "I couldn't say anything before. He'd hurt the children if I..." She sighed heavily, her shoulders sagging with defeat.

"I understand your position, ma'am," Shea said, trying to keep her voice gentle despite her frustration. She didn't want to arrest the woman for obstruction of justice, especially not when she had small children dependent on her. "But I need you to understand something. I want you to gather a few things and take the kids somewhere else to stay for a while. If I find you harboring your husband again, I will have no choice but to arrest you. Do you understand what I'm telling you?"

"Yes, ma'am. We'll be gone by morning." The woman's voice was resigned but grateful. "Cletus won't come back tonight, not with you watching the place."

"I'll send someone by tomorrow to make sure

you've followed my instructions." Shea turned and walked back to the patrol car, water dripping from her hair and clothes.

At least they'd confirmed that Cletus was still in the area and using his family home as a base of operations. Now they just had to figure out how to catch him before he escalated from psychological warfare to physical violence.

Chapter Seven

Shea drove back to the office through the winding mountain roads, her knuckles white from gripping the steering wheel so tightly that her hands ached. Anger simmered below the surface like molten lava, threatening to erupt at any moment. The fact that Mrs. Hodges would knowingly cover for a man like her husband—a man who was terrorizing an entire community—made her stomach turn with frustration and disgust. She understood the woman's fear, the impossible position she was in with small children to protect, but it didn't make the situation any less maddening.

Shea wasn't sure what she'd do if Mrs. Hodges didn't follow her orders to leave town with the children. The last thing she wanted was to arrest a frightened mother and leave those innocent kids without any parent at all, but she couldn't allow the woman to continue harboring a fugitive who posed a clear and present danger to everyone in Misty Hollow.

The storm had passed, leaving the night air crisp and clean with the scent of rain-washed earth and pine. Under normal circumstances, she would have found the drive calming, even restorative after a long day. Instead, every shadow seemed to hide potential threats, every bend in the road could conceal an ambush. The headlights carved narrow tunnels through the darkness, but beyond their reach lay an endless void where anything could be lurking.

Back at the office, the parking lot was nearly empty except for the night shift deputy's patrol car and a few vehicles belonging to the cleaning crew. She left Heidi in the truck with the windows cracked and retrieved her laptop from her desk, along with some case files she wanted to review at home. The building felt hollow and echoing after hours, every footstep seeming to announce her presence to anyone who might be listening.

She returned to her truck a few minutes later, her arms full of work materials. As she approached the vehicle, a white sheet of paper flapped at her from under the windshield wiper like a surrender flag in the gentle breeze. Heidi immediately began barking fiercely toward the road, her hackles raised and her entire body tense with aggressive alertness.

Shea's hand trembled as she reached for the scrap of paper, her heart already racing before she'd even read the message. You're next. She frowned, rereading the words in the dim glow of the parking lot's security lights. Next? For what exactly? As far as she knew, Cletus hadn't killed anyone yet—his brothers had been the ones with blood on their hands. What was she supposedly next for?

The handwriting was different from the previous notes, more erratic and angry looking. Had Cletus recruited someone else to help with his campaign of intimidation? The thought that there might be multiple people involved in stalking her made the situation feel exponentially more dangerous.

A sound came from her left, from behind a thick stand of bushes that bordered the parking lot. The rustle of leaves and crack of a small branch suggested someone moving through the undergrowth, trying to stay hidden while watching her. Feeling suddenly exposed and vulnerable under the bright security lights, she climbed quickly into her truck and sped away, her hands trembling on the steering wheel as she checked her rearview mirror repeatedly.

She now understood on a visceral level what hunted prey felt like. Every moment of normalcy was tainted by the knowledge that danger could materialize around any corner, at any time. The constant vigilance was exhausting, wearing her down both physically and emotionally.

When she reached her modest ranch house on the outskirts of town, she sat in the truck for several minutes, peering through the darkness at the trees swaying in the moonlight. What should have filled her with peace and relief—coming home after a long day—instead left a heavy weight of dread sitting in her chest like a stone. The familiar landscape seemed transformed, hostile. The trees that usually provided privacy and serenity now felt like they were pressing in on her, hiding unknown threats. The porch light flickered intermittently, casting ominous shadows that danced and shifted across the yard. Her home no longer felt like the sanctuary and refuge she'd hoped it would be when she'd first bought the property.

Shea wasn't used to being frightened, wasn't accustomed to backing down from anything. Throughout her law enforcement career, she'd faced danger head-on with confidence and determination. This psychological game of cat and mouse between her and Cletus left her nerves constantly on edge, her sleep disrupted, her ability to concentrate compromised. She felt like the relentless pressure was slowly wearing her down.

She opened the truck door and stepped out into the cool night air. "Come on, girl." She continuously glanced left and right as she approached the front porch, every shadow potentially concealing a threat. Her breath caught audibly at the faint crunch of dead leaves from somewhere around the side of the house. Was this it? Had Cletus finally decided to stop playing psychological games and make his move? Had he waited for darkness to fall before attempting to catch her alone, tired, and vulnerable?

Her entire body tensed, every nerve ending suddenly hyperaware. For a terrifying moment, she was completely paralyzed, her survival instincts battling against the wave of terror that threatened to overwhelm her. She felt as if she'd been thrust back in time to that rented cabin on the other side of Misty Mountain, except this time she didn't have the comfort and support of her friends' presence. This time, she was entirely alone with her fear. Her breath came in short, sharp gasps as she fumbled desperately in her jacket pocket for the rescue inhaler she hadn't needed to use in weeks.

Heidi growled low and menacing, her hackles raised as she stared intently toward the source of the sound. The German shepherd's protective instincts were in full alert mode.

The footsteps—for that's definitely what they were—grew gradually fainter, fading into the underbrush that surrounded her property. Whoever had been there was moving away, at least for now. She forced herself to move despite her shaking legs and unlocked the front door with fingers that trembled so badly she could barely manage to get the key in the lock.

Inside, she immediately engaged the deadbolt and took two quick puffs from her inhaler, leaning against the door with her eyes closed. With her back pressed firmly against the solid wood, she waited for the frightening wheeze in her lungs to subside and her breathing to return to something approaching normal.

Bright headlights suddenly pierced the darkness outside, the beams squeezing through a narrow gap in the wooden blinds covering her front window. The sound of tires crunching on the gravel driveway made her heart skip a beat before she recognized the familiar rumble of Trevor's truck engine. She moved quickly to the peephole and peered out, exhaling with relief as she watched him exit his vehicle and stride purposefully toward the house.

She opened the door before he could knock, not wanting to seem too eager for the company but unable to hide her relief at having another person nearby. "What's up?" She forced her voice to remain light and casual, though she suspected he could see right through the act.

His sharp gaze searched her face with obvious concern, noting details she wished she could hide. "I should be asking you that question. Doris mentioned that you took off out of the parking lot like you were responding to a five-alarm emergency."

"Everything is fine." The words came out automatically, but her lips trembled slightly, betraying the lie.

"Shea…let me in." His tone was gentle but firm, leaving no room for argument.

With a heavy sigh of defeat, she stepped back to allow him entry. He bent down and retrieved the threatening note she hadn't even realized she'd dropped in her haste to get inside. His brow furrowed deeply as he read the brief message. "When did you get this?"

"It was tucked under my windshield wiper when I left the office." She wrapped her arms around herself, suddenly feeling cold despite the warmth of the house.

He glanced pointedly at the rescue inhaler still clutched in her hand. "You're asthmatic?"

"Allergy and stress-related. It's no big deal." She quickly shoved the inhaler back into her pocket, embarrassed by this visible sign of weakness.

"You're visibly shaken, Shea. Did something else happen beyond finding this note?" His voice was full of genuine concern.

She shook her head, though the gesture felt unconvincing even to her. "Nothing more than the usual nightmare. I'm being followed, watched, hunted like an animal. The thing is, there's no way Cletus could have been at the station when I left and then here at my house so quickly. He must have people working for him, a network of accomplices who are everywhere, watching my every move." She turned and headed toward the kitchen, needing something to do with her hands. "I'll make some coffee. We might as well be comfortable if we're going to discuss this."

He followed her but stopped in the kitchen doorway, his expression serious and determined. "I'm staying here tonight."

"What?" She whirled around to face him, nearly dropping the coffee canister she'd been reaching for.

"I'm. Staying. Here." His expression left no room for argument or negotiation. "You're not going to face this alone anymore. It's too dangerous, and I won't stand by and watch you get hurt because of some misguided sense of independence. It'll be much harder for Cletus or his hired thugs to get to you if you have someone watching your back."

"I prefer being alone," she said automatically, though even as the words left her mouth, she knew they weren't entirely true. Maybe that had been the case, but the horror of that weekend with her friends on the mountain still hovered over her head like a dark cloud, changing her in ways she was still trying to understand. "Besides, I have Heidi for protection." She turned back to the coffeepot and began measuring grounds with hands that still shook slightly.

"Short of you pointing a gun at my head and pulling the trigger, I'm not leaving." His voice was calm but resolute. "You have two bedrooms, right? If not, I'll be perfectly comfortable on the couch. I can pick up some clothes and personal items from my place in the morning. Tomorrow's my day off anyway, so I'll have time to see about installing some proper security equipment around here."

She narrowed her eyes, though there was more frustration than real anger in her expression. "You've got it all figured out, haven't you?"

"Yes." A muscle ticked in his jaw, the only sign of tension in his otherwise calm demeanor. "Why are you being so stubborn about accepting help? You'd do the exact same thing for me or any of the other deputies if our situation were reversed. I know you would without question."

"Hmmph." She made a noncommittal sound because she knew he was absolutely right. She would move heaven and earth to protect any of her deputies if they were in danger. So why was it so impossibly hard for her to accept the same consideration from others? She'd stood on the porch just minutes ago and trembled like a young sapling during a fierce windstorm, literally losing her breath from panic and fear. Terror had snuck into her life, setting up deep roots in all the empty, vulnerable places. If she didn't regain control of her emotions soon, she'd be useless when the time came to face the real danger head-on.

Planting her hands flat on the kitchen counter, she took a slow, deliberate breath through her nose, held it for a count of five, then released it slowly through her mouth. The breathing technique her therapist had taught her helped calm her racing pulse. "Okay. You can stay."

"Great. I've got a change of clothes and some other things in the truck."

"Why?" She turned to face him with curious eyes.

"Emergency preparedness. You never know when you'll get caught in a sudden downpour, or spill coffee on yourself, or need to stay somewhere overnight unexpectedly." He flashed that dimpled grin that never failed to make her stomach flutter, the tension finally leaving his face now that she'd agreed to let him stay. "I learned to always be prepared from my Boy Scout days."

He darted out the front door to retrieve his belongings, leaving her alone with her thoughts and her dog. "What have I gotten myself into, Heidi?" she asked the German shepherd, who was watching her with those intelligent brown eyes that seemed to understand everything. The man already did things to her insides that she didn't want to think about too carefully. How would she handle him living under the same roof, even temporarily? Sleeping in the room right next to hers? Using her shower and kitchen? The domestic intimacy of it all felt both comforting and terrifying.

She was definitely in trouble, and not just from Cletus Hodges.

~

When Doris had casually mentioned how fast Shea had peeled out of the parking lot earlier, Trevor hadn't thought twice about following his instincts and speeding off to find her. His gut had told him something was wrong, and experience had taught him to trust those feelings. Luckily, she'd gone straight home, which was the first place he'd thought to look. The demand to stay in her house overnight had also come without conscious planning or deliberation. Still, he knew it was absolutely the right decision. With the way things were escalating, it was far too dangerous for her to be alone and vulnerable.

He grabbed the well-packed duffel bag he always kept behind the seats of his truck—a habit left over from his days in Houston when emergencies could come at any hour—locked the vehicle securely, then rejoined her in the house. He set his bag on the kitchen table next to a stack of mail and case files. The rich aroma of freshly brewed coffee greeted him, along with something that smelled like homemade cake. "Mind if I grab a quick shower first? It's been a long day, and I feel like I'm carrying half the mountain on me."

Her eyes widened slightly, but she shook her head. "Of course. The coffee will keep warm. Your room is the last door on the right. There are clean towels in the linen closet."

He showered quickly in her spotlessly clean bathroom, enjoying the luxury of unlimited hot water and decent water pressure. After days of dealing with the ancient plumbing in his rental house, this felt like paradise. He donned a comfortable pair of cotton lounge pants and a clean T-shirt, then returned to the kitchen feeling more human.

It wasn't until he saw the shocked expression on her face that he realized he'd forgotten to put on the shirt and was standing there shirtless. "Oh. I'll…uh, be right back to grab a shirt."

"No need." Her voice came out slightly higher than usual, and she cleared her throat. "I've seen a man without his shirt on before." She handed him a steaming cup of coffee and a generous slice of what looked like homemade pound cake. "The cake is from the freezer, but it should be thawed by now."

"I'm not picky when it comes to homemade cake." He settled into one of her kitchen chairs, noting how cozy and lived-in her home felt compared to his sterile rental.

She leaned against the kitchen island, her gaze inadvertently drawn to his chest before she caught herself staring. "How did you get those scars?"

He glanced down at the five distinct stab wounds dotting his torso—pale, raised marks that had faded over the years but would never completely disappear. "Knife attack."

"On duty?" She sat across from him at the small table, her expression serious. "I read through your personnel file when you were hired, but it didn't mention you being injured in the line of duty."

He stared at the ceiling for a long moment, gathering his thoughts and deciding how much to reveal. Then he focused on the cup of hot coffee in front of him, using it as an anchor. "You're aware from my background check that my brother Troy is a convicted serial killer?"

She nodded, her expression carefully neutral.

"I was his very first victim. His practice run, you might say."

"But you're still alive." Her voice was soft,

encouraging him to continue.

"I shouldn't be. By all rights, I should have died that night." He took a steadying sip of coffee. "He needed someone to test his methods on, to work out the kinks in his technique, so he decided to attack me when I was fifteen years old. He was eighteen, legally an adult, which made prosecution easier once they finally caught him." His gaze locked with hers, noting the compassion and understanding in her eyes. "You're not the only one who knows what it's like to be hunted by someone who wants you dead. He took me out to a remote area in the woods, gave me exactly a five-minute head start, then came after me with a hunting knife. I managed to stay ahead of him for most of the night, but he eventually caught up. I lay bleeding in those woods for hours before a deer hunter found me the next morning."

"I'm so sorry, Trevor." She reached across the table and gave his hand a gentle squeeze, her touch warm and comforting. "We both bear the scars from our experiences, don't we? Both physical and emotional reminders. The difference is, my attackers were strangers who chose me at random. Yours was family, someone who was supposed to love and protect you. Your parents must have been horrified."

"It destroyed their marriage and tore our family apart." He pressed his back against the chair, the memories still painful even after all these years. "They stayed together for appearances' sake, but they became like two strangers living under the same roof. Dad started drinking heavily to cope with the guilt and shame. Mom became emotionally numb, like a zombie going through the motions of life. They blamed themselves, blamed each other, blamed me for surviving when maybe I should have died."

He paused, studying her face. "My turn to ask why all the personal questions?"

"Just making conversation. Getting to know my deputy sheriff better." She gave him a ghost of a smile that didn't quite reach her eyes.

What would it be like to see a full, genuine smile transform her beautiful face? To see the persistent shadows flee from those amazing eyes that seemed to shift from blue to green and every shade in between, depending on her mood and the light?

She fell into contemplative silence, sipping her coffee and staring toward the window covered with wooden blinds. Outside, the wind had picked up, causing tree branches to scrape against the house with soft scratching sounds. After several minutes, she spoke again, her voice quiet and thoughtful. "Thank you for trusting me with what happened to you. I know it couldn't have been easy to share."

"It's only fair, considering what happened to you was plastered across every newspaper in Arkansas for weeks." He managed a rueful chuckle. "Makes us even, I suppose. Both survivors of attempted murder."

"Makes us more alike than I initially thought." She

stood and carried her empty cup to the sink, rinsing it carefully. "Good night, Trevor. Morning will come entirely too early."

Since the digital clock on the microwave showed nearly one in the morning, it would come earlier than either of them would prefer. "Good night, Shea. Sleep well."

With Heidi padding faithfully at her side, she headed down the narrow hallway toward her bedroom. Trevor finished his coffee and the excellent pound cake, then carefully placed both his cup and hers in the dishwasher. Before heading to the guest room himself, he methodically checked every door and window in the house, peering outside through gaps in the blinds for any sign of movement or surveillance. If Cletus or his accomplices had been watching the house earlier, they weren't visible now.

The moon shimmered like liquid silver on the surface of the small pond behind her house, creating a peaceful scene that belied the danger lurking in the shadows. Maybe, if he had time after installing security cameras and alarms later, he'd try a bit of fishing in that pond. Even if he didn't catch anything worthwhile, the quiet activity would at least help clear his head and relieve some of the stress.

He woke the next morning to the heavenly sounds and smells of bacon sizzling in a cast-iron skillet and fresh coffee brewing. The domestic normalcy of it was a pleasant change from his usual routine of grabbing something quick and unhealthy from a fast-food restaurant on his way to work. "I could get used to this kind of treatment," he said, entering the kitchen and stretching the kinks out of his back.

"Well, don't get too comfortable." Shea waved a spatula in his direction with mock sternness, though he caught the hint of a smile tugging at the corners of her mouth. "I like living alone and keeping my own schedule."

"Come on, I was no trouble at all last night. You probably barely knew I was here." In truth, he'd been hyperaware of her sleeping just on the other side of the thin wall, listening to every sound and wondering if she was having nightmares about her ordeal. Sleep hadn't come easily for either of them, he suspected.

"Sit down and eat. Breakfast is ready, and then I need to get to the office." She set a plate of perfectly cooked over-easy eggs, crispy bacon, and buttered toast in front of him.

"Do you ever take a day off? Even workaholics need to rest occasionally."

She poured herself a cup of coffee and leaned against the counter. "I'll take a few days off once Cletus is safely locked up—him and whoever he has working for him. Maybe I'll drive to California and spend some time at the beach, or head to Florida for some sun and relaxation. I don't have to decide right now."

He found himself hoping she might ask him to tag along on whatever vacation she chose, but he quickly shoved that inappropriate desire away. They were colleagues working together during a crisis, nothing more. She was his boss, his sheriff. They were together temporarily for safety reasons, not because they were developing any kind of romantic relationship. They were barely even friends, by her own admission.

After wolfing down her breakfast and feeding Heidi, Shea rushed toward the front door with her usual efficient energy, the German shepherd close at her heels. "Make yourself at home," she called over her shoulder. "I'll get an extra key made when I'm in town later. Let me know what all your security improvements will cost. I'd been planning to upgrade the security around here anyway, but I just haven't gotten around to it with everything else going on."

Once she'd left in a cloud of gravel dust, he walked the entire perimeter of her property, studying the angles and sight lines to determine the best placement for security cameras. His mind automatically catalogued additional improvements that needed to be made. He would install motion-activated alarms on both the front and back doors, add bright security lighting to the front porch and back deck, and maybe even set up some perimeter sensors in the woods surrounding the house.

After making a detailed list and sketching a rough diagram, he headed back to his rented house to pack a proper suitcase with enough clothes and personal items for an extended stay. Then he drove to the hardware store to purchase everything he'd need to turn Shea's home into a fortress.

He would do everything in his power to keep her safe from Cletus Hodges and his network of supporters.

He could only hope it would be enough when the real confrontation finally came.

Chapter Eight

"**Sheriff,**" **Doris called** out as Shea entered the building, her voice carrying a note of barely contained frustration. The morning sun streamed through the windows, casting long shadows across the worn linoleum floor of the sheriff's department. "We've got a whole lot of complaints this morning." She handed Shea a thick stack of pink message slips, shaking her head with obvious displeasure. "Stolen garden gnomes from Mrs. Peterson's yard, graffiti spray-painted on the side wall of the general store, and someone keeps breaking into Lucy's diner and stealing whole pies right out of the display case."

The distractions had started again with a vengeance, just as Shea had predicted they would. The brief respite had been nothing more than Cletus regrouping and planning his next wave of psychological warfare. "Thanks, Doris." Shea flipped through the messages on her way to the conference room for the daily morning briefing, noting the increasing creativity and boldness of the crimes. She tossed the stack of complaints onto the scarred wooden table with more force than necessary. "Everyone grab a couple. We're dividing these up."

The assembled deputies looked at the pile with expressions ranging from resignation to outright annoyance. They'd all been hoping the quiet period would last longer.

Bill Butler frowned, his weathered face creasing with concern. "You aren't going to personally handle any of these calls?"

"Nope." Shea settled into the chair at the head of the table, her posture radiating determination. "I'm going to focus exclusively on finding and apprehending Cletus Hodges. The man is hiding somewhere right under our noses, probably laughing at us, and I'm getting tired of his surprise visits and psychological games. I'll have my radio and phone with me at all times if someone absolutely insists on speaking with me directly about an urgent matter."

Heads nodded around the table with varying degrees of understanding and support. The deputies had all seen how the harassment was affecting their sheriff, and most of them respected her decision to prioritize the real threat.

"My first stop is going to be the Hodges place to verify that Mrs. Hodges followed my orders to leave town with her children. After that, I'll be back in the office working on strategy and reviewing all the intelligence we've gathered." She stood, ready to dismiss them. "Any questions before we get started?"

The same heads that had nodded moments before now shook in unison as the deputies stood, each grabbing a couple of complaint forms from the pile. They filed out with the weary resignation of people who knew they were being manipulated but had no choice but to play along.

Shea's phone rang almost immediately as she settled behind her desk, the shrill electronic tone cutting through the relative quiet of her office. She grabbed the receiver with perhaps more force than necessary. "Sheriff Callahan."

"How are you enjoying our little game so far?" The caller chuckled with obvious satisfaction, his voice carrying the distinctive accent and cadence she'd come to associate with the Hodges family. Cletus. "This is so much better than the crude approach my brothers favored, don't you think? A sophisticated game of cat and mouse between two intelligent adversaries."

She leaned back in her chair, trying to project calm she didn't feel. "Why not meet me face-to-face like a man and end all this childish nonsense?"

"And miss out on all the fun we're having? Tsk tsk, Sheriff." His tone was mockingly disappointed. "The game ends when I decide it ends, not a moment before. From here on out, things are going to start getting very interesting for you. Having that deputy staying at your place won't help you when the time comes."

How did he know about Trevor staying at her house? The thought that he'd been watching them so closely made her skin crawl. "I won the game against your brothers, Cletus, and I'll win against you too."

"Ah, but I'm considerably smarter than Darryl ever was. He grew careless, overconfident. Made too many mistakes." His voice hardened with genuine anger. "Besides, you have to pay for killing Bruce and destroying our family business. What are we supposed to do with that hunting cabin now? No one will rent it after you exposed our operations to the whole world."

"You're completely insane if you think what your family was doing was legitimate business."

He drew in his breath with a sharp hiss that sounded almost snake-like. "We're all entitled to our own opinions, my dear Sheriff. The difference is, mine is the only one that matters. Until we meet again." The line went dead with a harsh click.

Before she could even process the call fully, the phone rang again. She snatched it up, her nerves already frayed. "What?"

"Sheriff Callahan? This is Mayor Ferguson." The man's voice was carefully diplomatic, but she could hear the underlying tension. "The citizens of Misty Hollow have formally requested an emergency town meeting for tonight. We're hoping you can attend to address their concerns. It will be held at seven p.m.

sharp in the main assembly room at City Hall."

"My apologies for the brusque greeting, Mayor. I've been receiving some disturbing prank calls this morning." She pinched the bridge of her nose between thumb and forefinger, trying to ward off the tension headache that was building behind her eyes. "I'll be there tonight."

"Very good, Sheriff. And don't worry too much about the meeting. You're not being led to an execution." He chuckled nervously. "I'm still relatively new to my position, just as you are to yours. The people will come around once they understand the situation better. See you tonight."

The phone rang a third time before she could even set it down properly. "Sheriff Callahan speaking."

"Shea? You sound stressed. Everything okay?" Trevor's familiar voice carried genuine concern, and she felt some of the tension leave her shoulders at the sound.

"Just fine. Busy morning. What's the status on your project?"

"Security cameras are fully installed and operational. The motion sensors are active, and I've tested all the connections. How about I pick you up for lunch? You sound like you could use a break from whatever's going on there."

She glanced at the clock on her office wall, surprised at how quickly the morning had disappeared. Time seemed to move differently when she was under this much stress. "That sounds wonderful, actually."

"Great. I'm already parked outside." She could hear the grin in his voice, and despite everything, it made her smile slightly.

"Be right there." She patted Heidi affectionately and told her to stay put and guard the office, then grabbed her jacket and rushed out to meet Trevor.

The fresh air and autumn sunshine felt like a blessing after the claustrophobic atmosphere of the morning. As they walked the few blocks to the diner, Shea told Trevor about the town meeting scheduled for that evening. "I'm absolutely certain it's going to be nothing but a complaint session about my performance as sheriff."

"I'll be there to provide backup and moral support." He held open the door to the diner with a gallant flourish. "You're doing an excellent job under impossible circumstances, Shea. The townspeople will eventually realize that all this petty crime isn't your fault. Things could be significantly worse than stolen garden gnomes and missing pies."

True enough. Someone could already be dead. The fact that Cletus was limiting himself to harassment and property crimes was somewhat encouraging, though she suspected it was only a matter of time before he escalated to violence.

As they entered the diner, heads turned throughout the dining room, and openly hostile gazes followed their progress to their usual booth by the front window. The atmosphere was thick with suspicion and resentment. Doing her best to ignore the other customers and their whispered conversations, Shea settled into her seat and told Trevor about the disturbing phone call from Cletus.

"He knows you're staying at my house," she said quietly, leaning forward so her voice wouldn't carry. "I don't know how, but he's been watching us closely enough to know our personal arrangements. It's unsettling."

"That's concerning, but not entirely surprising given how organized he seems to be." Trevor's expression was grim. "I want this whole nightmare to be over as much as you do."

"That would be nice," she agreed as their server approached to take their order. The young woman's demeanor was noticeably cooler than usual, another sign of how public opinion was turning against the sheriff's department.

"Just a large garden salad for me," Shea said, her appetite diminished by stress and anxiety. "Italian dressing on the side, and the largest diet soda you have."

Trevor ordered a double mushroom Swiss burger with extra fries and onion rings. "Installing security equipment is hungry work," he explained with a wink. "The cameras won't keep out anyone who's really determined to get in, but at least you'll have advance warning of any approach to the house."

"That's all I'll need." Shea needed time to prepare for the inevitable confrontation with Cletus mentally. She couldn't allow the trauma and lingering effects of the mountain incident to interfere with her ability to fight for survival. In the end, she knew it would come down to a physical confrontation. That's how the Hodges family operated—they were predators who enjoyed the hunt and the kill. There would be no cowardly bullet to the back of the head. She'd killed Bruce in hand-to-hand combat after he'd underestimated her, and Cletus would want to prove he was stronger and more capable than his deceased brother.

"Is there a gym anywhere in town?" she asked, already knowing she needed to prepare physically as well as mentally.

"Yes, actually. There's an old barn about four streets over that's been converted into a decent fitness facility. Basic equipment, but functional. Why do you ask?"

"I need to keep up with my kickboxing training and general conditioning."

He narrowed his eyes with sudden understanding. "In preparation for facing Cletus?"

"Yes." She shrugged as if it were the most natural thing in the world. "A physical fight is inevitable, Trevor. I've accepted that reality."

"You won't be fighting him alone, Shea. I'll be right there with you."

"No, you absolutely will not." Her voice carried surprising steel. "I will not allow you to get between us when that confrontation comes. In Cletus's twisted view of the world, you're expendable. He'll kill you without hesitation just to get to me."

"And what am I in your view?" His question was quietly intense, loaded with meaning she wasn't ready to explore.

Her face heated at the unmistakable spark in his eyes and the implications of his question. "I will not let this family harm another friend. I've lost enough people already."

"Hmm." He sighed as their server arrived with their food, the moment of intensity broken by the mundane necessity of lunch. "Anything else you need me to work on at the house while I have the afternoon free?"

"No, you've done more than enough already. Go enjoy what's left of your day off. I'll be at the office until the meeting tonight, trying to make sense of all the intelligence we've gathered." An uncomfortable silence settled between them, heavy with unspoken words and unresolved tension. She'd said something to upset him, but for the life of her, she couldn't figure out exactly what.

~

The Misty Hollow town hall buzzed with barely contained tension and frustration when Shea entered that evening promptly at seven o'clock. The air was thick with angry murmurs and accusations floating around the packed room like storm clouds before a tornado. With Heidi walking calmly at her side, projecting an image of controlled confidence she didn't entirely feel, she marched down the center aisle and settled into a seat in the front row where everyone could see her.

Scattered complaints and criticisms about the recent crime wave drifted throughout the building like poison in the air. Shea kept her back straight and her head held high, projecting authority and competence even as doubt gnawed at her confidence.

Mayor Ferguson, looking nervous and slightly overwhelmed, took his place behind the wooden podium and called the meeting to order with several sharp raps of his gavel. The room immediately erupted into chaos despite his repeated requests for everyone to settle down and speak one at a time. Residents shouted over each other, their voices rising in volume and anger as frustration boiled over.

Shea took a deep, steady breath and stepped up to the podium, her movement commanding attention. "I'll take over, Mayor Ferguson."

Relief flooding across his pale face, the mayor gratefully relinquished the podium and sat in a chair to the side. "Good luck," he muttered under his breath. "You're going to need every bit of it."

Shea scanned the crowd until she located Trevor standing in the back of the room, his arms crossed and his expression supportive. Just seeing his familiar face made some of the tension in her shoulders ease slightly. She held up both hands in a gesture for silence, refusing to speak until the room quieted down. It would not serve her purpose to shout over the crowd like a carnival barker.

"We need real answers, not excuses," a middle-aged woman near the front shouted before the room had fully quieted. "First, someone breaks into my car and steals my purse. Then my husband's expensive tools disappear from our locked garage. What exactly are you planning to do about protecting law-abiding citizens?"

"Ma'am, did you file formal complaints about both incidents?"

"I'm doing that right now, in front of everyone!"

"I understand completely how frustrated and violated you must feel." Shea gripped the edges of the podium, her knuckles white with tension. "But I need you to file official complaints so one of my deputies can come to your property, document the crimes properly, and look for evidence that might lead us to the perpetrators."

"What about all the vandalism happening around town?" Another man stood up, his face red with anger. "My business was hit last night. I don't think this is just kids fooling around anymore. This looks like organized gang activity to me, and we don't want gangs establishing territory in our town."

Shouts of agreement arose from various parts of

the room, the crowd feeding off each other's fear and anger.

"Sheriff Callahan," a distinguished-looking older man in a suit stood up near the middle of the room. "What do you have to say about the apparent lack of arrests in these cases? The lack of accountability? The lack of visible progress? Don't you care about this community that voted you into office based on our former sheriff's recommendation?"

"Of course I care. I—" Her gaze swept over the increasingly hostile crowd, noting the angry faces and accusing stares. Despite all her hard work, all the long hours and personal sacrifice, this was how they saw her. Negligent. Incompetent. Shirking her responsibilities when they needed her most.

Trevor suddenly stood and strode purposefully down the center aisle, and to her surprise, former Sheriff Westbrook appeared at his side, the older man's presence immediately commanding respect. The room began to quiet, showing just how much reverence the townspeople still held for their longtime protector.

Shea swallowed past the enormous lump in her throat, wondering if she would ever earn even a fraction of the same respect and trust that Westbrook enjoyed.

Westbrook smiled encouragingly in her direction, then gently took her place at the podium. The room fell silent as if by magic, every person hanging on his words. "Folks, I want all of you to listen very carefully to what I'm about to say. Yes, I vouched for Sheriff

Callahan when I recommended her for this position. She's already done more for this town in the short time she's been here than most of you realize. She's prioritized public safety, addressed legitimate concerns promptly, and taken personal risks that most of you don't even know about. If you think baseless accusations and anonymous complaints will distract her from protecting Misty Hollow while there's a target painted on her back, you're sadly mistaken."

The silence was so complete you could hear a pin drop as Westbrook stepped back from the podium, yielding the floor back to Shea with a supportive nod.

"I won't stand here and deny that there's serious work to be done," Shea said, her voice stronger now. "But I want you all to know that I'm here for you, every single day. I took this job because I believe in this community and what it represents, and by God, I won't let it fall apart on my watch. We're always stronger when we work together as neighbors and friends, and that's exactly what I'm asking for here tonight."

The crowd murmured among themselves, the hostile tension beginning to dissipate like fog in sunlight. While not everyone looked thoroughly convinced, she could feel the tide of public opinion starting to turn slightly in her favor.

A large man in motorcycle leather and boots stood up near the back, his presence commanding immediate attention. "Sheriff Callahan, I want you to know that me and my club brothers have your back completely.

We'll help patrol this town day and night, keeping our eyes open for the troublemakers causing all this chaos. We've been there for this community and for Sheriff Westbrook for years, and we'll be there for you with the same loyalty." He turned to address the crowd directly, his voice carrying clear authority. "This is our town, our home. We work together like we always have, like our parents and grandparents did before us. Anyone not willing to do their part can pack up and move somewhere else. Now why don't you tell us what's really going on, Sheriff."

For the first time since taking the job, Shea didn't feel completely alone and isolated. She had allies, people willing to stand with her. She told the assembled townspeople about Cletus's direct threats and how he was orchestrating the crime wave from behind the scenes. "I have strong evidence that he's paying local young people to carry out his dirty work. So far, nothing severe has happened, but I don't believe that situation will continue indefinitely. I urge all of you to remain vigilant, patrol your own neighborhoods, and look out for one another. Don't hesitate to call the office if you have any concerns or if something doesn't feel right. I am your sheriff, and I will do everything in my power to make this a safe place to live and raise families."

The room erupted in genuine applause for the first time, the sound washing over her like a warm wave. Maybe, just maybe, she could earn their trust after all.

Mayor Ferguson resumed his place at the podium, looking relieved to move on to less contentious topics. "Now then, let's talk about more pleasant things, shall we? Like our annual fall festival that's coming up in two weeks."

Shea resumed her seat in the front row, Trevor settling beside her and giving her a playful bump with his shoulder that made her smile despite everything.

"You did great up there."

"Thanks to Westbrook and your friend in the leather jacket."

"That's Dave Morrison. His motorcycle club has helped law enforcement curb crime around here many times over the years. Having his public endorsement means a lot to these people." Trevor's voice carried genuine pride in her performance.

~

Hidden in the shadows outside the town hall, Cletus stepped back from the window where he'd been eavesdropping, rage rolling through him in powerful waves that made his hands shake with fury. He hadn't expected the town to rally around the sheriff so quickly and decisively. He also hadn't anticipated her being bold enough to speak his name publicly as the culprit behind the crimes, painting a target on his back.

His family had lived in these mountains for generations, long before most of these people had even heard of Misty Hollow. Now, thanks to that interfering woman, the whole town would be actively looking for him. His wife and children could never safely return home. The neighbors would turn into vigilantes, prepared to shoot him on sight without asking questions.

This would not do! These people needed to be reminded of the power and danger the Hodges family truly represented. What they were capable of doing to those who betrayed or opposed them. There were still men hiding in the remote mountain areas who remained loyal to the family name. Men who had escaped capture after the arrest of his brother. Men who were more than willing to play another, more deadly game if he asked them to.

It was time to escalate beyond petty harassment. Time to show Sheriff Callahan and the people of Misty Hollow what real fear looked like.

Chapter Nine

As the sun set over Main Street, painting the sky in brilliant shades of orange and pink, golden string lights flickered to life throughout the festival area. Wooden barricades that had blocked traffic all day were removed to let the growing crowd wander freely through vendor booths, colorful food carts, and inflatable entertainment structures for the children. Orange pumpkins and golden hay bales decorated every available sidewalk space, creating a picture-perfect autumn scene. A local country music band played enthusiastically from a makeshift stage constructed in front of the courthouse, their upbeat melodies drifting through the crisp evening air.

Shea smiled genuinely at the palpable happiness and sense of community celebration as she stood off to one side, positioning herself where she could observe the festivities while staying alert for potential threats. The positioning gave her clear sight lines down Main

Street in both directions while keeping her back to a solid brick wall.

The rich, mouthwatering aroma of caramel apples, warm spiced cider, and freshly baked pies filled the evening air, creating an almost intoxicating blend of scents that spoke of home and tradition. For a rare moment, she almost felt as if the town were truly at peace, as if the nightmare of the past weeks had been nothing more than a bad dream.

"Nice night for a festival." Trevor appeared at her side, materializing from the crowd with a soft pretzel in one hand and two cups of hot cider balanced in the other.

"So far," she replied cautiously, automatically scanning the crowd for anything out of place.

He chuckled and offered her one of the ciders. "Don't be such a pessimist and try to enjoy yourself for once." He tore off a piece of his pretzel and offered it to Heidi, who accepted the treat with dignified appreciation. "Eat some good food, buy some handmade trinkets, listen to the music...act like a normal person instead of a walking security system."

She frowned, though she accepted the warm cup gratefully. "I'm working, Trevor. This is my job."

"Doesn't mean you can't enjoy yourself while you're doing it." He gestured toward the crowd with his pretzel. "Between the sheriff's department, Dave Morrison and his motorcycle club, and about fifty other concerned citizens, there are plenty of eyes looking out for trouble tonight." He gave Heidi another bite, flashed Shea that dimpled grin that never failed to make her stomach flutter, then melted back into the crowd with a casual wave and a promise to check in with her later.

She shook her head in amazement. The man seemed as carefree as the hordes of children who were running and laughing through the streets, their faces painted like pumpkins and ghosts. How did he manage to maintain such a positive outlook after the traumatic childhood he'd survived? The abuse, the attempted murder by his brother—experiences like that would break most people.

Deciding she could learn something valuable from his attitude and approach to life, she kept her smile in place and began strolling casually through the crowd. Cheerful shouts of greeting from townspeople elicited friendly nods from her in return. After the successful town meeting and several days without any reported crimes, the citizens of Misty Hollow seemed to have genuinely warmed toward her. Maybe she really could make this job work after all.

The festival stretched the entire length of Main Street, with additional activities spilling over onto the side streets. Local artisans displayed handmade quilts, pottery, and carved wooden items. The volunteer fire department was selling barbecue dinners, while the high school booster club operated a dunking booth that proved surprisingly popular. Children darted between the booths with sticky fingers and chocolate-smeared faces, their laughter infectious.

She reached the end of Main Street, where the bouncy castles and a colorful row of carnival games had been erected in the large vacant lot that usually served as overflow parking for the courthouse. An old tobacco barn sat a few yards beyond the festivities, its weathered wooden walls strung with hundreds of twinkling holiday lights that shone through the numerous woodpecker holes and gaps between the boards. The effect was quite beautiful, creating patterns of light that danced across the surrounding area.

But it was something else about the barn that drew her attention—something that made her blood run cold.

Her steps faltered as she moved closer, pushing her way through a group of teenagers who were debating which carnival game offered the best prizes. Her stomach churned violently as she read the words that had been scrawled across the barn's side wall in bright red paint that looked ominously like blood in the artificial lighting: "Tick tock, Sheriff."

The message was fresh, the paint still glossy and wet in places. Whoever had written it had been here recently, maybe within the last hour. As she turned to leave and radio for backup, something metallic clicked ominously under her right foot. She glanced down and felt her heart stop as she saw her boot pressing on a small metal cylinder with wires protruding from both ends.

It took several terrifying seconds for her brain to

process what she was seeing. She was standing on an improvised explosive device—a bomb designed to detonate when pressure was released. "Stay, Heidi," she commanded, her voice remarkably steady despite the terror coursing through her veins.

The German shepherd whined anxiously, tilting her intelligent head as if sensing something was wrong with the situation.

Shea gave the stay command again, more firmly this time. She couldn't risk her beloved companion being hurt if the worst were to happen.

"Shea?" Trevor's voice called from somewhere behind her, probably wondering why she'd stopped moving.

She glanced over her shoulder as he approached, noting his relaxed posture and the half-eaten caramel apple in his hand. "Stay back!" she shouted, loud enough to startle nearby festivalgoers. "I'm standing on a bomb. It'll explode if I lift my foot."

For a split second, Trevor froze completely, his face going pale as the implications sank in. Then, instead of backing away to safety as any rational person would do, he dropped his snack and charged straight toward her. She watched in absolute horror as he flew through the air in a perfect football tackle, his shoulder connecting with her midsection and driving her sideways off the pressure plate.

The bomb exploded with a deafening roar just as they hit the ground hard, the blast sending chunks of dirt, metal fragments, and debris flying in all directions. The shock wave knocked several nearby people to the ground and shattered windows in the old barn.

She lay there gasping like a fish stranded on dry land, her ears ringing from the explosion and her lungs struggling to function. Trevor's solid weight pressed down on top of her, and she found herself staring up into eyes the color of a clear summer sky. His face was streaked with dirt, and there was a small cut on his forehead, but he was alive and conscious.

"Are you okay?" he asked, his voice sounding distant and muffled through the ringing in her ears.

"Can't...breathe," she managed to wheeze.

"What? Are you injured?" His gaze frantically scanned over her body, looking for apparent wounds or bleeding.

"You're squashing me," she gasped, shoving at his shoulders. "Get off."

He rolled away immediately, and she sucked in a grateful breath of smoke-tinged air. She did a quick mental inventory of all her limbs and major body parts. Everything seemed to be in working order, though she'd probably have spectacular bruises tomorrow. She called Heidi to her side and ran her hands thoroughly over the dog's body, checking for injuries. Relief flooded through her when she found nothing more serious than a few minor cuts from flying debris.

By now, a crowd of frightened onlookers had gathered in a rough circle around the blast site, keeping their distance but unable to resist their morbid curiosity. Mothers clutched their children protectively against their sides. Fathers wrapped their arms around their families as they scanned the area for additional threats. The festive atmosphere had been shattered in an instant, replaced by fear and uncertainty.

Shea struggled to her feet, brushing dirt and fragments of debris from her clothes. Her legs felt unsteady, but she forced herself to project an image of calm authority.

Her hand rested instinctively on the weapon at her hip as she addressed the crowd. "Go back to the festivities, folks. We're both fine, and the immediate danger has passed."

Was Cletus watching from somewhere in the crowd? Had he stuck around to witness his handiwork, to see whether he'd succeeded in blowing her to pieces? The thought that he might be standing among these innocent people, masquerading as a concerned citizen, made her skin crawl.

As the crowd gradually dispersed, many people casting worried glances back over their shoulders, she turned to face Trevor. "Are you completely insane? What were you thinking, pulling a reckless stunt like that?"

"It worked, didn't it?" He brushed dried grass and dirt off his jeans, wincing slightly as he discovered a scrape on his palm. "It seemed like the best option under the circumstances. Better to take the risk than to have some curious child wander over and trigger the device. A simple 'thank you' would be nice, Sheriff."

"Thank you." The words came out more emotional than she'd intended. "You saved my life, Trevor. There would have been no way to prevent my death if you hadn't acted so quickly." Her breath caught as the whole reality of how close she'd come to dying finally hit her. "Now let's find Cletus before he hurts anyone else."

As they made their way back toward the main festival area, the cheerful string lights no longer seemed welcoming and festive. Instead, the shadows they created between the booths and attractions lent a sinister, threatening atmosphere to what should have been a joyful community celebration. Shea's trained eyes swept continuously over the crowd, noting faces, postures, movements.

A middle-aged man in a cowboy hat leaned casually against a hay bale, flirting with a young woman holding a steaming mug of hot chocolate. A group of teenagers competed enthusiastically at a ring toss booth, their laughter carrying over the background music. A young couple held hands at the pumpkin-carving station, so absorbed in each other they seemed oblivious to the drama that had just unfolded. Somewhere out there, hidden among all these innocent people, was Cletus, watching with sadistic satisfaction as his plan unfolded.

"Do you think we should shut down the festival?"

Trevor asked quietly, his voice barely audible over the renewed chatter of the crowd.

"Not yet." Shea forced herself to appear relaxed and confident, though every nerve in her body was screaming danger. "If we panic and send everyone home, we give him exactly what he wants. Let's move through the crowd systematically and see if we can spot anything unusual or out of place. The man's arrogant and cocky—my instincts tell me he's here somewhere, watching and enjoying the chaos."

Her heart hammered against her ribs as she forced herself to stroll casually among the festivalgoers, projecting an image of calm authority while her sharp gaze caught every flicker of suspicious movement around her. Someone adjusting their hat could be signaling an accomplice. A man tying his daughter's loose scarf might be concealing his face. A vendor restocking his table of homemade jams could be positioning supplies for another attack.

Near the bobbing-for-apples station, where children squealed with delight as they dunked their faces into tubs of cold water, a man in a red plaid jacket stepped backward abruptly, colliding with Shea hard enough to knock her slightly off balance. He muttered what sounded like a genuine apology before quickly disappearing into the crowd, but the brief interaction set every nerve in her body on high alert. Was it truly an accident, or a deliberate ploy to get close enough to plant something on her?

She felt something crinkle in her jacket pocket that hadn't been there moments before. With trembling fingers, she slowly withdrew a folded slip of paper. The message, written in the same erratic handwriting she'd come to recognize, made her blood run cold: "That was a close call, wasn't it, Sheriff? Next time you won't be so lucky."

She whipped around frantically, trying to locate the man in the plaid jacket among the dozens of people moving through the area. He had to have been the one to slip the note into her pocket during their collision. How many other people at this festival were working for Cletus?

Trevor appeared at her side, having noticed her distress. He signaled subtly from across the small square, nodding toward the carnival games where a figure in a dark hoodie stood just beyond the edges of the bright lighting. The man's hands were shoved deep into his pockets, and his posture was rigid and alert, as though he was waiting for something specific to happen.

Another man, this one keeping his head down and face obscured, marched with obvious purpose down the sidewalk that bordered the festival area. Any one of the dozens of people around them could be Cletus himself, or one of the accomplices he'd recruited to carry out his campaign of terror.

She spoke quietly into her radio, requesting that all available deputies keep watch for the three suspicious individuals. One of them knew something important. One of them would make a move soon. The only questions were when and where the next attack would come.

~

Trevor did his best to keep Shea in sight while simultaneously watching for signs of trouble among the crowd. When she'd shouted that she was standing on a bomb, he'd acted purely on instinct, doing the only thing his training and protective instincts had suggested. Tackle her away from the device and hope they both survived the explosion. Fortunately, his desperate plan had worked, and they were both still among the living, though his ribs ached and his ears were still ringing.

Spotting the man in the dark hoodie again, he began following at a discrete distance, keeping several people between himself and his target. His gut—honed by years of law enforcement experience—told him something significant was about to happen. Something he needed to try to prevent or at least be prepared to respond to quickly.

But how could he effectively keep both Shea and the innocent festival attendees safe from a threat he couldn't clearly identify or locate? The enemy could be anyone, anywhere in this crowd. He strained to peer over the heads of the people around him, trying to track the suspicious figure's movements. The man in the hoodie had vanished again, melting into the crowd like smoke.

As he turned to head back toward Shea's last known position, a sharp crack split the air—the unmistakable sound of a high-powered rifle. The bullet ripped through the tail of his jacket as he pivoted, the fabric flapping dramatically. If he'd been standing just six inches to the left, or if he'd turned a split second later, the shot would have taken his head clean off.

Another shot rang out almost immediately, and a man who'd been smoking peacefully near the alley between the pharmacy and the hardware store collapsed to the pavement. Absolute pandemonium erupted instantly. Screams of terror cut through the night air as the panicked crowd surged desperately toward the festival's main entrance, trampling decorations and knocking over vendor tables in their frantic rush to escape.

Trevor drew his service weapon and spoke urgently into his radio, his voice barely audible over the chaos. "Shots fired near the pharmacy. At least one civilian down. Need all available backup immediately." Staying as low as possible while still maintaining mobility, he scanned the rooftops of the surrounding buildings, looking for any sign of the sniper's position.

"Where is he?" Shea appeared at his side, weapon drawn and eyes sharp with focus despite the chaos swirling around them.

"I can't pinpoint his location." Another shot rang out, this one striking an elderly man who'd been moving too slowly to escape with the crowd. Trevor rushed to help the wounded man to his feet. "Get inside the drugstore," he shouted, giving the man a firm push toward the building's entrance. "Take cover and stay down."

"There!" Shea pointed toward the flat roof of the First National Bank building. "I can see the rifle barrel."

The black metal barrel was just visible over the building's edge, angled down toward the street where people were still fleeing in terror. Trevor spotted a maintenance ladder mounted to the side of the building. "Follow me," he said, sprinting toward the alley with Shea close behind.

"Stay, Heidi." Shea gave the German shepherd a firm command, pointing toward a recessed doorway that would provide the dog with protection. "Guard."

They climbed the ladder quickly but carefully, knowing that one slip could be fatal. The metal rungs were slick with evening dew, and Trevor's hands were still shaking slightly from the adrenaline rush.

On the roof, a young man in a dark hoodie lay on his stomach behind a deer hunting rifle, his finger still poised over the trigger as he searched for new targets among the fleeing crowd below. He couldn't have been more than nineteen or twenty years old.

"Sheriff's department!" Shea announced, her weapon trained on the sniper. "Drop the weapon immediately or I will shoot you."

The young man turned toward them with a startled

expression, clearly not having expected to be discovered so quickly. The rifle clattered to the graveled rooftop as he raised his hands in surrender, though his face showed no signs of genuine remorse or fear.

"Shooting me won't stop him, you know," the boy said with disturbing calm. "There are plenty more of us waiting in line to take our turns at this game. This is just the beginning."

Trevor grabbed the young man roughly and yanked him to his feet, noting the gang-style tattoos visible on his neck and forearms. "At least you're off the streets for now. You'll be going to prison for a very long time, probably for the rest of your life."

"A price that's well worth paying for the cause."

"Why?" Shea's brow furrowed with genuine confusion and disgust. "What could possibly be so important that innocent people have to die? These are families, children, people who never did anything to hurt you."

"Revenge," the young man said with a chilling chuckle. "It's really that simple when you think about it. Our group believes in handing out its own form of justice. You killed one of ours, so now you have to pay the price. An eye for an eye."

"Shut up and save it for your lawyer," Trevor snapped, pulling plastic zip-tie restraints from his utility belt. "Good luck getting down that ladder with your hands secured."

The descent was slow and treacherous, with Trevor staying close behind the restrained sniper in case the young man decided to try something desperate. By the time they reached street level, the festival crowd had completely dispersed, and a patrol car was waiting with its emergency lights flashing.

"How many casualties?" Trevor asked Bill Butler, who was coordinating the response from street level.

"Three confirmed dead, several others trampled in the panic, but no serious injuries from the stampede." Bill glared at the young sniper with evident disgust, then turned his attention to Trevor. "Your jacket is torn. That bullet came pretty close."

"The first shot was meant for me. I turned to change direction at exactly the right moment." Trevor looked down at the hole in his jacket, realizing how close he'd come to joining the casualty count.

"Take this piece of garbage to the station for booking," Shea said, slapping the roof of the patrol car with her palm. "We'll finish processing the scene here and join you later for the interrogation."

When the squad car pulled away with its prisoner, Trevor and Shea walked solemnly to where three bodies lay on the sidewalk, covered respectfully with coats donated by festival volunteers. The man who'd been smoking, a middle-aged woman who still clutched a caramel apple in her death grip, and a teenage boy wearing a letter jacket from the local high school. Three innocent people targeted completely at random for no reason other than their proximity to the sheriff. The senseless loss made Trevor physically sick.

"I should have shut down the festival immediately after we found the bomb," Shea said, her shoulders slumping with the weight of responsibility and guilt. "This is my fault. These people died because of my decision."

"This is not your fault, Shea." Trevor pulled one of the coats higher over the teenager's face, his hands shaking with suppressed rage. "This is the fault of a madman and his army of brainwashed followers. All our focus and energy needs to be on stopping Cletus and his network before more innocent people die."

"I killed his brother in self-defense and helped put the other one behind bars where he belongs." She released a heavy, shuddering breath. "What clicks in a person's mind to make them think the hunting game on the mountain was somehow acceptable? I lost a dear friend in that nightmare. By Cletus's twisted logic, I have every right to seek revenge against him."

"That's exactly the difference between good people and evil ones," Trevor replied grimly, stepping aside as paramedics began the process of loading the covered bodies into a waiting ambulance. "Good people don't murder innocents to settle personal scores. Let's go see if we can get some useful information out of that kid."

"I'll follow you to the station in my truck." Shea whistled for Heidi to join her, and it was then that Trevor noticed the dark stain spreading across her right thigh.

"You're bleeding. You need medical attention immediately."

She glanced down at her leg with apparent surprise. "Didn't hurt at all until you mentioned it." She probed the wound gingerly with her fingers. "I think I landed on a piece of sharp wood when you tackled me off that bomb. I'll go to the emergency room once we finish questioning our suspect."

"At least let me bind it temporarily to stop the bleeding." He pulled a clean t-shirt from the emergency bag he kept behind the seat of his truck and wrapped it tightly around her thigh. "It's not perfect medical care, but it should help until you can get proper treatment."

They arrived at the sheriff's station to find a battered and bloodied Bill Butler being tended to by Doris, who was dabbing at his split lip with a damp cloth. He glanced up sheepishly when he saw them enter.

"Got ambushed right outside the building," he admitted with obvious embarrassment. "Soon as I got that punk out of the patrol car, five men in ski masks jumped me from behind those bushes. Threw some serious punches, knocked me around pretty good, then took off with the prisoner. I'm sorry, Sheriff. I won't stop looking until I find him and bring him back."

Who were these people willing to assault a law enforcement officer to free a cold-blooded killer? What kind of psychological hold did Cletus have over them that they'd risk their own freedom and safety? If they were brazen enough to attack a deputy right outside the sheriff's office, why hadn't they simply gone after Shea directly instead of playing these elaborate games?

Trevor rubbed his hands roughly over his face, feeling the weight of failure settling on his shoulders like a heavy blanket. People had died tonight, innocent people who'd just wanted to enjoy a simple community festival. He'd saved Shea from the bomb, but folks had died anyway, and the responsibility for their safety would ultimately fall back on her shoulders. The townspeople would blame her for what happened, regardless of the circumstances.

What if he failed to keep Shea alive when the final confrontation came? What if all his efforts weren't enough to protect the woman who'd somehow become the most important person in his world?

Chapter Ten

Fluorescent lights hummed overhead with their characteristic electrical buzz as Trevor and Shea sat across from each other in the sheriff's department break room. The harsh artificial lighting cast pale shadows under their eyes, highlighting the exhaustion that had become their constant companion. Tonight, they were both pulling the late shift, something that had become routine as they tried to stay ahead of Cletus and his network of followers.

The remains of their delivered supper sat scattered in the middle of the scarred wooden table—an empty pizza box with grease stains bleeding through the cardboard, two crushed soda cans, and crumpled napkins that spoke of a meal eaten more for necessity than pleasure. The pizza had been decent enough, but everything tasted like cardboard when you were operating on three hours of sleep and a steady diet of anxiety.

Three full days had passed since the festival massacre with no sign of Cletus or any of his accomplices. No threatening notes, no mysterious phone calls, no acts of vandalism or terrorism. The silence should have been reassuring, but instead it felt ominous, like the calm before a devastating storm. Shea grew more tired of the psychological games with each passing hour, and the uncertainty was wearing her down faster than any direct confrontation could have.

She sighed heavily and tossed her napkin on top of the empty pizza box with more force than necessary. "I'm supposed to be the one protecting people in this town, and I can't even keep myself safe from a hillbilly with a grudge. What kind of sheriff does that make me?"

Trevor leaned forward in his chair and placed his warm hand over hers, the simple gesture somehow grounding her in the moment. "You're human, Shea. That's exactly what makes you a good sheriff, not a weakness. People don't need some mythical hero who's invincible. They need someone who genuinely cares about their safety and well-being. Someone like you."

His words were like an anchor, rooting her in a brief moment of hope amidst the storm of self-doubt that had been raging in her mind. "Thank you for saying that. I needed to hear it."

He leaned back in his chair, crossing his arms over his chest, and stared at the water-stained ceiling tiles for several minutes before breaking the comfortable silence. "Did I ever tell you about my partner back in Houston?"

"No." She'd read in his personnel file that his previous partner had been killed in the line of duty, but the official reports had been frustratingly vague on details. "I saw the notation in your file, but there weren't many specifics."

He shifted uncomfortably in his seat, running his hand through his dark hair in a gesture she'd come to recognize as a sign of emotional distress. "His name was Johnny Martinez. Best guy I ever had the privilege of working with, and I mean that sincerely. We joined the Houston PD the same year, went through the academy together, and got paired up for patrol duties right from the start. He was the type of guy who always had your back, no matter what. Never hesitated to put himself in harm's way if it meant protecting his partner or innocent civilians."

He paused, his jaw working as he struggled with painful memories. "One night, we got called to what dispatch described as a routine domestic disturbance. Nothing unusual about the call—we'd handled dozens just like it. But when we arrived at the scene..." He cleared his throat roughly. "The guy was armed with a hunting rifle and holding his wife hostage. Johnny didn't make it out alive. I did."

"Survivor's guilt?" Her heart ached for the pain she could see written across his features.

"Maybe. Probably." He gave her a forced smile that

didn't reach his eyes. "I ask myself every day why I survived when he didn't."

"I'm so sorry you had to go through that, Trevor. Losing a partner is one of the worst things that can happen to a police officer."

"I should have had his back the same way he always had mine. We made the tactical decision to split up— Johnny went around to the back of the house while I created a diversion out front to keep the suspect's attention focused away from the hostage. We thought we were being smart, covering all the exits." His voice grew thick with emotion. "We didn't fool the perpetrator at all. He knew exactly what we were doing. He shot Johnny through an upstairs window with a clear view of the backyard, then turned the gun on his wife and finally himself."

The break room grew silent except for the persistent hum of the fluorescent lights and the distant sound of radio chatter from the dispatch area. The gravity of his words seemed to hang in the air like a physical presence. Finally, Shea spoke, her voice barely above a whisper. "I know exactly what that feels like. I couldn't keep one of my closest friends safe either."

She and Trevor had more in common than initially realized both of them carrying the weight of survivor's guilt, both questioning their worthiness to protect others. "It makes me afraid that I can't keep this town safe, that the people voting me in as sheriff was a horrible mistake that's going to get more innocent people killed."

"No mistake at all, Shea. From everything I know about Westbrook and his tenure here, he battled with the same emotions and self-doubt that you're experiencing. That's a big part of why this town loves and respects him so much. They could see that he genuinely cared that their safety kept him awake at night." Trevor's voice grew more confident. "They'll feel the same way about you once this nightmare is over. I know it with absolute certainty. They'll see your true worth once we capture Cletus and put an end to his reign of terror."

"Hmmm." The problem was that they had no solid leads, no concrete plan for finding and apprehending Cletus. He was out there somewhere in the mountains with a handful of devoted followers who were willing to kill on his command, and here she sat in the break room eating pizza as if she were on a dinner break from some ordinary job. How did that help anyone in Misty Hollow sleep safely at night?

She lunged to her feet with sudden determination. "I'm getting back to work. Cletus is somewhere close—I can feel it in my bones. Eventually, something will click when I'm studying that topographical map. There has to be something we're missing."

Trevor nodded and began cleaning up the remnants of their impromptu dinner. "I'll keep digging through the records and databases, too. We're bound to find something useful eventually. Maybe a property record we missed, or a connection we haven't considered."

Most of the time his relentless optimism didn't bother her—in fact, it was usually one of the things she appreciated most about working with him. Tonight, however, it irritated her like sandpaper on raw skin. The harsh reality was that they had a stronger statistical chance of not finding Cletus than they did of successfully locating him before he struck again. Sometimes working closely with a glass-half-full personality grated on her nerves, especially when she was running on caffeine and stubborn determination.

In her office, she settled behind her desk and stared intently at the satellite map of Misty Mountain displayed on her computer screen. She methodically placed an X over the cabin where her nightmare had begun months ago, and over each of the abandoned structures she and Trevor had already searched. That still left dozens of potential hiding places scattered across hundreds of square miles of rugged terrain. Finding someone who didn't want to be found was like looking for the proverbial needle in a haystack, especially when that someone knew the terrain better than his pursuers did.

She glanced down at Heidi, who was curled up in her usual spot beside the desk. "Any brilliant ideas, girl? Because I'm completely drawing a blank here."

The German shepherd looked up at her with intelligent dark eyes, then exhaled deeply and settled back down for another nap. Even her faithful companion seemed to understand the futility of their situation.

"Some help you are," Shea chuckled, though there was no real humor in it. She turned back to the computer screen and rubbed her burning eyes. What she needed was someone who knew every inch of Misty Mountain. This local guide was familiar with all the old mining operations, abandoned cabins, hunting camps, and natural caves that could provide shelter for someone trying to stay hidden.

She mentally ran through all the names of people she'd met since arriving in Misty Hollow, trying to identify someone who could serve as a knowledgeable guide. The problem was that she didn't know the long-term residents well enough yet to determine who might have the kind of intimate knowledge of the mountain that they needed. Most of her interactions had been professional rather than personal.

Frustrated with her lack of progress, Shea left her office and headed to the main bullpen area to see whether Trevor was having any better luck with his research. She found him hunched over his computer, surrounded by stacks of printed documents and legal files.

She explained her need for a local guide who knew the mountain intimately. "Know anyone who fits that description?"

"Not off the top of my head, but I haven't been here long enough to develop those kinds of connections." He looked up from his screen with tired eyes. "I'll send a text to Westbrook to see whether he can recommend someone reliable. In the meantime, take a look at this discovery."

Trevor tapped his computer monitor with evident excitement. She moved around behind his chair and peered over his shoulder, automatically catching a whiff of his masculine, woodsy cologne. The man always managed to smell appealing, even after a long day of police work.

"What exactly am I looking at?" she asked, trying to focus on the screen rather than his proximity.

"Tunnels and chambers in an old abandoned mine." He turned slightly in his chair, bringing his face close to hers with enthusiasm that made her pulse quicken. "It's about fifteen miles northeast of here, been closed for decades."

Her gaze fell involuntarily on his lips before she jerked her attention back to the computer screen with a mental reminder to stay professional. "You think Cletus might be holed up there?"

"It's possible." He shrugged. "Perfect place to hide if you don't want to be easily found. Multiple entrances and exits, natural shelter from the weather, and far enough from civilization that no one would accidentally stumble across you. I'd seriously consider hiding somewhere similar if I were trying to evade law enforcement. We could check out the mine first thing tomorrow morning, right after the daily briefing."

"Sounds like a solid plan." After making sure that any calls to the office would be automatically forwarded to her cell phone, Shea collected Heidi and locked up the building for the night.

When she arrived home, Trevor appeared from around the corner of the house, having completed his nightly security check. "Just making sure everything is exactly as we left it this morning. No signs of intrusion or surveillance."

"I appreciate your thoroughness." Although she checked the security camera feeds on her cell phone multiple times throughout each day, it never hurt to have someone physically inspect the perimeter. She unlocked the front door and punched her access code into the alarm keypad. Once Trevor was safely inside, she reset the security system.

"Goodnight. Morning will come entirely too early again." She paused at the entrance to the hallway. "You don't have to attend the morning briefing since you worked the night shift. I can meet you back here when it's over, and we'll head to the mine then. No sense in both of us being completely sleep-deprived."

"I'll be up and ready regardless." He unbuckled the leather belt that held his service weapon, flashlight, and radio as he headed toward his temporary bedroom. "I don't sleep well these days."

Shea did the same on her way to the master bedroom, then placed all her duty gear in the top drawer of her nightstand, where it would be within easy reach if needed during the night. She stripped down to her underwear, pulled an oversized sleep shirt over her head, and climbed gratefully under the warmth of her grandmother's hand-stitched quilt.

Despite her exhaustion, a small spark of hope flickered inside her chest as she settled into her pillow. Perhaps their luck would finally change in the morning, and they'd find concrete evidence of Cletus's hideout. Maybe this nightmare would finally come to an end.

~

Trevor stepped from the steaming shower the next morning to the heavenly aroma of pancakes and maple syrup wafting down the hallway. His stomach rumbled appreciatively despite the late dinner they'd shared the night before. He quickly buttoned his uniform shirt as he made his way to the kitchen, noting that Shea was already fully dressed and preparing what looked like a substantial breakfast.

"You're up early this morning," he observed, accepting the plate she handed him with genuine gratitude.

"Not particularly early for me. I need to be at the office in about an hour for the morning briefing." She gestured toward the stack of golden pancakes. "Since we'll be exploring that mine today, I thought you might need a hearty breakfast to sustain you. It could be a long day of hiking and searching."

"Thanks. You know the way to a man's heart." The words slipped out before he could stop them.

Pink color bloomed across her cheeks as she turned back to the stove, suddenly very busy with cleaning up. "Are you sure you want to get started so early today? It's supposed to be your day off, and you've been working way too many hours lately."

"I'm not much for lounging around doing nothing, especially not when there's important work to be done." He dug into his breakfast, marveling at the perfect fluffy texture of the pancakes. Everything Shea cooked seemed to turn out perfectly. "You're an excellent cook. These are restaurant quality."

"Cooking is one of my primary stress relievers," she admitted, settling into the chair across from him with her modest portion. "When I have time and energy, I usually spend an entire weekend cooking and freezing a month's worth of meals. Haven't been able to do that since this situation with Cletus started."

"I usually just order takeout or heat up something frozen from the grocery store." He stabbed another bite with his fork. "This kind of home cooking is a perk of staying here temporarily."

"Hopefully, you'll be able to get back to your normal life soon." Her tone was carefully neutral, but he thought he detected a note of something—regret, maybe?—in her voice.

Strange how the prospect of returning to his solitary routine didn't hold the appeal it once had. He'd grown to genuinely enjoy having someone to talk with over meals, someone to see first thing in the morning and last thing at night. His gaze fell on Heidi, who was watching them eat with patient hope. Maybe he should seriously consider getting a dog of his own when this was all over.

After they finished eating and cleaned up the kitchen together, they headed to the sheriff's office, where Shea efficiently doled out assignments and patrol routes for the other deputies. The meeting was brief and businesslike, with everyone understanding the urgency of the ongoing situation. Soon after, they climbed into Trevor's truck with Heidi and headed northeast toward the abandoned mine, following directions from an old geological survey map.

By the time they reached their destination, Trevor's phone showed it was just past ten in the morning. Based on what he'd seen in the online maps and satellite images, thoroughly searching the mine complex would likely take most of the day, assuming they didn't encounter any dangerous structural issues or cave-ins.

The weather had turned significantly colder overnight, with a sharp wind that bit at any exposed skin when they stepped from the relative warmth of the truck. Their boots crunched loudly over the carpet of dead leaves as they approached the mine entrance, the sound seeming unnaturally loud in the mountain silence.

A faded length of yellow crime scene tape fluttered forlornly from a nearby bush, and several wooden boards that had once been nailed across the mine's entrance now lay discarded and rotting to one side. Someone had been here recently and removed the barriers.

"What kind of crime happened here?" Shea asked, noting the remnants of the police tape.

"A kidnapping case from several years back, I think. Maybe a murder if you want to go back far enough in the records." Trevor studied the dark opening. "Kids used to like playing here until Westbrook put a stop to it for safety reasons. But it looks like people have been going inside again, judging by that wide-open entrance."

Trevor stopped at the threshold and stared into the yawning darkness that seemed to swallow their flashlight beams. The air inside hung heavy and damp, carrying the musty smell of mildew and decades of decay. He clicked on his powerful flashlight and tested the beam. "You okay with this? Some people don't do well in confined underground spaces."

Shea nodded firmly, though he noticed her hand unconsciously checked her weapon. "Let's do this. Cletus isn't going to catch himself."

The sound of water dripping echoed from somewhere deep in the mine's interior, a steady rhythm that seemed to emphasize the isolation and potential danger of their location. Trevor shined his light carefully, methodically scanning each corner and crevice of the carved-out entrance chamber. Ahead of them, a main tunnel disappeared into impenetrable darkness.

Shea stepped up beside him and added her flashlight beam to his. "Maybe we can see better with both lights working together."

The combined illumination did help somewhat, but as they moved farther into the abandoned mine, the darkness thickened, and their lights seemed less effective. Shea's breathing sounded harsh and slightly labored in the confined space, echoing off the rock walls. They stopped having unnecessary conversations, letting Heidi range ahead of them as their early warning system for potential dangers.

After what felt like an eternity of careful progress through the tunnel, they emerged into a larger chamber that had been carved out by mining equipment decades ago. This room showed unmistakable signs of recent human habitation. Fresh food wrappers were scattered across the floor, and a worn sleeping bag with visible patches had been rolled up in the corner of a small natural alcove. Most significantly, a crudely drawn map of Misty Hollow was pinned to the dirt wall with a rusty nail.

Trevor carefully pulled the hand-drawn map free and studied it by flashlight. Several key locations were circled in red ink: Shea's home address, the sheriff's office, and the town square where the sniper had killed innocent people during the festival. Cletus was planning additional attacks, and this map suggested he had specific targets in mind.

"Look at this," Shea said quietly, picking up something from the ground near the sleeping bag. She held out a grainy photograph that had been taken from a considerable distance with a telephoto lens. "It's me leaving the sheriff's office."

Trevor examined the surveillance photo, noting the details and the care with which it had been taken. Someone had drawn a crude bullseye directly across Shea's face with a red marker.

"Why doesn't he just make his move?" Shea paced the small chamber like a caged animal, her frustration finally boiling over. "He failed to blow me up at the festival, so why not come for me again directly? It's obvious from this surveillance that I'm not particularly difficult to get to or observe. Back in that rented cabin months ago, at least I knew exactly what my friends and I were up against. Darryl and his crew were brutal but straightforward with their attacks. I hate this psychological cat-and-mouse game that Cletus is playing."

"Let's call for a forensics team to come up here and properly process this scene, then seal the mine back up with proper barriers." Trevor stepped toward the entrance. "While we wait for them to arrive, we should search for other exits. I seriously doubt Cletus would choose to stay somewhere he couldn't escape if cornered by law enforcement."

He pulled out his cell phone to call the office, noting that he had only one bar of signal in the remote location. While he struggled to establish a clear connection, Shea wandered outside and began exploring the area around the mine entrance. To his alarm, she suddenly began climbing the rocky slope above the mine opening, moving as nimbly as a mountain goat despite the loose stones and treacherous footing. Heidi barked once and followed her up the incline.

Trevor's heart lodged firmly in his throat until Shea reappeared at the top of the rocky outcropping, waving down at him to indicate she'd found something significant.

"I found another way out," she called down to him.

He scrambled up the slope, loose rocks sliding dangerously from under his boots and threatening to send him tumbling back down. Grasping a sturdy young sapling for support, he managed to pull himself up the rest of the way to where she waited.

Shea parted the branches of a thick juniper bush to reveal a well-concealed opening. "This is his escape route." She pointed at a clear set of fresh footprints in the soft earth leading away from the hidden exit. "He must have seen us coming up the main road and fled through here. We probably missed him by minutes."

She let the branches fall back into place, her expression dark with frustration. "Cletus is always one step ahead of us, no matter what we do."

"We'll get him eventually," Trevor said, though the words sounded hollow even to him.

She spun around to face him, eyes flashing with anger and exhaustion. "Stop making promises you can't possibly keep, Trevor."

He opened his mouth to respond, then closed it again without speaking. He couldn't argue with her assessment—they might never catch Cletus. More innocent people might die while they chased shadows through the mountains. Either he or Shea could be killed before this nightmare ended.

"I'm sorry. You're right." He took a deep breath. "Let me rephrase that—we'll do our absolute best to get him, and we won't give up until we succeed or..."

"Or until it's too late and more people die because we weren't good enough." She slid down from the top of the mine opening and marched to his truck, then leaned against the tailgate with her arms crossed. "I'm heading home. I need some time to think."

Trevor nodded, understanding her need for space and time to process their latest failure. "I've got some errands to run before I head back to the house anyway."

His shoulders sagged under the accumulated weight of responsibility and the pressure of finding Cletus before more innocent people lost their lives. One of his planned errands was to dig deeper into public records and databases, searching for information about every known member of the extended Hodges family to identify any crucial details they might be missing. Another long night of research and investigation loomed ahead of him.

By the time the forensics team finally arrived from the nearby city of Langley in their specialized vehicle, the sun had already started its descent toward the western peaks of the mountain range, painting the sky in shades of orange and purple that would have been beautiful under different circumstances.

Chapter Eleven

Shea pulled onto the long dirt road that served as her driveway, the gravel crunching under her tires as she navigated the familiar path through the towering pine trees that formed a natural canopy overhead. When she reached the weathered barn that sat halfway between the main road and her house, she suddenly felt overwhelmed by exhaustion and frustration. She leaned her forehead against the steering wheel, closing her eyes for a moment as the weight of the day's failures pressed down on her shoulders.

She should not have snapped at Trevor back at the mine. None of this nightmare was his fault—he was doing everything humanly possible to help her catch Cletus and protect the town. Her anger and frustration were misdirected, born from her sense of inadequacy and the mounting pressure of knowing that people's lives depended on her ability to stop a madman.

She grabbed the bag of fast-food burgers from the

console, the greasy paper already growing cold in the evening air. "Come on, girl. I bought an extra patty just for you," she said to Heidi, forcing a smile despite her dark mood.

Her steps faltered abruptly, and her heart leaped into her throat at the sight of her front door hanging wide open, moving slightly in the evening breeze. She distinctly remembered locking it and setting the alarm system that morning before leaving for the office. She knew she had—it was part of her ingrained routine, especially given the current circumstances.

Through the open doorway, the thick, acrid odor of fresh spray paint drifted out into the night air, mingling with something else that made her stomach turn. The house sat in complete darkness, with only the pale moonlight filtering through the windows to provide any illumination.

She carefully set the bag of burgers on the porch railing and drew her service weapon, the familiar weight of it somehow comforting in her trembling hands. Using the toe of her boot, she pushed the door the rest of the way open while staying behind the frame for cover. "Clear the house, Heidi."

The German shepherd woofed once in acknowledgment and entered with her nose to the ground, immediately going into the search pattern they'd practiced countless times during training exercises. Shea remained in the doorway, weapon ready, as her faithful companion systematically moved from room to room.

What she could see of the living room made her stomach clench with rage. Sofa cushions had been thrown onto the floor and slashed open, their stuffing scattered like snow across the hardwood. Her grandmother's antique books had been knocked from their shelves and lay sprawled open with their pages torn. Through the dining room archway, she could see overturned chairs, several with broken legs, and her mother's china cabinet tipped over with shattered porcelain gleaming in the moonlight.

The destruction spoke of pure malicious anger rather than any search for valuables. This was personal, designed to hurt her emotionally as much as materially.

In her bedroom, clothes had been pulled from drawers and closets, scattered across the floor like confetti. Someone had taken a knife to her mattress, leaving deep gashes that exposed the springs underneath. The framed photographs on her dresser—images of her parents, her college friends, happier times—lay face-down in pieces of broken glass.

She moved down the hall to check Trevor's temporary room and found the same senseless destruction. While they'd been searching the abandoned mine for clues, Cletus or his accomplices had been here, violating her sanctuary and destroying everything that made the house feel like home.

Heidi returned with her tail wagging, the signal that no intruders were currently hiding anywhere in the house. Shea holstered her weapon and quickly snapped photographs of the damage with her phone, documenting the scene for evidence before stepping back outside to retrieve her forgotten dinner.

She scanned the open lawn stretching from the house to the tree line, looking for any sign of movement or surveillance. Nothing stirred except the soft evening breeze that rustled through the pine needles overhead. She'd missed the intruders again, and she fought back the urge to shout a challenge into the darkness in case Cletus was still watching from the shadows.

How had someone managed to get inside despite all of Trevor's security improvements? She glanced at the camera mounted under the porch overhang and frowned. The red power light, which should have been glowing steadily, was dark. She pulled the flashlight from her duty belt and clicked it on as she made her way around the corner of the house with Heidi padding silently beside her.

Several electrical wires hung loose from the main power box on the side of the house, clearly cut with wire cutters or a similar tool. That explained the lack of electricity throughout the house. Still, the cameras should have recorded whoever had tampered with the power supply, assuming they'd acted quickly enough after cutting the lines. She hoped the laptop battery in her office hadn't completely died during the power outage.

She was heading back toward the front door when

a loud thud sounded from somewhere behind the house. She spun toward the noise, her hand automatically flying to the gun at her hip as adrenaline flooded her system.

Heidi's hackles rose immediately, and the dog growled low in her throat while staring intently toward the source of the sound. Whatever had made that noise was large enough to concern her well-trained companion.

Shea quickly clicked off her flashlight, though she realized she'd probably already given away her position to anyone watching. Should she stay inside the house and risk being trapped in the confined space, or step outside where she'd be exposed but have room to maneuver? Was she dealing with a single intruder or multiple attackers?

She pulled her cell phone from her pocket with trembling fingers and sent Trevor a quick text: "Intruder at house. Need backup."

Another sound broke the tense silence—the distinctive creak of the front porch boards groaning under weight that was too heavy to be a small animal. The old wooden planks had a particular sound when someone stepped on them, and she'd heard it countless times over the months she'd lived here.

Then came a low whistle, soft but deliberate. A signal between accomplices.

Shea's stomach turned to ice as the implications sank in. She wasn't dealing with a single person—

multiple intruders were surrounding her home, coordinating their movements. She tightened her grip on her weapon and tried to steady her breathing for whatever confrontation was coming.

Moving as quietly as possible, she placed a calming hand on Heidi's head and slowly backed away from the office until she reached the kitchen. This central location gave her clear lines of sight to both the front door and the back exit, providing two potential escape routes if she needed them. She stepped into the small alcove that housed her pantry, using the shadows for concealment while she waited to see what the intruders would do next.

The sudden sound of tires crunching on gravel outside made her heart race. Heavy footsteps thundered across the porch and around the house as the intruders fled at the approach of a vehicle.

"Shea?" Trevor's familiar voice called out as he entered through the kitchen door. "Are you all right?"

"I'm okay," she replied, stepping out of her hiding place. "The power's been cut. I haven't had a chance to check the security camera footage yet, but someone was here." She holstered her weapon, noting how her hands were still shaking slightly. "Thank you for coming so quickly."

"I was already on my way back when I got your text message." His concerned gaze searched her face in the dim moonlight. "Did you see anyone, or just hear them?"

"The front door was standing open when I arrived home. I sent Heidi to clear the house—it's been thoroughly ransacked. I had just gone into my office to check the camera recordings when I heard someone moving around outside." She cleared her throat, trying to stop her voice from trembling with residual fear and anger. "I took cover and prepared to wait for them to come inside, but then you arrived and scared them off."

Trevor moved to the window and peered through the blinds into the darkness. "I don't see anyone out there now. Let's check that security footage while we still can."

The laptop computer in her office had little battery power remaining, but it stayed operational long enough for them to review the recorded surveillance footage. The grainy black-and-white images clearly showed three young men dressed in dark clothing entering through the front door after easily picking the lock. They immediately began throwing furniture around and destroying everything they could reach, laughing and joking as if they were at a party rather than committing serious crimes.

After several minutes of systematic destruction, one of the intruders went outside while the other two continued their vandalism inside. Moments later, the house lights went out as the electrical system was sabotaged.

"I don't recognize any of them. Do you?" She glanced at Trevor, hoping his longer experience in law enforcement might help identify the perpetrators.

"No, but they all look pretty young, probably teenagers or early twenties." He captured still images of their faces from the video recording. "I'll check with the high school administration tomorrow and see if anyone recognizes them. Look at their behavior—they're laughing and having a good time. These are kids who were hired to create chaos and destruction. Just another part of Cletus's psychological game."

A game that could easily get innocent people killed. "If they had tried to come inside while I was here waiting for them, I would have been forced to shoot one or more of them." The thought made her stomach turn. Even justified, she couldn't bear the idea of shooting someone so young. "These are probably just misguided kids who don't understand what they've gotten themselves into."

~

Harsh floodlights and the low rumble of multiple large engines suddenly filled the night air, drawing Trevor to the front window. He carefully peered through the wooden blinds, his heart sinking at what he saw outside. Three massive pickup trucks, the type equipped with hunting spotlights and light bars, had parked in a semicircle in front of the house, their powerful beams turning night into day.

"It's the cabin on the mountain all over again." Shea's eyes widened with recognition and barely controlled panic as she joined him at the window.

"You aren't alone this time," Trevor said firmly, reaching for her hand and giving it what he hoped was a reassuring squeeze. "I'm calling for backup immediately." He pulled out his phone and began dialing with urgent fingers.

"I wasn't alone back then either," she replied quietly, her voice carrying the weight of painful memories.

"No, but I'm trained law enforcement, not a civilian. Things will have a very different outcome this time." He turned his attention to the phone as it connected. "Doris, this is Trevor. The sheriff and I are trapped at her house, surrounded by at least six armed men in pickup trucks. We need all available backup units here immediately...I don't care if they're officially off duty! Get everyone here now and contact the state police for additional assistance."

"There you go making promises you might not be able to keep again," Shea said, though there was no real criticism in her voice as she checked the ammunition in her service weapon.

"Don't worry about backup—they'll come. The entire department would walk through fire for you." He paused. "Sorry about the promise thing. Old habit from trying to reassure victims."

He peered through the blinds again, taking note of new details about their situation. "I can see at least six men out there wearing hunting camouflage and flannel shirts, all carrying what look like deer rifles. No sign of

Cletus himself, but he's got to be out there somewhere directing this operation."

Loud country music suddenly blared from the truck radios, creating a surreal party atmosphere. The sound of beer cans being opened punctuated raucous laughter and crude taunts directed at the house.

"I'm going to check the back of the house," Shea announced, moving swiftly through the kitchen toward the rear exit.

She returned within moments, her expression grim. "Two more men positioned behind the house, both armed. We're surrounded with no way out."

Trevor studied her face, noting the controlled fear mixed with determination. "How did you manage to escape from the cabin on the mountain?"

"The rental cabin was built on stilts and hung out over a cliff edge. There was a large tree growing next to the back deck that I was able to climb down, though I had to booby-trap it with broken glass from the sliding door to prevent them from following." She rolled up her sleeve to show him a pale scar on her forearm. "After that, it came down to hand-to-hand fighting for survival. But we don't have any trees to climb down here, Trevor. We're stuck on level ground with no upper floor to retreat to and no natural advantages."

"What about your storm shelter? I remember you mentioning it before."

"It's only about twenty yards from the house, but we'd have to cross open ground to reach it. They'd pick us off before we made it halfway there."

"Let's think through our options carefully." He stepped away from the window, his mind racing through tactical possibilities. "So far, all they've done is surround us and try to intimidate us with lights and noise."

Just then, the front window exploded inward in a shower of glass and wooden frame fragments as a rifle bullet shattered it completely.

"Okay, they're escalating beyond intimidation tactics now," Trevor muttered, pulling Shea down below the window line.

Shea began pacing frantically between the living room and dining room areas, her usually smooth brow furrowed in deep concentration. "One of us might be able to squeeze through the master bathroom window and take out the two men positioned behind the house. Then the other person could exit through the back door, and we could try to reach the woods for cover."

"I'd never fit through that bathroom window—it's barely big enough for you. And I'm not letting you go out there alone to face armed men in the dark."

"It wouldn't be the first time I've had to do something like this, Trevor." Her voice carried steely resolve. "All this waiting around is just going to make me more anxious and give them time to organize a coordinated assault. I'm the sheriff of this county, and you're technically required to follow my direct orders."

"Actually, no, I don't have to follow your orders

right now." He managed a grim smile. "I'm officially off duty, remember? We could try a different approach—start shooting back and pick them off one by one. After a couple of their friends fall, the others might decide this isn't worth the risk and flee."

"Or they could all start shooting at the house simultaneously and turn it into Swiss cheese." She hurried down the hallway toward her bedroom. "I have a hunting rifle in my bedroom closet. I'll be right back."

She returned moments later, carrying a .243-caliber rifle with a break-down barrel action. "It's designed for deer hunting rather than self-defense, but I'm an excellent shot with it. Won plenty of target competitions back in college."

"Good. Start by shooting out their floodlights and headlights. Take away their night vision advantage."

Shea knelt beside the shattered front window, carefully avoiding the broken glass, and slowly raised the rifle to her shoulder. The armed men outside scattered like startled deer when her first shot rang out, extinguishing one of the powerful spotlights in a shower of sparks. She worked the bolt action smoothly, reloading and firing again and again until all the floodlights and vehicle headlights were nothing but darkened, useless shells.

"Take cover!" she shouted.

A tremendous barrage of return gunfire immediately erupted from multiple directions, peppering the cabin walls with rifle bullets and creating a deadly crossfire pattern. The two of them crawled rapidly down the hallway on their hands and knees while wood splinters and plaster dust rained down around them. Heidi yelped in terror and bolted for the relative safety of the master bedroom.

"I have to check on her and make sure she wasn't hit," Shea said, following her beloved companion down the hall.

Trevor took up position with the hunting rifle, pressing his back against the hallway linen closet for cover while keeping the weapon aimed at the front door. "Close all the bedroom doors when you come out. We need to limit their angles of fire if they try to rush the house."

Shea emerged from the bedroom a few minutes later with Heidi close beside her, carefully pulling the door shut behind them. She systematically closed the doors to the other bedrooms and the bathroom as well, creating additional barriers and concealment. "Now we wait and see what they do next."

"Now we wait," Trevor agreed, though his voice betrayed his doubts about their chances.

Her shoulder pressed warm against his in the narrow hallway. "I'm glad to have you here with me, Trevor. I don't think I could face this alone again."

"Me too. I can't imagine being anywhere else right now." He managed a brief smile before it faded as quickly as it had appeared. He didn't hold out much hope for surviving the night if backup didn't arrive soon, but at least they were together.

"It looks like Cletus is doing his absolute best to recreate the night his brother Bruce died. There's no way he would miss the opportunity to witness my capture or death firsthand. He's out there somewhere close by, watching and enjoying every minute of this."

"I seriously doubt those men have orders to kill you, Shea." Trevor rested his head against the wall behind him, trying to think through Cletus's likely strategy. "He'll want that honor for himself as revenge for Bruce's death. No, they'll probably focus their fire on me to eliminate the threat I represent, then try to take you alive to deliver to their boss."

"Here's a promise I can keep," Shea said, bumping his shoulder with hers. "I promise not to leave you behind, no matter what happens. We stick together through this, whatever the outcome."

"I like that promise a lot better than my usual optimistic nonsense."

Another devastating barrage of bullets sent him instinctively shielding Shea with his own body while she did the same for Heidi, who was trembling against them. "I guess they've decided to shoot their way in rather than try to rush us," he observed when the gunfire finally stopped. "Blow enough holes in the walls and doors, and they can just walk in without resistance."

"I hate sitting here passively waiting for them to breach the house," Shea said, keeping her arms protectively around her terrified dog. "Every instinct I have is telling me we need to take the fight to them somehow."

"I'm completely open to tactical suggestions. What do you have in mind?"

~

Cletus cursed creatively as the return gunfire from the house sent his hired men scrambling for cover behind their vehicles like scared rabbits. He quickly punched numbers into his cell phone with angry, impatient fingers. "Get back to your positions immediately! I don't care if she's shooting back—that's exactly what we expected. Get me that sheriff by any means necessary!"

"What about the deputy?" came the nervous reply from one of his men.

"He's of no use to me whatsoever. My dispute is with the woman who killed my brother." He shoved the phone back into his jacket pocket and lifted the military-grade binoculars to his eyes again, scanning the darkened house for signs of movement.

The young fools he'd hired to ransack the sheriff's house had performed their assigned task adequately; now it was time for their fathers and older brothers to prove their worth to the Hodges family name. The family reputation used to mean something significant around Misty Hollow, commanded respect and fear in equal measure. He fully intended to mean something again, regardless of the cost.

No woman, sheriff's badge or not, was going to destroy everything his family had built over generations in these mountains. What kind of man would he be if he didn't seek proper justice for Bruce's violent death and Darryl's imprisonment? The natural order of things demanded retribution.

He'd seriously contemplated joining his men in the direct assault on the house, but common sense had prevailed. Accidents happened all too easily in firefights, and it was only a matter of time before law enforcement backup arrived to complicate the situation. He couldn't risk being caught in the crossfire before accomplishing his primary objective.

Cletus shivered in the growing chill of the mountain night air, pulling his jacket tighter around his shoulders. Now that his temporary hideout in the abandoned mine had been discovered and would undoubtedly be under surveillance, he needed to find another secure place to stay while he planned his next moves.

He made another call to one of the men currently positioned outside the sheriff's house. "I'm going to need to stay with you and your family for a while until I can make other arrangements. Make up some believable story for your wife—tell her that me and my woman are temporarily separated and I need a place to crash. Anything that sounds reasonable."

He could house-hop among his supporters for weeks if necessary. The sheriff didn't know the identities of the men surrounding her house, so there would be no way to trace them back to him. When Cletus inevitably spotted backup units responding to the scene, he'd simply order his men to drive away and disappear into the night. He had contingency plans for every possible scenario.

This was just the beginning of his campaign of justice. Before he was finished, Sheriff Shea Callahan would understand precisely what it felt like to lose everything that mattered.

Chapter Twelve

The wind outside picked up in intensity, carrying with it the distinctive smell of approaching rain and the promise of a mountain storm. Shea zipped up her jacket against the growing chill, her mind racing as she considered their rapidly dwindling options. A storm might give her and Trevor the tactical advantage they desperately needed to escape this siege. Hopefully, the men outside would be forced to take shelter inside their trucks when the weather turned truly nasty, right?

"The approaching storm will make it much harder for us to hear anyone trying to approach the house," Trevor observed, shifting his weight uncomfortably on the hard floor where they'd taken cover. "It's getting significantly darker out there, too. Could work for us or against us."

Shea arched a brow in surprise at his tone. "Are you showing signs of being pessimistic for once? That doesn't sound like you."

He shrugged, wincing as another volley of bullets thudded against the exterior walls with deadly persistence. "Just trying to be realistic about our situation. We're outnumbered, outgunned, and surrounded."

"Are you okay?" Her anxiety increased exponentially at the thought that Trevor might be losing hope. His optimism had been one of the few constants keeping her grounded throughout this nightmare. If he was starting to doubt their chances of survival, what did that say about their actual prospects?

"Remember when I told you about my partner Johnny and how he was killed while responding to that domestic disturbance call?"

She nodded, then, realizing he couldn't see her clearly in the darkness, said aloud, "Yes, I remember."

"I didn't tell you the complete truth about what happened that night. Yes, he went around to cover the back of the house while I was supposed to create a diversion at the front. But I was also supposed to follow him around back once I had the suspect's attention focused on me." His voice grew thick with emotion. "I hesitated when the woman inside screamed. The sound froze me in place—reminded me too much of my own mother's screams when my father would lose his temper. By the time I snapped out of it and the first shot rang out, it was already too late to save Johnny."

"We all freeze sometimes, Trevor. It's a normal human reaction to traumatic situations."

"I bet you didn't freeze on the mountain when your friends were counting on you."

"No, I couldn't afford to," she admitted quietly. "The other women were depending on me to get them out safely. Sarah and Jenna were counting on me to be strong when they couldn't be." Would that terrifying weekend ever become such a distant memory that it no longer conjured up bone-chilling fear and guilt? "Speaking of backup, shouldn't our people be here by now?" She glanced at her phone to see whether she'd missed any calls or text messages. Nothing. The screen showed no signal bars. "I'm going to try calling Bill on the radio."

She keyed the microphone. "This is Sheriff Callahan. Deputy Butler, what's your status?"

"Good to hear you're still alive, Sheriff," came Bill's voice through heavy static and the sound of gunfire in the background.

More bullets slammed into the house, causing Shea to pull the radio handset away from her ear. "What's your current situation, Deputy?"

"We're having a bit of trouble ourselves out here. Doris managed to get the whole department mobilized to come help you and Bolton, but apparently, our response was anticipated. About halfway to your location, we got ambushed by another group of armed men blocking the road. Sorry, Sheriff, but you and Trevor are going to be on your own for the time being."

"Understood. Keep yourselves safe out there." She

hung up the radio with a growing sense of dread. "I guess you heard that conversation."

"Yeah." Trevor banged his head back against the wall in frustration. "We can't keep sitting here waiting for them to either burn us out or shoot the house to pieces around us."

"If this storm would hurry up and arrive with some real intensity, we could slip out the back door and make a run for the woods." Shea studied the darkness beyond the shattered windows. "It's really our only viable option that I can see. There's a creek that cuts through the forest behind the house. If we follow it downstream, the banks are low enough to provide us with decent cover from anyone trying to follow our trail."

"We can't afford to wait for the storm to provide natural cover. We need to create a diversion, and we need to do it soon before they decide to rush the house."

Shea ran through her mental inventory of anything in the cabin that they might be able to use as an improvised weapon or distraction device. "We could make an explosive device. Nothing too sophisticated, but effective enough to create chaos."

"You don't think your home has been damaged enough already?" Trevor asked with dark humor.

"There's nothing we can do about the destruction right now. Staying alive is more important than preserving property." She kept her voice practical and determined. "There's a small propane tank under the kitchen sink—the kind people use for camping stoves and portable grills. We could rig it to detonate near the front door, then escape out the back while they're distracted. Hopefully, the two men positioned behind the house will abandon their posts to see what happened at the front."

It could work. It had to work. Staying here any longer would be nothing short of suicide.

Staying as low as possible to avoid the broken windows, Shea crawled to the kitchen and retrieved the propane tank from under the sink, hoping it contained enough pressurized gas to create an effective explosion. She'd never actually used the camping equipment before—it had been left behind by the previous owner, along with most of the furnishings, which were now destroyed beyond repair. From a kitchen drawer, she pulled out a box of wooden matches and a dish towel that she quickly tore into strips.

Moving carefully back to the front of the house, she positioned the propane tank near what remained of the front door, which now resembled Swiss cheese more than an actual barrier. She rigged one of the fabric strips as a makeshift fuse, estimating the burn time as accurately as possible. "We'll have about thirty seconds once I light this thing, maybe less. Are you ready?" She glanced over her shoulder at Trevor.

"Let's do this." Trevor rose to a crouch, gathering their weapons and preparing to move.

Shea struck a match and lit the improvised fuse, watching as the flame began to crawl along the fabric toward the propane tank. Then she sprinted toward the back door as fast as she could move while staying low.

Two men were indeed standing outside the back door, both smoking cigarettes and taking little active part in the drinking and shooting that was going on at the front of the house. They seemed relaxed, confident that their prey was trapped inside with no way out.

The front of the house exploded in a tremendous blast after exactly twenty-five seconds, sending debris flying in all directions and creating a massive fireball that lit up the night sky. The two men guarding the back immediately tossed down their cigarettes and rushed toward the front to investigate the explosion.

"Come, Heidi." Shea flung open the back door and bolted toward the tree line with everything she had.

The heavy thud of Trevor's footsteps behind her provided reassurance that he was keeping up. Angry shouts and confused yelling erupted from Cletus's men as they realized their quarry had escaped.

She splashed into the creek without hesitation, the frigid mountain water immediately soaking through her shoes and the bottom of her uniform pants. The shock of the cold was intense, but she forced herself to keep moving. "The main road is in this direction. We won't use it unless we can link up with Bill and the others, but at least we'll know where we are. There's no reason to make it easier for Cletus's men to track us through the woods."

Heidi seemed utterly oblivious to the mortal danger

they were all facing. Instead of showing stress or fear, the German shepherd ran back and forth in the shallow creek water, splashing joyfully and treating this as some kind of exciting game. Every time she bounded past Shea, cold water sprayed in all directions. Despite the urgency and terror of their situation, Shea found herself smiling at her dog's carefree behavior. She wished that, even for just a few seconds, she could be as blissfully unaware of danger as her faithful companion.

A sharp crack of a breaking twig came from somewhere to their right. Heidi immediately stopped her playful splashing, her entire demeanor changing as her hackles rose and her ears perked forward in alert mode.

"Shh." Shea placed a firm hand on the dog's muzzle to keep her quiet, then reached for the hunting rifle that Trevor had thankfully remembered to grab before they fled the house.

Trevor moved closer to her side, his service weapon already in his hand. His eyes glittered in what little moonlight managed to escape the gathering storm clouds as he studied the dark shadows among the trees. When no additional sounds came from that direction, they continued their escape, moving inch by careful inch through the shallow water without making any noise.

When the creek made a sharp turn to the left, they climbed up the muddy embankment and back onto solid ground. Shea shivered against the increasing night chill as a light but steady rain began to fall, soaking through her jacket and making the footing treacherous. They had successfully escaped from the house, but they were far from being out of danger.

The sound of pursuit was growing closer—voices calling to each other through the trees, the snap and rustle of men pushing through undergrowth. How many were following them? How well did they know these woods compared to her limited familiarity with the area?

~

"What do you mean they got away?" Cletus's hand curled into a tight fist as rage surged through him like molten lava. "I specifically told you to watch that house and not let anyone escape. Find them immediately and bring me the woman alive."

"Boss, they went into the woods, and it's starting to rain pretty hard now. We can barely see ten feet in front of us."

"Have you idiots been drinking while you were supposed to be doing a job?" He'd cheerfully throttle the incompetent fool if he were standing in front of him right now. "Go after them through the woods. You won't melt from a little rainwater." He wished desperately for an old-fashioned telephone, one with a heavy receiver that he could slam down with satisfying force. Instead, he threw his cell phone onto the passenger side floor of his truck with disgust.

He couldn't be everywhere at once. Couldn't do

everything himself, no matter how much he wanted to oversee every aspect of this operation personally. He'd thought the situation at the sheriff's cabin was completely under control, so he'd driven to a nearby vantage point to watch the firefight between the responding deputies and his other team of men. Apparently, no one could be trusted to follow simple instructions and complete basic tasks.

He threw the truck into reverse and backed quickly from his hiding place, then sped toward the cabin as fast as the mountain roads would allow. Someone was definitely going to pay for this latest screw-up and pay dearly.

Cletus pulled up close to the smoldering remains of what had once been the front of the sheriff's house. The explosion had been far more effective than he would have expected from whatever improvised device they'd managed to construct. Only the steady rain kept the entire structure from becoming a raging inferno. He grabbed his pistol from the glove compartment, checking to make sure it was fully loaded.

This is precisely what he got for hiring people from outside the family. Complete imbeciles with no loyalty and no understanding of what was at stake. He strode purposefully up to the man he'd placed in charge of the operation, the one who was supposed to have ensured the sheriff didn't escape.

Without hesitation or warning, Cletus raised the gun and pulled the trigger. The man collapsed instantly, a look of shock and betrayal frozen on his face. As the other hired men watched with stricken expressions and growing fear, Cletus calmly walked back to his truck and sped away into the night.

Maybe now the survivors would understand that failure was not an acceptable option.

~

A dark shadow suddenly emerged from behind a large tree directly in front of them. This time, there was no hesitation in Trevor's response. He immediately raised his weapon and fired two quick shots. He rushed to where the man had fallen and kicked the attacker's rifle well out of reach, then knelt to check his condition.

"Are you traveling alone out here?" Trevor demanded, pressing the barrel of his gun against the wounded man's chest.

The man clutched his bleeding shoulder, his face twisted with pain and anger. "You'll pay dearly for shooting me. The boss doesn't like it when his people get hurt."

"I asked you a direct question—are you alone?" Trevor shifted his aim toward the man's uninjured leg. "I've got plenty more bullets, and I'm not feeling particularly patient right now."

"Others are coming through these woods. We spread out in a search line when we heard you splashing around in that creek. I heard voices and came to investigate, hoping to win some points with Cletus by capturing you myself."

"All you've managed to accomplish is getting yourself arrested and shot." Shea pulled a pair of handcuffs from her duty belt and secured the wounded man to a sturdy tree trunk. "We'll send someone back for you once this is all over, assuming you don't bleed to death first."

A string of creative cursing erupted from the man's lips as Shea and Trevor quickly moved away from the area.

"Good reflexes back there," she commented as they put distance between themselves and their prisoner.

"I acted without thinking this time instead of freezing up." He felt genuinely proud of himself for the first time in years. Maybe he really could move past the overwhelming sadness and regret of Johnny's death. Perhaps he could become the kind of deputy he'd always aspired to be. Maybe he really could keep Shea safe through this nightmare.

A rifle bullet suddenly kicked up the wet leaves at Shea's feet, missing her by mere inches. She spun around and returned fire in the direction the shot had come from. Trevor did the same, and they heard a scream of pain as another of Cletus's hired men fell somewhere in the darkness.

"We're giving away our position every time we shoot," Trevor observed, scanning the trees around them. "But listen—do you hear that gunfire in the distance? I think we've found our backup."

"Let's move toward the sound," Shea decided. "But

carefully."

Leaving the wounded attackers where they had fallen, Shea led the way through the dense forest toward the distant sound of what was a significant firefight.

Trevor caught her arm as they neared the main road. "We need to scout the situation before we go charging in. Could be a trap."

"I wasn't planning on running into the open blindly." She pulled free of his grip, though she appreciated his caution. "But I do want to get close enough to see what's happening. The sound of all that gunfire should mask any noise we make moving through the underbrush."

Shaking his head at his protective instincts, Trevor carefully parted the thick foliage between their position and the road. Three sheriff's department squad cars were positioned in a defensive formation with their doors open as improvised shields, facing off against two pickup trucks similar to the ones they'd left behind at the cabin.

Shea motioned for them to circle and approach from behind the trucks, where they could take out the attackers from an unexpected direction. Trevor nodded his agreement and followed her lead through the woods.

Moving into position behind the enemy vehicles, Shea carefully aimed with her hunting rifle and fired, dropping one of the gunmen instantly. The second attacker turned toward the unexpected threat, only to be taken down by Trevor's precise shooting. The remaining four men quickly changed their tactics and began directing their fire toward Shea and Trevor's position.

They dove back into the protective cover of the thick bushes, hoping they'd created enough of a diversion for the deputies to regroup and gain the tactical advantage. However, the sounds of the firefight seemed to intensify rather than diminish.

A man suddenly sprang from concealment and tackled Shea to the muddy ground, knocking the rifle from her hands and sending it skittering out of reach. She wrestled desperately to reach her holstered handgun as her attacker tried to pin her arms.

Heidi growled ferociously and clamped her powerful jaws around the man's arm, shaking her head violently as she'd been trained to do.

The attacker yowled in pain and terror, trying frantically to shake the determined dog off his bleeding arm.

Trevor grabbed the fallen hunting rifle and delivered a devastating blow to the back of the man's head with the heavy wooden stock. The attacker grunted once and rolled off Shea, unconscious or worse.

"Are you hurt anywhere?" Trevor asked urgently, running his gaze over her for signs of injury.

"No, I'm fine." She pushed herself to her feet and immediately wrapped her arms around her dog's neck in gratitude. "You're such a good girl, Heidi. Yes, you are. The best partner a sheriff could ask for."

"Hey, I was the one who actually knocked him out," Trevor protested with a grin, trying to lighten the mood.

"You're a very good boy too," Shea replied, and for the first time in hours, the ghost of a genuine smile teased at the corners of her lips. "Now let's go save the others."

When they emerged from the forest cover again, the remaining attackers had been overwhelmed and were being handcuffed and loaded into squad cars. Bill Butler approached them with his hand extended.

"Thanks for the tactical assistance," he said, shaking both their hands vigorously. "Sorry we couldn't make it to your location in time to help. They were ready for us."

"There are several wounded men back in the woods, and probably others still waiting at what's left of my cabin," Shea reported efficiently. "Let's round up all of Cletus's people and get them properly booked. We can sort out the charges in the morning."

"Later today, you mean," Trevor corrected, glancing at his watch in surprise. "The sun will be coming up soon."

The adrenaline rush of the last several hours was finally starting to fade, leaving him acutely aware of his complete exhaustion and the lack of sleep, food, and water over the past day. Deputy Bombeck noticed his condition and handed him an unopened bottle of water.

"Thanks, Richard. You read my mind."

"You and the sheriff look like spit out gum, no

offense intended."

"None of you look particularly fresh either. Anyone seriously injured in the firefight?"

"Billings took a bullet to the arm, but it's just a graze. Nothing that won't heal completely. Cutter has some cuts from flying glass when his windshield got shot out, but he'll be fine, too. Considering how outgunned we were, we're fortunate to all still be breathing." Bombeck clapped Trevor on the shoulder, then gestured toward a squad car. "Come on, I'll give you two a ride back to the sheriff's place so you can assess the damage."

"That's the best offer I've heard all night," Trevor said gratefully, waving to get Shea's attention.

She finished giving instructions to Bill about processing the crime scenes, then climbed into the back seat of the patrol car, somehow managing to squeeze Heidi in beside her, and leaving the front passenger seat for Trevor.

"I don't want to see what my house looks like in the full light of day," she said quietly, the exhaustion finally showing in her voice.

"We'll get everything fixed and set to rights," Trevor promised. "I'll help with whatever needs to be done."

"You've already done more than enough, Trevor. I should probably just hire a contractor to deal with the damage." She was quiet for a moment. "If you hadn't arrived when you did tonight, I'd either be in Cletus's hands right now or dead. I owe you my life."

The thought of either possibility sent ice water through his veins. He silently vowed never to leave her side again, not until Cletus was safely behind bars where he belonged. "That's what partners do for each other."

"You're the best partner any sheriff could hope to have," she said with a tired but genuine smile, though weariness was settling heavily in her words and posture.

He'd do absolutely everything in his power to make sure she never had reason to regret those words.

Chapter Thirteen

Bingo. Another promising lead at last. Thanks to an old friend and former colleague in New York—a retired Dallas detective who'd moved north after twenty-five years on the force—Shea finally had a comprehensive list of Cletus's known relatives and associates in the tri-county area. She'd spent the better part of three days after the siege at her cabin working the phones, calling in favors, and cross-referencing database records to build a complete picture of the Hodges family network.

She punched the first address from her handwritten list into her phone's GPS system, then closed her laptop with satisfaction. Progress felt good after so many dead ends and false leads.

She headed to the bullpen in search of Trevor, hoping to coordinate their approach to checking these new locations, only to discover from Doris that he'd been called out to handle an early morning traffic accident on the interstate. A jackknifed semi had collided with several passenger vehicles, creating a major scene that would require hours of investigation and cleanup.

Not wanting to lose momentum while the trail was still warm, she scribbled him a detailed note listing all the addresses she planned to visit that morning, left Heidi sleeping peacefully in her office, and headed for one of the department's squad cars. Time was of the essence—every hour they delayed gave Cletus more opportunity to plan another attack or disappear altogether.

The drive took her off the main highway onto increasingly narrow back roads that wound deeper into the mountains. She exited onto a poorly maintained two-lane road, then turned onto what could generously be called a dirt track, overgrown with weeds and dotted with potholes large enough to swallow a tire. The jarring impacts made her teeth clank together painfully every time she hit a bottomless hole.

Dense woods towered menacingly on each side of the rough path, their interlocking canopy blocking out most of the morning sun and creating an artificial twilight that made her instinctively check that her weapon was easily accessible. This was exactly the kind of isolated location where someone could disappear without a trace.

A magnificent twelve-point buck suddenly bolted from the undergrowth directly in front of her vehicle.

Shea slammed on the brakes, her heart jumping into her throat as the massive deer froze in the middle of the narrow road. For several tense seconds, the animal stared at her through the windshield with liquid brown eyes before bounding gracefully into the trees on the opposite side.

Shea's heart threatened to hammer completely free of her chest at the unexpected close call. She took several deep, steadying breaths before putting the car back in drive and proceeding more cautiously. There was probably only a small chance she'd find Cletus at any of these locations, but she couldn't afford to leave any stone unturned. Eventually, persistence would pay off, and she'd catch him at one of his hiding places.

The closer she got to the GPS coordinates, the more her well-honed law enforcement instincts whispered that something felt distinctly off about this entire situation. She trusted her contact in New York—after all, Detective Martinez had been her mentor during a training exchange program years ago—but something about this felt too convenient, too easy.

She finally stopped in front of a weathered log cabin that had clearly seen much better days. The structure was solid enough, but the paint was peeling, several windows were cracked, and the front porch sagged ominously. From the trampled grass and weeds scattered throughout the yard, it is evident that someone lived here recently, but the place had an abandoned feel that set her nerves on edge.

She studied the surrounding area carefully through her windshield for several minutes, looking for any signs of movement, surveillance, or potential threats. When no one emerged from the house to investigate her arrival—and most mountain folks were curious about unexpected visitors—she slowly opened her door and stepped out onto the uneven ground.

Moving cautiously toward the cabin with her hand resting lightly on her holstered weapon, she tried to project authority while remaining alert for any signs of ambush. The crunch of dried leaves under her boots sounded unnaturally loud in the forest silence. "Hello? Anyone home? This is Sheriff Callahan."

Her voice echoed slightly in the surrounding trees, but no one responded from inside the cabin. She stepped carefully onto the sagging front porch, wincing as the weathered planks creaked ominously under her weight. She'd knock once or twice to be thorough, and if no one answered, she'd move on to the next address on her list.

She rapped her knuckles firmly on the solid wooden door, then moved to the side to peer through a grimy window into the dim interior.

Empty beer cans and whiskey bottles littered a small table set for two people. Dirty dishes sat stacked on the counter next to an overflowing ashtray. Someone had lived here recently, but where were they now?

She backed carefully off the porch and decided to check the rear of the property before leaving. Behind the house, she discovered an ancient blue tick hound lying motionless near a bone-dry water bowl inside a makeshift pen constructed from rusty wire fencing. The sight of the apparent animal neglect made her stomach turn with disgust.

"Sorry, I don't have any food with me, buddy," she said softly, filling the empty bowl from a nearby garden hose. The poor animal barely lifted its head to acknowledge her presence, too weak from dehydration and starvation to show much interest in the fresh water.

A sharp crack of a breaking twig sounded directly behind her. Shea spun around instantly, her hand flying to her weapon as Cletus Hodges stepped into the small clearing with a large hunting knife clutched in his right hand.

"Well, well, well. Look what we have here—a pretty little sheriff has walked right into my carefully prepared trap." He displayed a predatory grin that reminded her uncomfortably of a shark preparing to attack. "I was hoping we could have a civilized conversation about recent events, but honestly, pummeling you into complete oblivion sounds like a lot more fun."

It wasn't difficult to see the family resemblance between Cletus and his deceased brothers. They all shared the same brutish facial structure, heavy brows that seemed permanently lowered in anger, and an arrogant swagger that spoke of men who'd never faced real consequences for their actions.

"I'm delighted that you decided to come here without that deputy of yours or your faithful dog." He took a deliberate step forward while she automatically took one back, her mind racing through tactical options. "This confrontation should be just between the two of us, the way nature intended. May the best person win."

"I'm not going to fight you, Cletus." She kept her voice steady and controlled while waiting for him to make the first aggressive move.

"Oh, I'm quite certain you will." His grin widened with malicious anticipation. "You see, I've already given very specific orders to eliminate both the deputy and your beloved dog if you refuse to cooperate with my plans. All it will take is one simple phone call from me, and everything you hold dear in this world will be gone forever." He chuckled with obvious satisfaction. "I hear the repairs on your house are progressing nicely. Such a shame you won't be around to enjoy the renovations."

"I defeated your brother Bruce in hand-to-hand combat. I'm pretty confident I can do exactly the same thing with you."

"Ah, but you see, I'm considerably smarter and more experienced than Bruce ever was." His expression hardened with genuine menace. "Now put down that gun and show me what you're made of. Let's keep this confrontation as close as possible to what happened with my dear departed brothers."

Hand-to-hand combat was the absolute last thing

she wanted to engage in. She'd already experienced more than enough violence and trauma to last several lifetimes. But seeing no viable alternative that wouldn't result in Trevor and Heidi's deaths, she reluctantly placed her service weapon on the weathered back deck of the cabin.

"I don't have a knife," she pointed out, hoping to create some delay while she assessed her options.

"I came fully prepared for every contingency." He reached behind his back and pulled a second knife from his belt, tossing it casually at her feet. "Can't have an unfair fight, after all."

She bent to retrieve the weapon from the dirt, testing its weight and balance in her hand. The blade was well-maintained and razor sharp—Cletus had planned this confrontation down to the smallest detail. She could do this. She had to do this. With a heavy exhale, she settled into a defensive stance and prepared for his inevitable attack.

Cletus lunged forward with surprising speed and agility for such a large man. Shea sidestepped his charge at the last possible second, using his momentum against him while simultaneously moving closer to where her gun lay on the deck. If she could somehow reach her weapon, she could end this fight before it truly began.

Seeing exactly where her desperate gaze had fallen, Cletus quickly grabbed the pistol and hurled it into a thick patch of weeds and thorny undergrowth near the corner of the house. "No cheating allowed, Sheriff. We're going to settle this the old-fashioned way."

For such a large and seemingly clumsy man, he moved with surprising grace, bouncing easily on the balls of his feet like a boxer before springing at her again with renewed aggression.

She raised her arm to block his downward knife strike, then drove her elbow hard into his ribs with all the force she could muster. He grunted in pain but immediately retaliated with a vicious backhand that sent her stumbling backward. Before she could regain her balance and footing, he roared with rage and tackled her to the hard ground, driving all the air from her lungs.

The impact was devastating, but Shea managed to roll out from under his crushing weight and leap back to her feet with desperate energy. She slashed at him with her knife, catching the blade in his thick flannel shirt and opening a shallow cut across his chest.

He laughed at the minor wound and jumped back out of range, then came slashing at her again with renewed fury. This time his blade found its mark, cutting deep into her arm just below the shoulder. She gasped as white-hot pain shot through her entire body like an electric shock. Blood immediately began running down her arm, making her knife hand slippery and increasingly difficult to control.

"First blood goes to me," Cletus sang out with

obvious satisfaction, clearly enjoying every moment of her pain and struggle.

The man's insufferable arrogance only spurred her determination to keep fighting despite the burning agony in her wounded arm. She began dancing around him in a circle, looking for any opening or weakness she could exploit. At one point, he turned too slowly to follow her movement, and her powerful roundhouse kick connected solidly with his midsection, sending him crashing to the ground.

With a string of creative curses, he jumped back to his feet and wiped blood from his split lip. "Should've known you'd have some fancy martial arts training. Figures a woman sheriff would need extra help."

"Basic karate and kickboxing," she replied, continuing to search for another opening while trying to ignore the steady flow of blood from her arm. The wound was deeper than she'd initially thought, and exhaustion was beginning to threaten her coordination and reflexes.

Fighting through the increasing pain and weakness, she feinted to the left as if preparing to attack from that direction.

Cletus took the bait and staggered off balance as he tried to counter her expected move.

Taking advantage of his momentary vulnerability, Shea dropped to her knees and grasped a large rock about the size of her fist from the ground beside her. With all her remaining strength, she hurled it directly at his face. The impact struck him squarely in the temple, stunning him long enough for her to land a solid kick to his stomach that doubled him over.

He cursed violently and clutched his bleeding head with both hands, his knife momentarily forgotten.

"This ain't over by a long shot, Sheriff," he snarled, his face twisted with rage and humiliation. "Not at all." He staggered backward toward the tree line, then turned and disappeared into the dense woods.

Shea's entire body began trembling uncontrollably as the adrenaline started to fade from her system. She sank to the ground as her legs finally gave out, no longer able to support her weight. Blood continued to stream steadily from the deep gash on her arm, soaking through her uniform shirt. She removed the garment and tied it tightly around the wound as a makeshift bandage. The sports bra she wore underneath provided little protection from the growing chill of the mountain air.

She fumbled for her radio with increasingly clumsy fingers, only to find empty space where it should have been clipped to her belt. She must have lost it during the violent struggle. Her cell phone lay several feet away, apparently knocked from her pocket when Cletus had tackled her. Crawling over on hands and knees, she retrieved the device with shaking hands, then leaned back against the cabin wall for support.

"Stay awake," she muttered to herself, fighting against the waves of dizziness and nausea. "If you fall asleep and he comes back with reinforcements, you're dead."

~

Cletus would kill her the next time they met, and he would derive immense pleasure from the act. Back in his concealed truck, he pulled a wad of fast-food napkins from the glove compartment and pressed them against the gash on his head where the rock had connected. Once he managed to get the bleeding stopped or at least slowed to a manageable level, he'd drive back to the cabin with his rifle and finish off the troublesome sheriff once and for all.

He had seriously underestimated her fighting skills and physical conditioning. He hadn't expected her to fight with the intensity and technique of a trained male combatant. Despite the fact that Cletus outweighed her by at least fifty pounds and had several inches of reach advantage, she'd more than held her own in their confrontation. Next time, he'd know exactly what to expect from her. Who was he kidding? The next time, he'd bring his gun and end this personal vendetta quickly and efficiently.

He picked up his cell phone from the passenger seat and dialed a familiar number. "I want you to take out Deputy Bolton immediately. Use whatever method you prefer, but get it done today."

"Hold on there, Cletus. I didn't sign up to kill any law enforcement officers. That's a whole different level of trouble than anything we've done so far."

"You signed up to follow my orders without question. Do exactly what I tell you, or say goodbye to that wife of yours. Your choice entirely." He hung up without waiting for a response.

Where was the loyalty he'd expected from his extended family? He'd anticipated some resistance from the outsiders he'd promised payment to—especially since he had no intention of actually paying them anything—but from his blood relatives? He had expected nothing but complete and unquestioning obedience.

~

Trevor glanced in his rearview mirror for the third time in as many minutes. The rusty white Ford pickup truck was following him as he drove away from the scene of the highway accident involving a jackknifed semi and a passenger van. Fortunately, no one had been killed when the truck had lost control and the van had slammed into its trailer, but there had been multiple injuries requiring ambulance transport.

Now he had an entirely different problem to deal with. His phone suddenly buzzed with an incoming text message containing only an address and the single word "Help." Shea was in serious trouble and needed immediate assistance.

He quickly entered the address into his GPS system, activated his emergency lights and siren, and pressed the accelerator to the floor as he sped toward her location.

The Ford truck behind him kept pace easily, eventually gaining ground and pulling closer to his rear bumper. He didn't have time for whatever game this was. Trevor had to reach Shea before it was too late.

When he pulled onto an exit ramp to leave the highway, the Ford deliberately rammed into the back of his squad car with significant force. Trevor's head jerked forward painfully from the impact, and he had to fight to maintain control of his vehicle. The driver then attempted to run him entirely off the road by swerving into the side of his car.

Trevor tried to get a clear look at the driver's face, but the man wore a baseball cap pulled down low over his eyes and kept his head turned away. Deciding that two could play this dangerous game, Trevor yanked his steering wheel hard to the right, slamming into the truck with the same force he'd received. Metal screeched against metal as the pickup ran down the guardrail designed to protect drivers from the steep drainage ditch below.

Another deliberate swerve of his steering wheel sent the truck careening over the guardrail and down into the ditch, where it rolled twice before coming to rest on its side.

He immediately called in the accident to dispatch, then increased his speed dramatically toward Shea's location. His patrol car bounced violently down the rough dirt road, bottoming out several times on the deep ruts before finally reaching the isolated log cabin.

He threw open his door and shouted, "Shea! Where are you?"

A faint "here" came from somewhere behind the house.

Trevor raced around the building and dropped to his knees beside her, his heart nearly stopping at the sight of so much blood. "What happened? Who did this to you?" He examined the makeshift bandage around her arm with growing alarm.

"Cletus set up a trap using false information. We fought hand-to-hand with knives. I managed to bash his head with a rock, and he retreated into the woods." She was shivering uncontrollably from shock and blood loss.

"Hold on. I'm getting you out of here." He scooped her carefully into his arms and rushed back to the patrol car. Once he'd settled her into the passenger seat, he turned the heater on full blast and retrieved a thermal blanket from the trunk to wrap around her trembling form.

"My service weapon is somewhere near the back deck," she said weakly, closing her eyes against the pain.

"I'll retrieve it."

"The dog, too. It's been seriously neglected and needs veterinary attention."

"Understood." What she planned to do with another dog was beyond him, but he would honor her wishes.

The poor animal barely looked up when he opened the makeshift pen, forcing Trevor to carry the emaciated creature back to the car once he'd located and secured Shea's weapon. "I honestly don't think this guy has much time left."

"We'll let a veterinarian make that determination," she whispered.

"What made you think following a lead alone was a good idea?" He carefully turned the car around and headed back toward civilization. "After everything we've been through together?"

"You were handling the highway accident. I didn't expect to find Cletus at any of these locations. I have several more addresses to check."

"Most likely all of them are dead ends designed to lure you into more traps." He shot her a sharp look of concern and frustration. "How many times do I have to tell you that you don't have to face this alone?"

"He specifically threatened to kill you and Heidi if I didn't cooperate."

"I'm perfectly capable of taking care of myself." He told her about the white truck that had tried to run him off the road. "I didn't stick around to check on the driver's condition, but I did call it in to dispatch. I'd like to make a quick stop at the scene before taking you to get proper medical treatment."

"A couple of butterfly bandages will be sufficient for this wound." She opened her eyes with effort.

"We'll let a qualified doctor make that

determination." When they arrived at the location where he'd forced the truck off the road, Trevor left Shea secure in the patrol car and approached Bill Butler, who was coordinating the accident investigation.

"Sorry, I had to leave the scene of that highway accident so abruptly." He quickly explained how he had found Shea injured and the circumstances surrounding it.

"No worries at all. The truck driver is alive and on his way to the hospital under guard. That's one more of Cletus's hired thugs off the streets." Bill glanced toward Trevor's car. "Is the sheriff going to be all right?"

"She'll need stitches for a knife wound on her arm, but she should recover fully. We also confiscated a very old, neglected dog that needs immediate veterinary care."

"The vet will probably just recommend putting the poor thing down humanely. I'll take him home with me and give him whatever time he has left in comfort."

Trevor clapped the deputy on the shoulder with genuine appreciation. "You're a good man, Bill."

He returned to the car and his injured partner. "Let's get you some professional medical attention. While I drive, why don't you come up with a realistic plan to ensure you don't head out on dangerous calls alone again?"

"Fine. I promise I won't go alone again in the future."

For some reason, he didn't entirely believe her promise, but it was a start.

Chapter Fourteen

Shea's contact in New York vehemently denied knowing anything about the address she'd provided to Shea, claiming she'd never heard of the location and had certainly never recommended it as a place to search for Cletus. The revelation that someone had been impersonating her trusted colleague sent chills down Shea's spine and confirmed her worst suspicions about yesterday's trap.

In addition to that disturbing news, her New York friend had recommended that Shea meet with a criminal profiler in Little Rock who specialized in obsessive stalkers and violent predators. Dr. Nora Hensley now only worked part-time cases due to a vicious assault she'd suffered at the hands of a suspect the previous year. However, she still maintained her reputation as one of the best behavioral analysts in the region.

Shea had sent the woman all their case files the night before via encrypted email, but she gathered up the physical evidence they had accumulated on Cletus anyway and met Trevor in the break room early that morning.

"Feel like making a road trip to Little Rock today?" She explained about the profiler and her potential insights into Cletus's psychological patterns. "I'm willing to try anything at this point. We need a fresh perspective on this case."

"Absolutely. Sounds like exactly what we need." Trevor flashed that familiar grin and playfully snatched the keys from her hand before she could protest. "I'll drive. You can use the time to organize your thoughts before the meeting."

The autumn sun hung high in the clear blue sky by the time they reached their destination in the state capital. The drive had taken them through some of Arkansas's most beautiful countryside, with rolling hills covered in trees displaying their full fall colors. Under different circumstances, Shea might have enjoyed the scenic route.

As they pulled into the parking lot of the professional building that housed Dr. Hensley's office, Shea took a deep breath and turned to Trevor. "I'd like to speak with the profiler alone, if you don't mind."

Hurt flickered briefly in his eyes, but he nodded with understanding. "Any particular reason?"

"My contact warned me that Dr. Hensley rarely speaks to anyone outside of immediate family since she was attacked last year. The assault left her with some significant trust issues." Shea touched his arm gently. "She might be more comfortable and open to sharing information if she's only dealing with one person initially, especially another woman in law enforcement."

"That makes perfect sense." Trevor's smile returned, the momentary pain in his expression completely gone. "I'll be right here in the waiting area when you're finished."

Shea walked through the heavy glass doors into the sterile, fluorescent-lit office building. Her boots echoed against the polished marble floor as she made her way to the elevator. The seventh floor housed several medical and professional offices, giving the hallway a clinical atmosphere that reminded her uncomfortably of a hospital.

Dr. Hensley's office was located at the end of the corridor. Sitting at the far end of a long metal conference table was a composed woman in her late forties with neatly styled, gray-streaked hair and piercing blue eyes that seemed to take in every detail instantly. A distinctive scar ran from just behind her left ear down to the corner of her mouth, pulling one side of her face into what appeared to be a perpetual frown.

"Sheriff Shea Callahan." Shea crossed the room and extended her hand. "Thank you so much for agreeing to meet with me on such short notice."

"Dr. Nora Hensley, but please call me Nora." The woman's handshake was firm and confident, belying any weakness her scars might suggest. "I'm always willing to help bring down dangerous predators. They destroyed enough of my life already." She gestured toward the chairs. "Please, have a seat and let's get started."

Shea settled into the chair across from her and spread photographs, handwritten notes, and evidence bags across the polished table surface. "You've had a chance to review the files I sent last night? Including the details of my initial confrontation with the Hodges brothers on the mountain?"

"Yes, I've read everything thoroughly, but I'd like to hear the entire story directly from you. Sometimes the emotional context and personal details don't come through in written reports." Nora pulled out a legal pad and an expensive pen. "Start from the beginning and don't leave out anything, no matter how insignificant it might seem."

Shea took a steadying breath and began recounting the events in chronological order. The girls' weekend that had turned into a nightmare. Cletus's escalating campaign of psychological warfare. The threatening notes and surveillance photos. The deadly ambush at her home just days ago. The sniper attack at the Fall Festival killed innocent people. Yesterday's trap and their brutal knife fight behind the isolated cabin.

Dr. Hensley scratched detailed notes as she listened, her sharp gaze constantly flicking between the evidence spread across the table and Shea's face, as though she were piecing together an intricate psychological puzzle. After Shea finished her account, the profiler leaned back in her chair thoughtfully, then removed her wire-rimmed glasses and cleaned them slowly.

"Sheriff, I'll be completely blunt with you because sugarcoating the situation won't help anyone." Her voice carried the authority of someone who'd spent decades studying the darkest aspects of human behavior. "Based on everything you've told me, and the evidence patterns I've observed, Cletus Hodges isn't simply angry or seeking straightforward revenge. He's developed a dangerous obsession with you that goes far beyond normal grief or family loyalty."

She leaned forward, her blue eyes intense and focused. "This man blames you not only for the death of one brother and the imprisonment of another, but also for his own failures, his personal pain, and most dangerously, his deep-seated sense of worthlessness and inadequacy. In his twisted perception, you've become the embodiment of everything that's wrong with his life."

Shea felt her jaw tighten involuntarily. "How far do you think he's willing to go to hurt me?"

Dr. Hensley's voice dropped to a more serious tone. "People like Cletus don't see their victims as separate, independent individuals with their rights and lives. To him, you're a symbol of everything he desires but believes he'll never achieve. Power, respect, authority, success. He doesn't just want revenge against you—he wants to completely destroy you emotionally, psychologically, and ultimately physically."

"What's his ultimate endgame?" Shea asked, though she suspected she already knew the answer.

"To make you suffer extensively before he finishes what his brothers started on that mountain. He wants to see you completely broken, stripped of everything that makes you strong and confident. The psychological torture is just as important to him as the eventual physical confrontation." The profiler's expression grew even more grave. "And Sheriff, he's absolutely willing to hurt or kill innocent people to achieve his goals, as you've already witnessed."

Shea's breath caught in her throat. "So how do I stop someone like that?"

Dr. Hensley steepled her fingers, her tone measured but firm with professional conviction. "You need to control the narrative of this confrontation. This man thrives on feeling powerful and superior, on believing he consistently outsmarts law enforcement and stays one step ahead. You need to anticipate his likely moves and cut him off at every turn before he can act."

She paused, studying Shea's face carefully. "Set traps for him, but make them subtle enough that he doesn't realize he's being manipulated into making mistakes. Use his arrogance and obsession against him.

However, you must be prepared to put yourself in significant harm's way as bait."

That wouldn't be an easy task with Trevor constantly shadowing her every move for protection. Putting herself directly in Cletus's crosshairs was a risk she was willing to take if it meant ending this nightmare, but the thought of anyone else getting hurt because of her decisions made her stomach churn with guilt and anxiety.

The profiler continued, her voice softening slightly with what might have been sympathy. "Sheriff, you're going to need to rely completely on your team and trust them to hold the line when things get dangerous. You absolutely cannot do this alone, no matter how much your protective instincts tell you otherwise." She began gathering her papers and files. "One more thing, Sheriff. Don't let him get inside your head with his psychological games. That's his most potent weapon, and once he breaks down your mental defenses, you'll be vulnerable to making fatal mistakes."

Shea let out a short, sarcastic laugh that held no humor. "That's much easier said than done, especially when he's already demonstrated how thoroughly he's researched my life and routines."

"I understand completely. But remember, you have advantages he doesn't. Training, backup, resources, and most importantly, you're fighting for justice while he's driven by hatred and obsession." Dr.

Hensley stood and extended her hand again. "Good luck, Sheriff. I hope you catch this monster before he hurts anyone else."

Heaving a deep sigh, Shea gathered up her files and evidence materials, then returned to the waiting area where she found Trevor reading a magazine and periodically checking his watch.

She filled him in on the key points of her conversation with the profiler as they walked back to the patrol car.

"I like her already. She agrees with me about you not going anywhere alone anymore." Trevor smiled as he opened the driver's door. "Professional validation of my protective instincts."

"Don't think for one second that I'm going to start playing the helpless damsel in distress," Shea warned, though there was no real bite in her tone.

"Wouldn't dream of suggesting such a thing. I know you too well by now." His expression grew more serious. "Just remember that we're a team in this fight. This isn't just about you anymore—it's about protecting the entire town, the department, and anyone else Cletus might target to get to you. He's already tried having me run off the road, remember?"

As if she could forget that terrifying incident. "So, what's the plan? I'm sure your brain was working overtime while you were sitting out here waiting."

"We set an elaborate trap for him, just like the good doctor recommended." Trevor slid into the driver's seat and started the engine. "But we do it smart, with backup plans and safety measures."

As they drove back toward Misty Hollow through the late afternoon sunlight, Shea's radio suddenly crackled to life with a report of a disturbance near the eastern edge of town. Without hesitation, Trevor gripped the steering wheel tighter and turned in that direction, activating the emergency lights.

The disturbance turned out to be nothing more threatening than a group of teenage boys shooting at a dilapidated old barn with paintball guns, covering the weathered wooden walls with splotches of bright colors. Shea took down all their names and addresses, then ordered them to head home immediately.

"You boys will be responsible for properly repainting that entire barn," she informed them sternly. "I don't care how run-down it looks—it's not your property to destroy. The owner is an elderly widow who doesn't need this additional expense."

The teenagers mumbled apologies and promises to make things right as they gathered up their paintball equipment and trudged toward their cars.

If only all emergency calls could be resolved so easily and harmlessly.

~

The sheriff's station was tranquil that evening except for the persistent hum of the overhead fluorescent lights and the occasional crackle of radio chatter from dispatch. Trevor could see Shea sitting at her desk across from his in the main bullpen area, the blue glow from her computer monitor illuminating the exhaustion and stress etched on her face.

She'd been working for hours without a break, poring over case files, crime scene photographs, and witness statements, searching for any detail they might have missed that could give them an advantage over Cletus.

Trevor pushed back from his desk and headed to the break room to make a fresh pot of coffee. When it finished brewing, he didn't announce it or ask if she wanted any—he filled two mugs and set one carefully on her desk, being mindful not to disturb the crime reports and photographs spread across the surface.

After a long moment of comfortable silence, he settled into the chair across from her desk. "You're running yourself into the ground again, Shea. It's past nine o'clock. Let's go home and get some rest."

"I don't have a choice in the matter. People are counting on me to solve this and keep them safe." She didn't look up from the file she was studying.

"People are counting on us, on the entire department. Not just on you carrying the whole burden alone." He leaned forward, studying her tired face with growing concern.

She finally rubbed at the heavy fatigue weighing down her eyes. "Dr. Hensley said that Cletus wants to see me completely broken down. The worst part is that he's winning this psychological war. Every time I think about what he might do next, every time I catch myself looking over my shoulder or jumping at unexpected sounds, it feels like he's already gotten inside my mind."

Trevor leaned forward further, resting his elbows on the edge of her desk. "That's exactly what he wants—to make you feel isolated and like you're fighting this battle completely alone. But you're not alone, Shea. I'm here, and I'm not going anywhere no matter how dangerous things get."

"But what if someone gets seriously hurt or killed because of me?" Her voice wavered with emotion she usually kept carefully controlled. "What if my decisions get innocent people hurt?"

"Stop." He reached across the desk and placed his hand over hers, noting how cold her fingers felt. "You're a good sheriff—an excellent sheriff—but you can't control everything that happens. Yes, Cletus is dangerous and unpredictable, but so are you. You're smart, tough, well-trained, and you have an entire department full of people who believe in you and trust your judgment."

The hard, defensive expression on her face gradually softened. "Why are you so determined to stick by me through all this? You know better than anyone how much danger is involved."

His gaze searched hers, looking for any sign of how she might respond to honesty. "Because I know exactly what it feels like to be in over your head, facing something that seems impossible to overcome. And because..." He paused, choosing his words carefully. "Because I care about you, Shea. More than I probably should, if I'm being frank with myself."

"Thank you. For everything you've done and everything you're risking." She shut off her computer and began locking the sensitive files away in the secure filing cabinet. "You're right. Let's go home. I've left Heidi alone long enough today, and it's been far too long since I've had a decent night's sleep."

So, she had chosen not to respond to his admission of feelings for her directly. That was probably for the best, he told himself. A romantic relationship between coworkers, especially between a sheriff and her deputy, didn't sound like the smartest professional decision either of them could make.

Trevor cleared off his desk and secured his paperwork, then followed her back to the cabin through the quiet mountain roads. He stood watch on the front porch as she let Heidi out into the yard to sniff around and take care of her business, the German shepherd clearly happy to see her master after a long day.

Trevor felt like an overprotective helicopter parent hovering constantly, but after Shea's knife fight with Cletus, he refused to let her out of his sight for any length of time. The man was like a cockroach, somehow managing to squeeze into any small opening to cause maximum destruction.

He methodically scanned the tree line and

surrounding property, his trained eyes looking for any sign of surveillance or potential threats. His gaze finally settled on Heidi, who didn't seem worried or alert in the slightest. Instead, the dog was happily chasing the tennis ball that Shea tossed for her across the yard, her tail wagging with pure joy.

Trevor had arranged for the electricity to be completely repaired the day after the siege at the cabin. All the security cameras were operational again, and the monitoring system was even more sophisticated than before. The bullet-riddled front door and all the broken windows had been replaced with reinforced materials, and every hole in the walls had been properly patched and painted. Looking at the house now, no casual observer could tell what kind of violence had occurred there just a few days earlier.

His mind kept running over what the profiler had said about setting an elaborate trap for Cletus. A trap would necessarily put Shea in significant danger, serving as bait to draw him out of hiding. A trap would also mean that Trevor would have to stay entirely out of sight, potentially too far away to provide immediate assistance when things inevitably turned violent. It wasn't that he doubted her ability to handle herself— she'd proven repeatedly that she was more than capable—but if something went wrong and he wasn't close enough to help...

He shook his head firmly, refusing to let his mind dwell on worst-case scenarios and what-if situations. A schoolteacher had once told him that today had enough troubles of its own without borrowing worry from tomorrow. The quote came from the Bible, he thought, though he couldn't remember the exact book or verse. Either way, it remained excellent advice that had served him well over the years.

He stood as Shea and Heidi approached the porch, the dog panting happily from her exercise. "I noticed some eggs and other ingredients in the refrigerator. I could make us some omelets for dinner if you'd like."

"That sounds absolutely wonderful." She flashed one of her rare, genuine smiles as they entered the house together. "It's definitely too late to order takeout from anywhere."

While he cooked the eggs and added diced ham and shredded cheese, she fed Heidi and refreshed the dog's water bowl. "Here you go." He set the perfectly prepared omelets on the kitchen table, relieved to see that playing with her beloved companion had removed much of the visible stress and tension from Shea's face.

"Thanks, Trevor. This smells incredible." She dug into the food with evident hunger. "I'm much hungrier than I realized. I don't think I ate anything for lunch."

"Are you planning to pull the entire department together first thing in the morning to devise a comprehensive plan for luring Cletus out of hiding?" He settled into the chair across from her at the small table.

She nodded while chewing. "Absolutely. But let's

not talk about work tonight. I've had more than enough police business for one day."

"What would you like to talk about instead?"

She studied his face thoughtfully as she took another forkful of the omelet. "Have you always wanted to pursue a career in law enforcement?"

"Ever since the police officers saved me from my brother that night, I've wanted to be a hero to someone else who desperately needed help." He sipped his coffee, remembering that terrible time with surprising clarity.

She leaned back in her chair. "Have you ever actually felt like a hero?"

"Once." He laughed at the memory. "I rescued a little girl's kitten that had gotten stuck high up in an oak tree. She stopped crying immediately and gave me a piece of lint-covered candy from her pocket as a reward."

Shea laughed with genuine amusement, the sound musical and warm. "That's incredibly sweet."

"Do you realize that's the first time I've heard you really laugh?" The sound was like music to his ears, low and melodic and completely natural. He desperately wanted to make her laugh and smile more often.

"I haven't had very many reasons to laugh lately."

"Not even when you're with your college friends?"

She set down her fork and wiped her mouth with a

napkin. "I do laugh when I'm with my girlfriends, but I've always been considered the serious, responsible one of our group."

"Tell me about them. I'd like to know more about the people who matter to you."

"Okay." She settled back in her chair, her expression softening with fond memories. "Becky is my absolute best friend and the typical soccer mom with her color-coded lists and schedules for everything. Emma is the eternal cheerleader, always optimistic and encouraging. Deborah can actually be more serious than me sometimes, which is saying something. Rachel is the pessimist of the group, always expecting the worst possible outcome." She paused, her smile fading slightly. "The others—Tessa, Lauren, Melanie, and Annie—are all hardworking career women with demanding jobs. At least Melanie was before she was murdered on the mountain." The familiar shadows returned to her eyes. "I would die for any one of them without hesitation."

"It sounds like you almost did die protecting them. How often do you all manage to get together?"

"Not nearly often enough. We always aim for at least once a year, but sometimes two or three years will pass between visits because of work and family obligations. After what happened last time..." She trailed off, staring into her coffee cup. "We haven't even mentioned the possibility of getting together again."

"Maybe you should plan something once this nightmare with Cletus is finally over. It would do you good to get away and spend time with people who care about you after everything he's putting you through."

"Maybe I will." She carried their dirty dishes to the dishwasher, clearly signaling that the conversation was over. "Goodnight, Trevor."

"Goodnight, Shea."

As he watched her disappear down the hallway with Heidi close behind, Trevor found himself hoping that whatever plan they developed in the morning would finally put an end to Cletus and his deadly games once and for all.

Chapter Fifteen

The day after meeting with her deputies to formulate a comprehensive plan to lure Cletus out of hiding, Shea glanced at the clock on her office wall for what felt like the hundredth time in the past hour. Waiting had never been one of her virtues, and the anticipation was eating at her nerves like acid. It was becoming increasingly difficult to sit still when she knew that tonight could finally bring this nightmare to an end.

The plan they'd developed was deceptively simple but required precise timing and coordination. She would head to an abandoned mill on the outskirts of town—a location that Bill Butler had scouted extensively and declared perfect for their purposes. The old structure was isolated enough that Cletus would feel confident approaching, but it also offered multiple concealment positions for backup teams to remain hidden until needed.

Word about Shea's supposed plans to visit the mill had spread through Misty Hollow faster than she'd thought possible, which was precisely what they'd hoped for. All she'd had to do was casually mention to the chatty server at Lucy's diner that she intended to spend some alone time exploring the supposedly haunted old mill after work. She'd explained that she was fascinated by local ghost stories and paranormal activities and had heard the mill was a hotspot for supernatural encounters.

The waitress had eaten up every word of the fabricated story, her eyes wide with concern and excitement. By evening, half the town would know that their sheriff was planning to spend hours alone at the mill, apparently in search of ghosts. It was the perfect bait for someone like Cletus, who wouldn't be able to resist the opportunity to catch her isolated and vulnerable.

"It's time." Trevor poked his head into her office, his expression a mixture of determination and barely concealed worry. "You ready for this?"

"As ready as I can be." She checked the ammunition in her service weapon one final time, then holstered it and followed him outside. The other deputies from her department, along with several borrowed officers from Langley, were gathered in the parking lot as the sun began its descent toward the western peaks of the mountains.

The late afternoon air carried the crisp bite of

autumn, and the trees surrounding the station displayed their full fall colors—brilliant reds, oranges, and golds that would have been beautiful under different circumstances. Tonight, however, the approaching darkness felt ominous rather than peaceful.

Since Bill Butler knew the terrain around the old mill better than anyone else on the team, he had volunteered to lead the convoy and coordinate the positioning of personnel. The mill itself stood in a small clearing, surrounded by dense forest and thick undergrowth that would provide excellent concealment for the backup teams. The narrow gravel road they'd use to reach the location was the only vehicle access to the site, unless someone was willing to hike several miles through rugged mountain terrain on foot.

The vehicles were parked strategically out of sight behind a sagging, weather-beaten barn that sat about two hundred yards from the mill. From there, the teams could respond quickly if needed while remaining completely invisible to anyone approaching the target location.

The tactical plan was straightforward but thorough. Shea would position herself inside the mill with a concealed earpiece hidden beneath her jacket collar, allowing her to maintain constant communication with the backup teams. Trevor would lead the primary response unit stationed in the woods nearby, splitting his personnel into two distinct groups for maximum coverage and flexibility.

One team would monitor the access road with spike strips already deployed and ready to deploy if Cletus attempted to flee by vehicle. The second team would position themselves strategically throughout the surrounding forest, prepared to close in from multiple directions on Trevor's signal. Everyone involved understood their roles and responsibilities.

It should have been a foolproof plan. So why did cold fingers of dread walk slowly up her spine as she approached the entrance to the abandoned mill?

"You okay?" Trevor placed his hands gently on her shoulders and searched her eyes with obvious concern. "Your face has gone ashen."

"I'm fine. Just pre-operation nerves." She tried to project confidence she didn't entirely feel.

"It's not too late to let me take your place inside. Cletus won't be able to tell who's waiting for him in a dark building until he's close enough for us to take him down."

"No, absolutely not. It has to be me." Her voice carried unwavering determination. "He's obsessed with me specifically, and if he senses any kind of deception, he'll disappear back into the mountains. Besides, if something goes wrong, I don't want any of my team members getting hurt because of my decisions."

She knew that Cletus would be highly wary of any situation that seemed too convenient or easy. The man might be obsessed beyond rational thought, but he wasn't stupid. He would almost certainly suspect that some kind of trap was being set, and his intimate knowledge of these mountains gave him significant advantages over the law enforcement officers trying to capture him.

"Here." Bill approached with supplies, handing her a water bottle and an energy bar. "We have no idea how long you might have to wait in there. Could be minutes, could be hours."

"How long should we realistically plan to maintain position?" She glanced around at the assembled group of officers, noting the determination on their faces. "The story I spread around town was that I'm planning to spend several hours at the mill, potentially late into the night."

"Trying to spot the ghost of some miller who supposedly died there a century ago." Trevor managed a slight smile despite the tension. "You sold the crazy sheriff angle."

"The girl at Lucy's completely bought the story about me having some kind of mental breakdown." Shea took a sip of water to combat her dry throat. "Nothing draws gossip and attention in a small town like the local sheriff going a bit unstable." She straightened her shoulders and checked her equipment one final time. "Okay, let's do this."

She started toward the mill entrance, then stopped halfway and turned back to the group. "Wait. Cletus will expect to see my personal vehicle here. If my truck isn't visible, he'll know immediately that something's wrong."

"Good catch." Trevor quickly ordered one of the Langley deputies to move Shea's truck from the hidden parking area and position it conspicuously next to the mill building, as if she'd driven there alone and planned to spend the evening exploring.

Inside the mill, she located the concealed position that Bill had prepared for her during his reconnaissance mission the previous night. The spot offered good sight lines to all the entrances while providing cover from multiple angles. She settled onto the portable stool he'd hidden there and leaned her head back against the cold brick wall.

"I don't want to have to kill again," she whispered, the words barely audible even to herself.

Trevor's voice came through the earpiece, soft but firm with conviction. "We'll do absolutely everything in our power to prevent that outcome, but if it comes down to a choice between you and him..." His tone hardened with protective steel. "You choose yourself. Every single time."

The last rays of sunlight gradually disappeared behind the trees, casting the interior of the mill into almost complete darkness. Shea activated the battery-powered camping lantern that Bill had left strategically positioned nearby during his setup work. Its pale glow cast long, dancing shadows across the dust-covered floor, making her wish desperately that she'd brought Heidi along for emotional support and companionship.

Her earpiece crackled with Trevor's voice. "All teams report in. Confirm positions."

"Road team in position," came the first response. "Spike strips deployed and ready."

"Woods team Alpha positioned," reported another voice. "Good sight lines to the mill."

"Woods team Bravo ready," added a third officer. "Northern approach covered."

"Sniper Delgado in position," came the final report from the borrowed Langley officer positioned in the old barn. "Clear view of all approaches. No movement detected."

"Copy all teams. Maintain radio discipline from this point forward. Sheriff, keep your movements to an absolute minimum. Don't make yourself an easy target and stay well away from the windows. Remember, Delgado has overwatch and will take the shot if necessary."

"Understood." Shea fought to keep her voice steady despite the tightness building in her chest and the rapid beating of her heart. She positioned herself carefully on the stool with her service weapon resting across her lap, finger near but not on the trigger.

The minutes seemed to crawl by agonizingly slowly, every slight sound amplified by the silence and her heightened state of alertness. A field mouse darted across the floor, stirring up small clouds of dust that made her nose itch. She fought the urge to fidget or shift position, knowing that any unnecessary movement could give away her location or create noise that might alert Cletus to the trap.

After what felt like an eternity, she made the tactical decision to extinguish the lantern. She wouldn't be easily spotted in the dark corner where she waited, and the darkness would give her a significant advantage if Cletus did appear. If he came—and she was increasingly convinced that he would—she would have the element of surprise on her side.

"Nothing yet on any front," Trevor reported through the earpiece. "Road remains clear. Sniper reports no movement in the surrounding trees. Hold your position and stay alert."

Radio chatter from the various team members began filling her ears as the waiting continued.

"If this guy's as psychologically unstable as the profiler described, he's probably not going to approach quietly or cautiously."

"Let's hope we're wrong about that. A quiet approach would make our job much easier."

"Intelligence suggests he might not come alone. Could have hired muscle with him."

"Then we take down whoever shows up. The important thing is ending this tonight."

But Shea knew better. Her instincts told her that Cletus would come, and he would come alone. The other deputies were wrong about his likely approach. He wouldn't arrive like a ghost or try to sneak up on her. This had become too personal, too much about his obsession with her specifically. He would want to face her directly, to look her in the eyes when he made his move.

She slipped her hand into her jacket pocket, curling her fingers around the small digital recorder she'd placed there as a precautionary measure. She'd insisted on bringing the device in case she could somehow coerce Cletus into confessing to his crimes or making incriminating statements. Shea wasn't taking any chances of having evidence thrown out on technicalities. This man needed to be locked away for the rest of his natural life.

"Delgado reporting from overwatch position," came the sniper's voice through the communication system. "Main entrance remains clear. No movement detected in any direction. Continuing to monitor."

Shea rechecked her ammunition supply, a nervous habit that helped calm her nerves. Sitting completely motionless was making her hypersensitive to every sound—the rustle of wind through the dead leaves outside, the scratch of a tree branch rubbing against the exterior wall of the mill, the distant call of a night bird. Each noise sent fresh perspiration running down her back despite the cool temperature of the autumn evening.

She was beginning to think she preferred direct, face-to-face confrontation to this nerve-wracking waiting and uncertainty. At least in a direct fight, she could take action and influence the outcome. This passive waiting felt like torture.

Based on everything she'd learned about Cletus's psychology, she was confident he wouldn't bring accomplices tonight. That part of his campaign was over. The hired help, the coordinated attacks, the psychological warfare—all of that had been building up to this moment. Now it was strictly between the two of them, and the man would eliminate anyone who tried to interfere with what he saw as his vendetta.

The faint crackle of gravel being disturbed on the access road was almost imperceptible at first, barely audible over the ambient forest sounds. But Shea's trained ears caught it immediately. She stiffened and leaned forward slightly, straining to hear more details.

"Trevor, do you copy? I think I hear something on the road."

"Confirmed. Road team, report status immediately."

"We have movement on the access road," came the tense response. "Single vehicle approaching with headlights extinguished. Appears to be an older model pickup truck, possibly dark colored."

Shea's pulse quickened dramatically. She took a deep, steadying breath and forced her hands to remain steady on her weapon. Her gaze locked onto the mill's main entrance, where the faint outline of the doorframe was barely visible in the darkness.

"All teams, stay sharp and maintain positions," Trevor commanded with quiet authority. "Woods teams, hold your positions until my signal. Sniper, keep continuous eyes on the target."

This was it. Everything they'd planned and prepared for was about to unfold. Shea felt a mixture of relief that the waiting was finally over and intense anxiety about what the next few minutes would bring.

"Target is exiting the vehicle," Delgado reported from her elevated position. "Single male subject, definitely armed with what appears to be a long gun. Moving on foot toward the mill. Approach is slow and extremely cautious."

Shea adjusted her grip on her service weapon, her finger hovering just off the trigger guard. "How close is he now?"

"Approximately forty yards from your position and closing steadily," Trevor answered. "Remember the operational plan. Do not engage unless necessary for your safety. Let him make the first move."

The sound of boots crunching on gravel grew progressively louder and more distinct. She could hear each careful footstep as he approached, could almost sense his hyperalert state and suspicious nature. A dry twig snapped under his weight, the sound sharp in the night air.

Shea's heart was racing now, but she forced herself to remain completely motionless and focused on the task ahead.

"Ten yards from the entrance," Trevor reported. "He's stopped and appears to be scanning the area carefully. All teams stay ready for rapid deployment."

A dark shadow passed across one of the broken windows on the side of the building. She quickly wiped her sweaty palm on her jeans before retightening her grip on her weapon, making sure her hands wouldn't slip at the crucial moment.

"Road team, maintain maximum alertness," Trevor continued. "This situation could deteriorate very quickly."

"Target appears increasingly agitated," Delgado added from her sniper position. "He's systematically scanning the entire area around the mill. I'm holding fire and waiting for your signal."

The mill's front door creaked ominously as Cletus finally pushed it open, revealing his silhouette in the doorway. He clutched what looked like a pump-action shotgun in both hands and stepped cautiously across the threshold into the dark interior.

"Shea," Trevor whispered through the earpiece. "Wait for my signal. Do not move until I tell you."

"Copy that." Her response was barely above a whisper, almost inaudible even through the sensitive microphone.

~

Trevor kept his gaze fixed intently on Cletus from his carefully chosen vantage point in the abandoned barn. In the hayloft directly overhead, he could hear the faint rustle of straw as Delgado made minor adjustments to her sniper position for the best possible shot angle.

"Give me the green light, Deputy," Delgado requested through the communication system. "I have a clear shot on the target."

"Negative. Not yet. He needs to make verbal contact with Sheriff Callahan first." Trevor prayed silently that he wasn't making a catastrophic tactical error. Shea was trusting him completely to keep her safe and make the right decisions at the critical moments.

"I'm losing visual contact as he moves deeper into the building."

"Not yet," Shea whispered through her earpiece. "If we move too early, he could flee back into the mountains, and we'll never get another chance like this."

"I need to relocate to maintain sight lines, Sheriff. Otherwise, I won't be able to engage if he moves further into the mill."

"Do it quickly and quietly," Trevor authorized. "Shea, stay completely silent. Let him discover your presence naturally."

The air around the mill seemed to grow thick with tension and anticipation. All radio communication ceased as everyone held their breath.

What was Cletus doing in there? He'd remained motionless since entering the building, probably listening for any sounds that might indicate a trap. After several long moments, he took a deliberate step backward and exited the mill entirely, emerging into the moonlight.

Trevor watched through his night vision scope as Cletus turned in a slow, complete circle, obviously expecting an ambush to materialize from the surrounding darkness. When nothing happened and no one revealed themselves, he took a deep breath and reentered the mill with renewed determination.

"Sheriff?" Cletus called out, his voice echoing in the empty space.

Trevor's grip tightened involuntarily on his weapon as his pulse spiked with adrenaline.

The trap was set perfectly. The next few minutes would determine whether this night ended in victory and justice, or in violence and tragedy.

Chapter Sixteen

Cletus entered the mill for the second time, his footsteps echoing ominously in the cavernous space. Shea slowly rose from her concealed position on the stool, one hand gripping her service weapon tightly, the other reaching for the tactical flashlight clipped to her duty belt. Her heart hammered against her ribs as adrenaline flooded her system.

"You here, Sheriff?" His voice, while deliberately kept low, seemed to boom and reverberate in the oppressive silence of the abandoned mill. The acoustics of the empty building amplified every sound, making even his breathing audible. He muttered something unintelligible to himself, then appeared to hesitate before starting to turn back toward the entrance.

"I'm here," Shea called out from the protective shadows where she'd been waiting, her voice steady despite the fear coursing through her veins.

"Didn't think you were stupid enough to come out

here alone just to look for some mythical ghosts." There was dark amusement in his tone, as if he found her supposed paranormal interests both ridiculous and pathetic.

"It sounded like it might be fun," she replied, carefully staying in the darkest corner of the mill while slowly beginning to skirt around the perimeter to move closer to his position. "I'm surprised it took you this long to join me. I've been here for hours."

"Had some important business to take care of first." His answer was deliberately vague, but she could hear the underlying threat in his casual tone.

"I've lost visual contact," Delgado reported through the communication system, frustration evident in her voice.

"Maintain position and stay alert," Trevor responded immediately.

Cletus suddenly took several deliberate steps backward, his head tilted slightly as if he were straining to hear something. Could he somehow detect the faint radio chatter through Shea's concealed earpiece? The device was supposed to be virtually undetectable, but Cletus had proven to be more observant and cunning than anyone had anticipated.

"Shh." Shea cleared her throat loudly, hoping to mask any potential electronic sounds. "So what happens now, Cletus? What's your grand plan?"

"Come out of hiding where I can see you properly, and I'll be happy to show you exactly what I have in mind." His voice carried a predatory quality that made her skin crawl.

Shea clicked on her tactical flashlight and immediately directed the powerful beam straight into his eyes, hoping to temporarily blind and disorient him.

He staggered backward, cursing violently as he raised his free hand to shield his face from the intense light. Then, to her surprise, he laughed—a sound completely devoid of humor or sanity. "You got me there; I'll give you that. But you're still a stupid woman if you thought I'd walk into an obvious trap without being fully prepared for every contingency."

With fluid, practiced movements, he pulled what appeared to be a homemade Molotov cocktail from inside his heavy coat. The glass bottle was stuffed with a cloth wick that he quickly ignited with a disposable lighter. "See you in hell, Sheriff," he snarled, hurling the improvised incendiary device in her general direction.

He immediately darted toward the rear of the mill and dove headfirst through one of the broken windows, glass shards raining down around him as he made his escape.

Shea lunged desperately out of the path of the flaming bottle, which shattered against a pile of discarded cardboard boxes and yellowed papers that had been left behind when the mill ceased operations decades ago. The aged materials caught fire instantly, and flames began spreading rapidly across the debris-littered floor.

"He's getting away!" she shouted into her microphone while scrambling to her feet. "The building is on fire!"

"Delgado, be ready for any target that emerges," Trevor's voice held unmistakable urgency. "All teams converge on the mill."

"I can't see anything through all this smoke," the sniper reported, frustration clear in her transmission.

"He escaped through the back window," Shea called out, already moving toward the same opening. "I'm going after him immediately."

"Negative! Meet us outside. Do not pursue alone," Trevor ordered firmly.

"You'd better move fast then, because I'm not letting him slip away again." Without waiting for a response, Shea sprinted toward the rear of the burning building and climbed through the same window Cletus had used for his escape route.

Outside, crushed grass and broken vegetation clearly showed which direction the fugitive had fled. "All teams spread out in a search line," she commanded through her radio. "He's headed directly for the tree line."

The sound of Trevor's boots thundered against the ground as he rounded the corner of the building at full speed. Side by side, he and Shea immediately gave chase into the dark forest, their flashlight beams cutting narrow paths through the dense undergrowth.

What little natural moonlight had been available became almost completely nonexistent once they plunged into the woods. The thick canopy overhead, still heavy with autumn leaves that hadn't yet fallen, created an oppressive, claustrophobic environment that seemed to press in around them from all sides. Fallen branches, dense undergrowth, and the occasional small animal scurrying away from their approach made the terrain both treacherous and disorienting. Yet Cletus seemed to navigate through it all with the confidence of someone who knew every inch of these mountains.

Shea's breathing quickly became labored and ragged. The muscles in her thighs screamed in protest at the sudden intense exercise after spending more than an hour perched motionless on the small stool. Beside her, Trevor appeared to have no trouble maintaining the demanding pace, his longer stride and superior conditioning giving him a clear advantage.

On each side of their position, though well out of sight, came the sounds of the other pursuit teams also crashing through the forest in hot pursuit. With so many officers converging from multiple directions, Cletus couldn't possibly escape this time. The net was closing around him.

For several heart-stopping moments, Shea completely lost sight of their quarry in the darkness. Then she spotted him again as he veered sharply to the left, darting between the massive tree trunks with the agility and grace of a deer that had been startled from cover. The blue and white plaid flannel shirt he wore provided just enough contrast against the dark shadows, making him visually impossibly difficult to track.

Trevor stumbled over an unseen obstacle but managed to catch himself before falling, muttering something about Cletus being as slippery and elusive as a greased eel. Shea ignored his commentary, keeping her focus entirely on her breathing technique and maintaining visual contact with the man who had brought so much terror and chaos to her peaceful town.

Cletus suddenly paused in his flight long enough to spin around and fire a shot from his shotgun. The blast echoed through the forest like thunder, and the bullet struck a large oak tree just inches from Shea's head, sending fragments of bark flying into her face. She instinctively put her fingers to her cheek, bringing them away with small droplets of blood on the tips.

Somewhere to their right, someone screamed in pain. Shea's steps faltered momentarily as she contemplated breaking off the pursuit to render aid to the injured officer. No, that would allow Cletus to escape once again into the vast wilderness. The wounded deputy would have to wait for medical attention.

As they continued their ascent up the steep mountainside, the air grew noticeably colder and thinner. Shea's lungs burned as she struggled to draw enough oxygen, desperately needing a rest but refusing to give up ground on their target.

The chase led them dangerously close to a rocky ravine where loose stones created treacherous footing. Trevor slipped on the unstable gravel and nearly fell over the precipice. Shea grabbed his jacket and hauled him back from the edge. "Watch your step," she gasped.

"Thanks for the save," he panted.

"Anytime, partner." They continued following Cletus's trail to the right, eventually splashing through an ice-cold mountain creek that soaked them up to their knees. Nothing was worse than trying to run in waterlogged boots and pants that clung to her legs. The further Cletus led them through this nightmarish obstacle course, the angrier Shea's stomach boiled.

The fugitive seemed to zigzag randomly to the right and left, then suddenly run straight ahead for long stretches. What kind of twisted game was he playing now? He knew these mountains like the back of his hand, yet his movements seemed almost random and without any clear destination in mind.

Shea suddenly tripped over something stretched across the path, sliding across the muddy ground on her stomach with her hands stretched out in front of her to break the fall. "What did I trip over?" she asked, spitting dirt from her mouth.

"Looks like a tripwire stretched between two trees at ankle height," Trevor observed, helping her struggle back to her feet. "Classic booby trap. Are you injured?"

"Just scraped up and angry, but I'm fine. Come

on, we can't afford to stop." They couldn't lose momentum now, not even for scraped hands and knees. "Everyone keep your eyes open for more booby—"

A bloodcurdling scream of agony suddenly came from behind them and off to their right, cutting through the night air like a blade. "All units, watch your footing," Shea broadcast urgently into her radio. "Suspect has set traps throughout this area and is deliberately leading us into them."

"Both Langley officers are down, but injuries appear non-fatal," Bill Butler reported grimly. "One officer took a sharpened stake through the leg. The other stepped into what looks like a modified bear trap. Cletus is systematically picking off our people one by one."

"All remaining units pull back to safe positions," Shea commanded. "Deputy Bolton and I will continue the pursuit alone." She couldn't risk losing any more of her officers to Cletus's deadly games. Next time, someone might not survive their injuries. If anyone had to pay the ultimate price tonight, it needed to be Cletus Hodges.

"Get those wounded officers immediate medical attention," she added.

She lost sight of their target again as he seemed to vanish into the darkness ahead. The forest fell silent except for the sound of her and Trevor's labored breathing and the distant calls of night birds. After several tense minutes that felt like hours, a twig snapped audibly somewhere to their left, and the deadly chase resumed with renewed urgency.

"Miss me yet?" Cletus called out mockingly.

Shea spun around, trying to locate the source of his voice.

He stood prominently on top of a large rock formation that appeared to conceal a cave entrance, his teeth flashing in a predatory grin that was visible even in the dim available light. "Getting tired already? I could keep this up all night long if necessary."

"Come down from there and let's finish this once and for all," Shea called back, her eyes narrowing with determination. Her service weapon wouldn't be accurate enough to do significant damage at that distance.

"I can circle and approach from behind," Trevor whispered urgently.

"Absolutely not. We stay together." Separating would make them both too vulnerable to Cletus's traps and superior knowledge of the terrain.

Cletus ducked out of sight behind the rocky outcropping.

Shea holstered her weapon, grabbed onto a sturdy young sapling, and began pulling herself up the steep side of the rocky formation. Trevor followed her lead, and they climbed together. When they finally reached the top, she immediately drew her gun again. Cletus was nowhere to be seen.

Her shoulders sagged with exhaustion and frustration. They couldn't have allowed him to escape again, not after coming this close.

~

"He wants us to follow him deeper into his territory," Trevor observed, leaning against a tree trunk to catch his breath. "This is all part of his plan. He'll show himself again when he's ready."

He'd no sooner finished speaking when Cletus appeared again, this time standing on a small ridge about a hundred yards ahead. The trees had thinned considerably the farther up the mountain they'd climbed, and the moon provided a perfect dramatic backdrop for his silhouette. "There he is, bold as brass."

Cletus waved at them in a mocking gesture.

"We're being led into an elaborate trap," Trevor said, exhaling heavily. "This whole chase has been choreographed."

"We don't have any choice in the matter. One way or another, this nightmare ends tonight." Shea moved forward with grim determination, leaving Trevor to follow in her wake. "How often do you think this kind of thing happens—chasing dangerous criminals across these mountains?"

"Probably more than most people realize. There are plenty of places to hide up here, and folks could go completely off the grid and never be seen again if they wanted to disappear." Now that they understood Cletus wouldn't simply vanish on them, and that prolonging the chase was part of his twisted plan, they reduced their pace to a more sustainable quick walk. Trevor didn't like being led around like a dog chasing a bone, but he also understood they had little choice.

Whatever Cletus had planned at the end of this deadly game would most likely mean the end of one of them, or quite possibly both him and Shea. He couldn't allow that to happen. The only person who would be going down permanently tonight was Cletus Hodges.

"This is ridiculous," Shea muttered, shoving a low-hanging branch away from her face. "We set up an elaborate trap, and now we're the ones being manipulated and coerced."

"We could turn around and walk away, let him come to us again on our terms," Trevor suggested.

"No." She glanced over her shoulder with fierce determination. "This ends tonight, here and now. You don't have to be part of this anymore, Trevor. This is ultimately between me and Cletus."

"It stopped being just about the two of you a long time ago," he replied firmly. "I'm staying until the end." Even though his feelings for her had grown far beyond simple professional respect, he was still a sworn deputy with a duty to uphold the law and protect innocent people.

"I can't have you becoming a distraction when things get violent." She continued moving forward through the undergrowth.

"I won't be a distraction. I promise."

"Over here, Sheriff!" Cletus's voice suddenly rang clearly through the trees. "How about picking up the pace a little? I don't have all night to waste on this."

"I'm going to cut out his arrogant tongue," Shea growled. The fugitive's constant taunts were becoming extremely irritating.

"As satisfying as that sounds, I'd much rather see him stand trial and go to prison for the rest of his natural life," Trevor replied. "Maybe he can be cellmates with his brother Darryl."

They eventually found Cletus waiting for them in front of a small cabin that appeared to be well-maintained despite the overgrown yard and gardens. In his right hand, he brandished a large hunting knife with obvious confidence, clearly prepared for the final confrontation. "I was beginning to think you'd never find your way here."

"Drop your weapon immediately," Shea commanded, raising her gun to aim directly at his center mass. "This is over. You can't win."

"Oh, but I absolutely can win," he replied with that same predatory grin. "And I will."

"There's nowhere left to run, Cletus. You're surrounded and outgunned."

While Shea kept the man's attention focused entirely on her and their verbal exchange, Trevor began moving carefully around them in a wide circle, hoping to position himself behind Cletus for a tactical advantage. If the fugitive made even the slightest aggressive move toward Shea, Trevor was prepared to shoot him without hesitation.

When he felt he was close enough, Trevor suddenly rushed forward and tackled Cletus to the ground with all the force he could muster.

Cletus maintained his grip on the hunting knife and slashed viciously toward Trevor's exposed throat. Trevor rolled desperately to the side, barely avoiding the razor-sharp blade.

"Move away from him, Trevor!" Shea still had her weapon trained on Cletus, but she couldn't risk taking a shot with Trevor so close to the target.

"This is going to be even more fun than I planned," Cletus snarled. "I only intended to fight the sheriff tonight, but you'll make an excellent warm-up exercise." He thrust the knife forward in a deadly arc.

Trevor lunged to the side again to give Shea a clear shooting angle, but his foot caught on a protruding tree root, and he tumbled hard to the ground, the impact knocking the wind completely out of his lungs. Cletus immediately leaped on top of him like a predator pouncing on wounded prey.

The hunting knife found its mark, sliding between Trevor's ribs with sickening ease. Cletus twisted the blade deliberately, eliciting a cry of pain from his victim. Trevor managed to shove the larger man off him, but Cletus jumped right back into the attack, using Trevor's body as a shield between himself and Shea's gun.

"Drop your weapon right now, Sheriff, or I finish him off," Cletus threatened, pressing the bloody knife against Trevor's throat. "It would be a real pity, since my actual beef isn't with him at all."

"Don't do it, Shea," Trevor managed to grind out through clenched teeth, trying to push down the white-hot pain radiating from his wounded side.

Indecision flickered across her face as her gaze darted frantically from Cletus to Trevor and back again. After a moment of agonizing hesitation, she slowly lowered her gun hand.

"Drop it completely and kick it toward me," Cletus ordered with obvious satisfaction.

Shea reluctantly did as she was commanded, her service weapon sliding across the ground to stop at Cletus's feet.

"Now get yourself into that cabin," he continued. "I'm going to bring my new friend here inside with us, and you're going to tie him securely to a chair. Try anything clever or heroic, and I'll kill him slowly and painfully."

"He needs immediate medical attention," Shea protested. "Let him go, and this can stay between you and me."

"I need him as leverage, Sheriff. You're far too strong-willed and stubborn to cooperate just because I ask nicely." Cletus kept the knife pressed against Trevor's throat while he forced him to stand. "Now get moving."

Trevor's knees threatened to buckle as Cletus shoved him roughly toward the cabin entrance. Inside, he collapsed gratefully into a wooden chair, his vision blurring from blood loss and pain.

"There's rope on that kitchen table," Cletus said, gesturing with his knife. "The owners of this place don't stay here during the colder months, so we have complete privacy. Now we can finally have some real fun."

"No more games," Shea said firmly. "Let's just end this."

"I'm in complete control now, Sheriff," he replied with obvious satisfaction. "Now tie him up properly. Make sure those knots are tight, because if he manages to escape, he's a dead man."

With apparent reluctance and apologetic eyes, Shea wrapped the rope around Trevor multiple times, then secured it with knots tied behind the chair where he couldn't reach them. "At least let me put some kind of bandage on that knife wound," she pleaded.

"Fine. Use a dish towel from the kitchen," Cletus said, lowering himself slowly onto the leather sofa with a satisfied sigh. "I'm looking forward to finishing you off nice and slow, Sheriff Callahan. You didn't just murder my brother in cold blood—you destroyed my entire family."

"Nothing personal about it," she replied, returning with a clean towel that she carefully positioned under the rope to press against Trevor's wound. "I was just doing my job."

Trevor hissed involuntarily at the pressure but

managed to give her an encouraging look.

"That's not true at all," Cletus said, his face darkening with anger. "You weren't even officially the sheriff yet when you killed Bruce."

"Actually, yes, I was. I just hadn't started working in the office yet," she corrected, her worried eyes meeting Trevor's. "The election was already over."

"I'll be fine," Trevor assured her quietly. "This is just another scar to add to the collection of five I already have from my brother."

He forced a weak smile, trying to project more confidence than he felt.

"I'll find us a way out of this mess," she whispered, gently cupping his cheek with her hand.

"Now who's making promises they might not be able to keep?" he replied softly.

Chapter Seventeen

"Finally. I have Shea Callahan, the mighty sheriff, exactly where I want her." Cletus sneered with dark satisfaction, savoring the moment he'd been dreaming about for months. "Let's relive that memorable time on the mountain, shall we? Only this time it won't be a Hodges brother who ends up lying dead in the dirt."

The mention of the mountain incident sent Shea's mind reeling backward in time to that awful weekend that had changed everything. The bone-deep fear she'd felt for her friends' safety. The loud, taunting music blared from the hunters' camp. The terrifying sound of random gunfire echoing through the forest. The moments when those evil men had stormed their rented cabin with murderous intent. Her desperate hand-to-hand combat with Bruce Hodges, fighting for her very life. Then the harrowing journey through the dark woods as she led her surviving friends to safety, never knowing if they would make it out alive.

She could still remember sitting in the back of Sheriff Westbrook's squad car afterward, the crushing weight of having taken a human life washing over her like a devastating tsunami. She continued to have vivid nightmares about that terrifying weekend, waking up drenched in cold sweat and gasping for air. Now she was facing a frighteningly similar circumstance. If she somehow managed to survive this confrontation again, there would undoubtedly be many more sleepless nights filled with trauma and guilt.

She pushed herself to her feet with deliberate slowness and turned to face Cletus directly, quickly redoing her hair into a tight ponytail to keep it entirely out of her face during the inevitable fight. "I'm certain you're wrong about that prediction."

"Looks like your faithful deputy might be the first one to go." Cletus grinned with malicious glee, gesturing toward Trevor with obvious satisfaction. "Just look at him, bleeding out slowly like a stuck pig at slaughter time."

Shea's gaze snapped instantly from Trevor's pale, pain-etched face back to Cletus, her fists clenching involuntarily with righteous fury. "You don't get to talk about him. You don't get to talk about anything worthwhile."

Cletus roared with rage and lunged forward aggressively, swinging his hunting knife in a wild, deadly arc intended to disembowel her. Shea had anticipated his crude attack and sidestepped with practiced grace, immediately delivering a powerful roundhouse kick to his exposed ribs. He grunted in pain but recovered his balance with surprising speed.

Grabbing a heavy metal camping lantern from a nearby wooden table, he swung it toward her head with brutal force.

She ducked low, narrowly avoiding the potentially skull-crushing blow, and immediately countered with a lightning-fast jab to his jaw that sent him staggering backward into the wall.

"You've definitely gotten tougher since our last encounter," Cletus acknowledged, wiping fresh blood from his split mouth with the back of his free hand. "But you're still just a scared little girl trying to play hero in a man's world."

"You don't know the first thing about me," she replied, her words dripping with ice-cold contempt.

"Don't...let...him get...into your head, Shea." Trevor's strained words came from behind her, each syllable obviously costing him significant effort. "Remember all your training. You've absolutely got this."

Keep your focus completely centered, Shea! As much as she desperately wanted to rush to Trevor's aid and tend to his wounds, she couldn't afford to be distracted. Not until she permanently finished with Cletus. Hold on just a little longer, Trevor.

Cletus began pacing slowly in a deliberate circle

like a predator trying to position himself for the killing blow, constantly seeking the perfect angle of attack. The razor-sharp blade in his hand glinted menacingly in the flickering light of the single lantern still burning on the kitchen table.

Shea attempted to land another swift kick to his midsection, but he anticipated her move this time and delivered a brutal punch to her side that completely knocked the wind out of her lungs. She stumbled but somehow managed to keep her footing through sheer determination.

His next vicious punch sent her crashing backward into the heavy wooden table, the sharp edge digging painfully into her ribs and knocking the lantern to the floor where it shattered. Cletus loomed over her menacingly, his shadow falling across her like a dark omen. "All talk and no bite, Sheriff."

Summoning every ounce of her remaining strength, she swept his legs out from under him with a perfect martial arts technique and scrambled several feet away before delivering a devastating kick to his chest that sent him crashing violently into the cabin wall. "You should be very scared of my bite, Cletus."

He pushed himself away from the wall with apparent effort, shaking his head to clear the cobwebs. "You think this is just about survival? You're completely wrong. This is a final showdown between you and me, and only one of us will walk out of this cabin alive." He began dancing lightly on the balls of his feet, taunting her with exaggerated boxing movements. "This is my revenge for you completely ruining my family's legacy."

"Your so-called family consists of murderers who prey on innocent people for sport, hunting them like helpless animals for your twisted entertainment."

"It was just a game, nothing more serious than that."

"A deadly game that you and your brothers need to pay for with your lives. How many innocent people have you killed, Cletus? For how long has this been going on?" She kept her gaze locked intently on his, ready to spring into action the instant he made another aggressive move.

"You really want to have a philosophical discussion while your precious deputy lies there bleeding to death?" His eyes narrowed with cruel amusement.

"I'm perfectly fine," Trevor managed to say, though his voice was growing noticeably weaker.

Shea desperately hoped that was true. Eventually, backup would arrive to help them. They only had to survive long enough for reinforcements to reach this remote location. "Yes, I'd very much like to know the truth before I silence you permanently."

"Stalling for time, I see. Very intelligent strategy." He shrugged with apparent indifference. "Very well, I'll indulge your curiosity. We purchased that hunting cabin on the mountain exactly ten years ago with money we'd saved from various criminal enterprises. The first time we decided to rent it out for extra income was to a couple of businessmen wanting a weekend away from their nagging wives."

His expression grew dark with remembered anger. "When Darryl went up there to check on them and see whether they needed anything, they told him rudely to butt out and leave them alone. They paid for that disrespect with their lives."

Cletus grinned with obvious pride at the memory. "Darryl didn't take kindly to rudeness from city folks and came up with the hunting game as punishment. It turned out to be so much fun and so profitable that we decided to keep it going indefinitely. Maybe your deputy there, if he manages to live through his injuries, can do some research and find out just how many missing persons cases will never be solved." The man's eyes absolutely reeked of madness and complete moral bankruptcy.

"How many innocent people did you murder?" She ground the words through clenched teeth.

"I'm honestly not sure of the exact count, but I believe your group of friends might have brought the total number up to around twenty-five victims over the years. Sadly, I didn't personally participate in every hunt. I have a wife and children to support, after all."

"Don't you dare pretend to have even an ounce of human decency. You're evil to your very core."

Genuine anger sparked dangerously in his eyes.

"You're a cold-blooded murderer, exactly the same as I am."

"Mine was legitimate self-defense to protect innocent lives." Seeing a brief opening in his defenses, she lunged forward aggressively, her knife managing to catch and tear the hem of his flannel shirt.

Cletus's hunting knife grazed her side before she could completely free herself from his grasp, opening a shallow but painful cut. "Now things are finally getting interesting. No more dancing around each other like amateurs, Sheriff. Let's finish this properly." He leaped forward with renewed aggression.

She whipped away from his attack only to be jerked backward when he grabbed her ponytail and yanked with brutal force. Her head snapped back violently, exposing her vulnerable throat to his blade. She immediately stomped down hard on his foot with her boot heel, then drove her head backward into his nose with all her strength. She smiled grimly at the satisfying sound of cartilage crunching and managed to yank herself free.

Blood spurted freely from his broken nose as he cursed creatively. "So, you want to play dirty now?"

"You're the one pulling hair like a little girl having a tantrum." Shea tilted her head mockingly and wiggled her fingers in a taunting come-here gesture.

Cletus charged forward like an enraged bull, wrapping his powerful arms around her waist and lifting her completely off the ground. He slammed her down onto the coffee table with devastating force. The furniture shattered completely under the impact, sending splinters of wood flying in all directions. She managed to kick him off her and rolled quickly back to her feet despite the pain.

The fight intensified dramatically from that point forward. One minute Shea had the upper hand with superior technique and training, the next minute Cletus dominated through brute strength and sheer viciousness. The man's deep, personal hatred of her made him a far more formidable and dangerous opponent than his brother Bruce, who had merely been playing a twisted game for entertainment.

"Take him down, Shea!" Trevor urged her on from his position tied to the chair, his voice growing weaker but still filled with determination and faith in her abilities.

She screamed with primal fury and threw her knife with perfect accuracy. The blade embedded itself deeply in his shoulder muscle. With a cry of rage and pain, he charged at her one final time. She planted her feet firmly and landed a fierce uppercut to his jaw with every ounce of strength she possessed. His head snapped back violently, and he collapsed like a felled tree.

Yanking her knife free from his shoulder, Shea straddled his unconscious form and raised the bloody weapon to deliver what should have been the killing blow. Rage and the desire for permanent vengeance clouded her vision like a red mist.

Cletus suddenly opened his eyes and laughed weakly. "Go ahead, Sheriff. Finish it properly. Prove to everyone watching that you and I aren't so different after all."

"No, Shea." Trevor's voice trembled with urgent concern. "You've already won this fight. There's no need to kill him in cold blood."

She shook her head vigorously to clear her vision and the bloodthirsty rage, then stood up slowly, glaring down at the defeated man with obvious contempt. "You don't get to control me or my actions anymore." Instead of using the blade, she brought the heavy hilt of her knife down hard on his skull.

His eyes rolled back as he lost consciousness. Shea retrieved her handcuffs from where she'd placed them next to her confiscated gun and secured his hands behind his back with practiced efficiency.

Rushing immediately to Trevor's side, she dropped to her knees and quickly worked to untie the ropes binding him to the chair. "Stay with me, Trevor. I refuse to lose my partner now."

"You won't lose me," he replied with a weak but genuine smile. "It's not a mortal wound by any means. Nothing that a few stitches and some rest can't fix completely."

"Don't be ridiculous and try to downplay this." She carefully pulled the blood-soaked dishtowel away from his side to examine the knife wound. "This is going to require much more than simple stitches. Let me find you a clean towel to help control the bleeding."

By the time she located a fresh towel in the kitchen, the welcome sounds of her backup team could be heard approaching the cabin from outside. Heavy boots thundered across the wooden porch.

"Sheriff? Deputy Bolton?" Bill Butler's familiar voice called out.

"We're in here, Bill." Shea quickly applied firm pressure to Trevor's wound with the clean towel. "We're going to need an ambulance here immediately."

"Way ahead of you on that, Sheriff." Bill appeared in the doorway and quickly assessed the chaotic scene—the destroyed furniture, the blood, and the unconscious Cletus. "I figured at least one of you would need serious medical attention." He glanced down at the slowly reviving Cletus with obvious disgust. "Want me to take out this piece of trash?"

"Yes, please. And make sure he's properly secured this time." She didn't want to have to hunt him down ever again. Turning her full attention back to Trevor, she asked, "Do you think you can walk if I help support you?"

"Just help me get to my feet." He grunted with obvious pain as she carefully placed his arm around her shoulders for support. "You're bleeding too."

"It's just a shallow graze. Nothing serious compared to your injury." She'd certainly had much worse wounds in the past.

She helped him slowly make his way onto the front porch, then carefully handed him over to the waiting paramedics who immediately informed her that both she and Trevor would need to be transported to the hospital to receive proper medical care. She nodded in agreement, then walked over to Bill, who was closing the back door of his squad car.

"How did you manage to find us way out here?" she asked with genuine curiosity.

"Deputy Bolton's cell phone," he replied with a satisfied grin. "We all have GPS tracking devices on our department phones for exactly this kind of emergency. Your phone too, but yours was turned off during the operation."

"What about the wounded Langley officers?"

"They'll both live and make full recoveries. Nothing that won't heal with time and proper medical treatment." He reached for the door handle. "Outstanding job tonight, Sheriff. I guess you do have what it takes to handle this position after all. I'll see you at the hospital."

"Thanks, Bill. That means more to me than you know." She stepped back as he drove away from the cabin with the captured Cletus secured in the back seat.

His professional approval probably shouldn't matter to her, but it did. She'd traveled a long, difficult road to gain acceptance from her deputies and the community. If fighting a dangerous man like Cletus Hodges was what it took to earn that hard-won approval from both the town and her fellow officers, she would gladly do it again without hesitation.

~

Trevor gradually woke from the post-surgery anesthesia to find Shea dozing fitfully in the uncomfortable visitor's chair beside his hospital bed. The stark white of a fresh bandage was visible through the cut in her shirt where Cletus had sliced her.

"Hey there." Her eyelids fluttered open as she sensed his movement.

"I needed surgery?" he asked, still feeling groggy from the medication.

"I tried to tell you that simple stitches wouldn't be nearly enough." She managed a tired but relieved smile. "Cletus missed hitting any vital organs, thankfully, but the knife wound went much deeper than the emergency room doctors initially liked. You'll be able to go home tomorrow morning if there's no sign of infection developing."

"What's the status on Cletus?"

"Broken nose, possible concussion, and a very long prison sentence ahead of him." She gave one of her rare, genuine laughs, then her expression sobered. "Thank you for preventing me from killing him when I had the chance."

"You didn't need the death of another human being weighing on your conscience," Trevor replied, though privately he wasn't entirely sure he wouldn't have killed Cletus himself if their roles had been reversed. He reached out and took her hand in his. "I'm thrilled you won that fight."

"So am I." A familiar shadow darkened her eyes, and she sighed heavily. "Trevor, I need to be honest with you. I don't have enough emotional capacity left in me for a romantic relationship right now. I'm too psychologically broken from everything that's happened. Maybe someday in the future, when I've had time to heal..."

"I'll wait as long as it takes," he replied without hesitation, gently squeezing her hand. "For now, we're friends and partners, and I'm perfectly content with that arrangement."

She nodded gratefully. "Bill Butler gave me his official approval to continue as sheriff. That's a big deal around here."

"It is a big deal coming from him." Trevor chuckled, deliberately refusing to dwell on his disappointment that Shea wasn't ready for anything more than friendship. He probably shouldn't want more either, given that they worked together with her as his direct superior. "The townspeople will give you their approval, too. You've earned your place here."

"Hopefully, now that Cletus will be locked away for the rest of his life, Misty Hollow will finally start to feel like home to me." She stood slowly, carefully slipping her hand free from his. "I'm going to head back to the house and get cleaned up. Check on Heidi and make sure she's okay. I'll be back first thing in the morning to take you home to my place until you're fully healed."

The pleasure of knowing he wouldn't have to stop seeing her every morning filled him with warm contentment. "I'll be right here waiting."

Someone suddenly screamed near the nurse's station, the sound echoing through the hospital corridor. "Stay right here in bed," Shea ordered firmly.

He would not lie there while she potentially faced danger alone. He flung the blanket off his body and carefully dragged his IV tower along with him as he followed her down the hallway, ignoring the sharp pain in his side.

"That Hodges man somehow escaped from custody!" One of the nurses pointed frantically toward the emergency stairwell.

"I'm completely serious, Trevor. Stay here where it's safe." Shea drew her service weapon from its holster and headed determinedly in the direction the terrified nurse had indicated.

Another piercing scream filled the air, and Shea whirled around just as Cletus suddenly jumped out from one of the patient rooms, wielding a stolen surgical scalpel in his hand with obvious murderous intent.

Without thinking or hesitating, Trevor lifted his IV tower and swung it with all his strength at Cletus's head. The metal pole connected with a solid thunk, and the escaped prisoner dropped to the floor like a sack of potatoes.

Trevor glanced at Shea and gave her a crooked, slightly embarrassed grin. "Like I've always told you, I've got your back no matter what."

Her eyes twinkled with amusement. "A lot of us have seen your back tonight, Trevor. I have to say, it's not a bad sight at all."

Heat rushed to his face as he suddenly realized the back of his hospital gown was gaping wide open, providing everyone with an unobstructed view. He quickly reached behind himself and held the fabric closed with his free hand. "It's not very ladylike to look."

She shrugged with obvious amusement. "I've never claimed to be a proper lady." She efficiently handcuffed the unconscious Cletus. "I guess I'll need to take care of getting him back into secure custody before I can head home."

"Back to bed immediately, Deputy," a giggling nurse instructed, leading Trevor back toward his room. "Next time you decide to leave your room for any reason, you might want to make sure you're properly tied in the back. Not that I and the other nurses are complaining about the view, mind you."

That was not a mistake he would ever make again. As the acute embarrassment gradually faded, he found himself laughing despite the pain in his side. He hadn't thought twice about coming to Shea's aid when she might have been in danger. Cletus could have attacked her before she had time to react appropriately.

He fell asleep with the deeply satisfying feeling of a job well done. He wasn't completely useless after all, and he'd been starting to feel that way while tied up in the cabin, forced to watch helplessly as Shea fought Cletus alone. Shea was right about one thing—they made excellent partners in every way that mattered.

Chapter Eighteen

The next morning, Shea and Trevor carefully exited the hospital only to be immediately confronted by an overwhelming barrage of camera flashes and microphones being aggressively shoved in front of their faces. The gathered reporters pressed forward like a pack of wolves sensing wounded prey, their voices overlapping in a cacophony of shouted questions.

"Sheriff Callahan! Can you tell us what happened in that cabin?"

"Deputy Bolton! How does it feel to be a hero?"

"Is it true that Cletus Hodges tried to escape from the hospital last night?"

"Want me to stay here while you go get the car?" Shea asked Trevor, glaring pointedly at an exceptionally aggressive reporter who had stepped far too close for comfort.

"And face these vultures alone? Absolutely not," Trevor replied firmly, wincing as the sudden movement aggravated his still-healing wound.

They were saved from the media frenzy by the welcome sound of Bill Butler pulling up in a patrol car, emergency lights flashing and siren giving short, authoritative bursts. The crowd of reporters reluctantly parted to allow the vehicle through.

"You folks need some assistance getting out of here?" Bill called through his open window, a knowing grin on his weathered face.

"You're an absolute lifesaver," Shea replied gratefully, opening the back door for Trevor and helping him ease into the seat without jarring his injury.

"Sheriff Callahan! What was it really like in that isolated cabin?" one persistent reporter shouted over the noise of the crowd.

"Intense," she replied curtly, not wanting to give them any material they could sensationalize.

"When will Cletus Hodges be released from the hospital and transferred to county lockup?"

"That information is classified pending the ongoing investigation." In reality, he'd already been moved to the station's holding cell early that morning according to the detailed report that had been waiting on her desk.

"Can you tell us anything more about the confrontation? Our sources say there was significant violence."

Shea slammed the car door firmly and turned to face the pack of reporters with barely controlled irritation. "There will be an official press conference held outside the sheriff's department building at exactly five p.m. today. No further comments will be made until then." Without saying another word in response to the continued barrage of questions being shouted at her, she quickly moved around the vehicle and climbed into the back seat beside Trevor. "Please get us out of here, Bill."

"My absolute pleasure," Bill replied, laying on the horn and slowly pushing through the crowd of media personnel who reluctantly moved aside. "Where would you like to go?"

"To my personal vehicle. I want to go home and get cleaned up properly before heading into the office." The hospital shower had been functional but hardly refreshing, and she desperately wanted to wash away the lingering stress and trauma of the past few days.

"I hate to be the bearer of bad news, but there are even more bloodsucking reporters waiting around your truck in the hospital parking lot."

"We'll manage somehow," she said with determination. She didn't want to have to make another trip back later to retrieve her vehicle, not to mention she'd left Heidi alone far too much over the last several days and the dog would be anxious. "What's the general mood in town since news of Hodges's arrest spread?"

Bill met her gaze in the rearview mirror, his expression thoughtful. "It's split down the middle. Some folks are genuinely happy that justice is being served. Others are conflicted since the Hodges family has been part of this community for generations, going back to the original settlers. You'll get a better sense of public opinion this afternoon during the press conference, I reckon."

Yes, she certainly would. Press conferences ranked somewhere near the bottom of her list of enjoyable professional activities, right above root canals and tax audits. She glanced at Trevor, noting the pale cast to his skin despite his attempts to appear strong. "How are you really holding up? Don't give me the tough guy routine."

"Honestly, I'm doing great considering everything we've been through," he replied, managing to produce that familiar dimpled smile that never failed to lift her spirits. "It's going to feel incredible to have all this violence and chaos finally behind us."

"It absolutely will," she agreed wholeheartedly. She never wanted to see another member of the Hodges family or even hear their name spoken aloud ever again.

Back at her cabin, she insisted that Trevor use the bathroom first to clean up and change his bandages while she took care of feeding Heidi and letting the dog out into the yard for some much-needed exercise and fresh air. Other than the looming press conference, the day ahead didn't appear to be particularly demanding or stressful. She could even bring her furry best friend to work with her for companionship.

She leaned against the front porch railing, coffee mug in hand, watching as Heidi stalked a large crow that had dared to land in her territory. The German shepherd's playful hunting instincts were on full display as she crouched low and approached the bird with exaggerated stealth. For the first time in weeks, Shea found herself yearning for simple, peaceful days exactly like this one. Days where she could go to work, serve her community with routine matters, then come home and spend quality time with her beloved dog. Evenings where she could curl up in front of the television with a glass of wine and temporarily forget about all the troubles and violence in the world until the next morning brought new responsibilities.

Right now, the prospect of a long string of mundane, uneventful days with little more to worry about than traffic violations and noise complaints sounded heavenly.

"All finished in there," Trevor announced, appearing in the doorway while rubbing his still-damp hair with a clean towel. "Want me to keep an eye on Heidi while you take your shower?"

"No, she's perfectly fine out here," Shea replied. With Cletus safely locked up behind bars, the immediate dangers that had plagued them for weeks were finally behind her. "There's fresh coffee in the kitchen if you want some."

She headed for the bathroom and turned the shower spray as hot as she could comfortably bear, letting the steaming water wash away not just the physical grime but also the lingering tension and fear that had become constant companions.

As she stood under the therapeutic hot spray, the full emotional weight of the past day's events suddenly flooded through her with unexpected intensity. Wrapping her arms tightly around her middle, she huddled under the cascading water and finally allowed the tears to flow freely. They were cleansing tears filled with overwhelming relief that she hadn't been forced to kill another human being. Tears of profound gratitude that both she and Trevor had survived their ordeal and were able to wake up on this side of the dirt this morning.

After the emotional release, she methodically washed her hair and body, got dressed in fresh clothes, and went to the kitchen for much-needed coffee. She felt significantly better and more emotionally stable than she had in many days. She filled her favorite mug, added vanilla sugar-free creamer, and positioned herself at the window to observe Trevor throwing a tennis ball for Heidi to chase across the yard.

He would be returning to his place now that the ordeal with Cletus was finally over. She was surprised to realize that she might miss having another person around the house. Her thoughts drifted to their brief but emotionally charged conversation in the hospital when she'd essentially rejected his romantic overtures. No, she remained far too psychologically broken and emotionally damaged to seriously contemplate getting that close to anyone, no matter how much she might want to.

As if he somehow sensed her watching from the window, Trevor turned and flashed that characteristic dimpled grin that always sent her stomach into flutters. She honestly didn't know how she would have survived her challenging transition to life in Misty Hollow without his steady support and partnership.

A quick glance at the kitchen clock sent her rushing toward the front door. "Time to head into town."

Trevor retrieved the tennis ball from Heidi and placed it carefully in a flowerpot on the porch for later. "I'm ready when you are."

In the truck, he clicked his seatbelt into place and turned to look at her with evident admiration. "I want you to know that I'm incredibly proud of you, Shea."

"For what specifically?"

"For dealing with Cletus and this entire situation with complete integrity and professionalism. I know you desperately wanted to plunge that knife directly into his heart when you had the chance."

"I'm so grateful that you talked me out of following through on that impulse," she replied sincerely, backing away from the house and heading toward town. "I would have regretted that decision for the rest of my life. It would have been entirely different if he hadn't been defeated and I'd had to react in immediate self-defense. Thank you for being my moral compass when mine was compromised."

"Anytime. That's what partners do for each other,

remember?"

She detected just a hint of something—resentment, perhaps, or disappointment—underlying his seemingly casual teasing tone. "Right. Partners."

As they approached downtown, it became immediately apparent that news vans had completely clogged Main Street. Reporters and curious town residents had converged on the sidewalks and were blocking the main entrance to the sheriff's office building. The scene resembled something from a major metropolitan news event rather than a small mountain town.

"Today is definitely going to be a complete circus," Shea observed with resignation, choosing to drive around to the back entrance.

"Just hang in there and stick to the facts," Trevor advised as he opened his door and then let Heidi out of the back seat. "The good news is that Cletus will be transported to the state facility in Little Rock later today. We won't have to face him again until the trial proceedings begin."

They rushed through the rear entrance before the gathered reporters could surround them and demand impromptu interviews. "I'll meet everyone in the conference room in exactly five minutes," Shea announced, heading directly for her office. After a quick review of urgent messages and emails, she made sure Heidi was comfortable in her usual corner spot, then headed to the scheduled meeting.

"Good morning, everyone," she said, nodding at each deputy in turn as she entered the conference room. "Thankfully, today appears to be relatively slow, which gives us adequate time to prepare for the press conference. I'll handle all the talking, along with Mayor Ferguson. None of you will be expected to answer questions or make statements, but I do need you to present a united front. Can you do that for me?"

She had honestly expected at least one of her deputies to bring up the topic of how long the Hodges family had been established in Misty Hollow, or to express some level of sympathy for the local connections. Pride filled her chest when none of them did. Her team clearly understood that justice had to be served regardless of the perpetrator's name or family history in the community.

By five o'clock that afternoon, she had donned her formal uniform jacket and stepped outside with her deputies flanking her in a show of solidarity and professional support. Mayor Ferguson turned from the temporary podium that had been set up in front of the department entrance and smiled encouragingly.

"Sheriff Callahan, the floor is yours."

Shea approached the microphone and held up both hands to quiet the restless crowd. "I understand the legitimate concerns of this community," she began, keeping her voice steady and authoritative despite the few openly hostile faces she could see in the crowd. "I want to assure all of you that the decision to pursue and arrest Cletus Hodges was not made lightly or without careful consideration. The evidence against him is overwhelming and irrefutable. Both Deputy Bolton and I bear the physical scars of our confrontation with him. Cletus Hodges was directly responsible for the sniper shooting at our fall festival that resulted in the deaths of three innocent community members. My sworn duty as your sheriff is to uphold the law and ensure justice, regardless of a person's social status or family influence in this town."

She still couldn't fully understand the apparent loyalty some residents felt toward such a criminal family.

"Do you fear potential retaliation from the remaining members of the Hodges family?" a reporter called out.

"No. With both Cletus and Darryl now behind bars, we have effectively cut the head off the snake. The criminal organization they led has been dismantled."

"What about those local residents who remain loyal to the Hodges family?" another journalist pressed.

"As I stated clearly, justice will be served regardless of who the person is or what their family connections might be."

"Some critics are saying this arrest will significantly tarnish Misty Hollow's reputation and hurt tourism. What's your response to those concerns?" the first reporter continued.

Shea cleared her throat and maintained her

composed demeanor. "This town has weathered its share of difficulties and challenges long before I arrived here as sheriff. It survived those previous storms, and it will certainly weather any future ones. The safety and security of our citizens must always take priority over concerns about reputation or economic impact."

She kept all her responses firm, clear, and unwavering in their conviction.

Some members of the gathered crowd clapped in obvious approval of her statements, while others muttered comments she couldn't clearly hear. All sounds suddenly ceased as a state prison transport van pulled slowly into the parking lot, its presence commanding everyone's immediate attention.

Two heavily armed guards in official uniforms exited the vehicle and marched with military precision toward Shea. "Ma'am, we're here to transport the prisoner to the state facility as scheduled."

Shea led them inside to the secure holding cell where Cletus had been placed under constant guard since before sunrise. The man immediately began spewing creative curses and detailed promises of future retaliation directed specifically at her as the two guards efficiently placed him in standard transport chains and shackles.

The crowd outside erupted into chaos when Cletus was led through their midst toward the waiting van. A few angry residents threw rocks and debris at the prisoner, while others actually called out encouragement for him to stay strong and fight the charges. Cletus managed to lift his shackled hands as high as the chains would allow and shuffled through the crowd like some sort of wrongly accused celebrity making a dramatic public appearance.

Shea shook her head in disgust and disbelief, feeling immense relief to finally have the dangerous man completely out of her jurisdiction and responsibility.

Mayor Ferguson stepped to her side as the transport van disappeared down the street. "You handled that entire situation with exceptional professionalism, Sheriff. This town is genuinely fortunate to have someone of your caliber and integrity. You faced an extremely dangerous opponent head-on, never backing down despite the personal risks involved."

"I couldn't have accomplished any of this without the complete support of my entire team," she replied honestly.

"It takes a truly good person to recognize and acknowledge that kind of contribution," he observed with approval. "There might be some minor political fallout from certain segments of the community, but I'm confident the town will come around to supporting you fully. The recent crime wave has completely stopped. Now the healing process can finally begin. This community is on the brink of positive change, and you're positioned right at the center of it all."

She stepped back to the podium and firmly told the

crowd to disperse peacefully. There would be no additional comments or statements from anyone. As the reporters and residents began to scatter, she motioned for her deputies to return inside the building and headed straight for the sanctuary of her private office.

A few minutes later, Trevor entered carrying a steaming cup of coffee. "You look like you could definitely use this."

"You're absolutely not wrong about that. Thank you so much." She gratefully accepted the mug and relaxed back in her chair for the first time in hours. "It's really and truly over."

"Yes, it is. You handled that press conference like a seasoned professional," he said, settling into the chair across from her desk.

"Thanks for the encouragement. I still feel like I probably made some new enemies out there today." She blew gently into the hot coffee.

"Yeah, maybe a few, but that inevitably comes with this job. You simply can't make everyone happy all the time."

"I'm genuinely glad to see you've managed to keep your natural optimism intact through all of this."

He shrugged casually. "It's just who I am at my core."

"Even despite everything you went through in your past."

"Actually, because of my past experiences. I faced death at a very young age at the hands of someone I loved and trusted, and I came through it alive and stronger. As a direct result of surviving that trauma, I consciously choose to look at life in the most positive way possible."

She chuckled appreciatively. "I want to be just like you when I finally grow up." Maybe someday in the future, she could leave behind the psychological weight of what had happened on that mountain with her friends. "I think I'll take a few well-deserved days off after the trial concludes and spend some quality time with my college friends."

"That sounds like an excellent plan."

"I know I'll be leaving this place in completely capable hands while I'm gone." She studied his face over the rim of her coffee mug.

His eyes widened in genuine surprise. "Bill Butler has significantly more seniority than I do."

"I'm choosing you to serve as acting sheriff whenever I'm not available. I've worked side by side with you through the most challenging circumstances, Trevor. You're a brave, honest man with an unshakeable moral compass and excellent judgment. I honestly couldn't choose anyone better qualified." She meant every single word.

"I'm deeply honored by your confidence in me," he replied, that familiar grin spreading across his face. "So, are you planning to leave tomorrow morning?"

"Don't be in such a hurry to get rid of me, my friend." She smiled warmly as she took another sip of her coffee, feeling emotionally lighter than she had in many months and significantly less lonely than usual.

"I guess I'd better start clearing my personal belongings from your place and return to my normal routine," he said, standing with obvious reluctance. "Are you ready to head home?"

The honest answer was no, but she couldn't say that. "Sure, let's go."

Later that evening, after sharing a simple but satisfying dinner of delivered pizza, Shea stood alone on her front porch and watched Trevor's truck disappear down the winding road. Her shoulders slumped with unexpected sadness as she placed a comforting hand on Heidi's head. "Well, it's just us girls again. The house sure seems empty without him around, doesn't it?"

Heidi whined softly, her intelligent gaze following the departing vehicle until it vanished from sight.

"Yeah, that's exactly how I feel too."

Epilogue

The crisp autumn air carried a sense of renewal over Shea's cabin and Misty Hollow. In the dawn of the morning, a fine mist hung over the valley lending a sense of fantasy. Heidi peered up through the branches of a cypress tree at a teasing squirrel.

"You ready, girl?" Shea locked the front door behind her. Since Cletus's trial where he'd received a life sentence, she liked going into town early to walk the streets and clear her head for the upcoming hours. It allowed her an opportunity to meet the townsfolk one-on-one if they chose to strike up a conversation.

This morning was no different. She pulled the collar of her coat high on her neck and strolled down the sidewalk of Main Street with Heidi at her side.

"Mornin', Sheriff." An elderly man tipped his hat as he passed.

"Good morning, Wilbur."

Another gentleman with a rolled newspaper under

his arm stopped and patted Heidi on the head, gave Shea a curt nod, and hurried across the street to the diner. Shea smiled at the familiarity of the morning.

The few weeks since Cletus's arrest had improved her acceptance in Misty Hollow a hundredfold. Even those who had frowned at the man's sentencing seemed to realize that Shea would always serve on the side of justice.

"A Doctor Hensley called." Doris handed her a handwritten message. "Said she was checking in."

"Thank you." Shea carried the note to her office and called the profiler. "Good morning, Nora."

"Sheriff. Thought you might like to know I spoke with Cletus Hodges."

"You did?" Shea lowered into her desk chair.

"The man is blinded by hatred over the killing of his youngest brother…the baby of the family, but I'm sure you already knew that. There's a history of mental illness in his family, and the killing of his brother took away the last semblance of stability he had. The man has spent over a week in the psychiatric ward of the prison."

"Thank you for keeping me up-to-date. I don't feel any sympathy for him, but this has given me some closure."

"You're welcome. I doubt you'll have any more problems with his family. With the three brothers taken care of, I believe the wind will have gone out of their kinfolk's sails, so to speak. Have a good day."

After hanging up, Shea leaned back in her chair, the vinyl squeaking under her weight. Mayor Ferguson peered into her office, sending Shea upright. "Mayor."

"I have some good news." He motioned to the chair opposite her.

"Please, have a seat."

"I'm sure you're busy, so this won't take long. I just want to let you know that the town has agreed, almost unanimously, to retain you as sheriff through the next year." He sat tall and patted his chest. "I'd like to take the credit, but it was your actions in taking care of Cletus that really cinched the deal. If you're willing, of course."

"Misty Hollow has become my home. I'm honored." Joy bloomed in her chest.

"Wonderful." He stood and thrust out his hand.

She did the same, sealing the deal, at least for another year.

"Heard you're taking a vacation. A well-earned one, I might add."

"Yes." She smiled. "I catch a flight out this afternoon. I'm spending the holidays with my best friend and her family." Becky had squealed with delight when Shea told her. "Deputy Broderick will handle things well in my absence."

"I'm sure he will." The mayor's grin remained in place as he left her office.

Later that afternoon, Trevor arrived to take her to the airport. "The place won't be the same without you."

"That's sweet." She clicked on her seatbelt. "Thank you for taking care of Heidi for me. You'll do great while I'm gone. It's only a little over a week."

"It'll seem like an eternity."

She laughed. "Where's your optimism now?"

"Leaving on a jet plane…with you." He gave her the dimpled grin she loved.

"Stop it." Her face heated. The man had an effect on her—something she'd never felt before.

When they reached the airport, she leaned through the window and hugged Heidi, her gaze locking with Trevor's. "Take care of yourself."

"You, too."

She withdrew, feeling as if she were leaving him to a fate he shouldn't face alone. As soon as she entered through the double doors, she shook off the feeling. Nothing more than remnants lingering from the last few weeks. She'd be in a much better place mentally when she returned.

She squared her shoulders and joined the line to check in.

The End

Keep reading for the first chapter of Evil Returns.

Dear Reader,

I hope you're enjoying the new sheriff of Misty Hollow. If so, you won't want to miss the next book, *Evil Returns*, coming soon. Trevor is faced with his past, alone, until Shea returns.

If you're enjoyed *The Threat*, please leave a review on Amazon. Reviews are priceless to authors.

God Bless,

Cynthia

Chapter One

Deputy Trevor Bolton trusted his instincts. Always. Trusting his instincts had kept him alive more times than he could count. But the last few days…something felt…off. A creeping sense of unease settled in his bones. Someone was watching.

He glanced at Heidi, Shea's German shepherd. The dog lay with her head on her paws, ears up, dark eyes focused on something Trevor couldn't see or hear through the falling rain.

It had all started a few nights ago during his evening run. The sensation of eyes tracking him from the tree line near his property. Then, the moving shadows appeared—dark figures just beyond his line of sight. Every time he turned to take a deeper look, they disappeared.

At first, he'd convinced himself it was nothing. A

side effect of missing Shea, a trick of the light, an overactive imagination. But when his motion-detector front porch light came on at three in the morning, then the next two mornings after that, he knew he wasn't dealing with an animal. At least not the four-legged kind.

The last two days had offered a little respite because of the rain, but now there was no doubt someone was watching him. Trevor set his empty tea glass on the small iron table next to his patio chair and moved to the porch railing. He squinted through the dark. Nightfall and rain made visibility nonexistent past a few yards. When his skin crawled, he glanced at the dog again. Heidi still seemed to be on alert but not agitated.

"Come on, girl. Let's go inside. I'll bring you back out later." Hopefully, the rain would've stopped by then.

Trevor spent the next hour trying to watch an action movie on the television. Instead, his gaze kept flicking to the window.

A creak sounded outside. Then, a crash of thunder. He relaxed, chalking up any unusual sounds to the storm. After a while, he drifted off to sleep.

Heidi's barking at the front door startled him awake. The dog's hair stood on end. She scratched at the door.

Trevor grabbed his pistol from the coffee table and peered out the window. The rain had stopped. A full moon played peek-a-boo with the clouds. He put a restraining hand on the dog's head, then he carefully opened the front door.

Heidi dashed off the porch and into the woods. Trevor took a step to go after her but stopped.

A knife lay in the center of the porch, its blade catching the light of the moon. Rust clung to the handle, but he recognized it immediately.

It was identical to the one his brother, Troy, had used twenty years ago. The same blade that had cut into Trevor's flesh when his brother stabbed him five times, leaving him to bleed on the forest floor. When he'd bent over him, Troy had whispered, "You won't be the favored one anymore."

Trevor's hand clenched at his side, his pulse hammering against his ribs. His gut told him this wasn't a message. This was a warning. From whom? Who would've known where Troy had hidden the knife he'd used not only on Trevor but on a handful of others?

Frowning, Trevor entered the kitchen and pulled a rubber glove from a drawer. Then, he returned to the porch and picked up the knife.

Troy was still in prison. Trevor had checked last week—something he did regularly. Why would someone leave the knife now? There were always crazies. A fan of his brother's?

After whistling for Heidi, he entered the house and placed the knife on the kitchen table where he studied it for several long minutes. Realizing he'd get no answers so late at night, he locked up the house and went to bed.

After a sleepless night, he sat at his desk, or rather Shea's desk, at the sheriff's office. The knife, now in an evidence bag, rested on the desk, the rusted blade as familiar as the scars in his side. Five deep wounds, five moments of agonizing clarity before he had collapsed.

His jaw tightened. The fact that someone had found the knife Troy had hidden all those years ago scared him more than he wanted to admit.

Coffee. He needed coffee. Leaving Heidi sleeping on a dog bed in the corner, he headed to the break room and poured a cup of sludge, which the department called coffee. Hoping to make it palatable, he added a healthy dose of cream and sugar, then returned to the office.

He paused in the doorway, his heartbeat speeding up.

Shea whipped around to face him. "What is this?" She pointed at the knife.

~

Shea's stomach had tightened the moment she saw the knife. Rusted. Worn. Used. Something about it felt wrong. Her gaze locked with Trevor's. "What is this?"

"Something someone left on my porch last night." He sat in a chair across from her. "Welcome back. You're early."

"Only a day. Vacation is nice, but a week is more

than enough time to spend following my friend to soccer games and swim lessons." She set her bag on the floor. "You look like you haven't slept in days."

"I haven't. Not much, anyway." He leaned forward, his voice low and controlled. "This is the same kind of knife my brother used to stab me twenty years ago."

"Are you sure?" She frowned. "What's its normal purpose?"

"My father used one like this to skin deer."

She tapped her fingers against the desk. "Your brother is still locked up, isn't he?"

"Last I checked. But, that's the next thing on my to-do list. Call the prison and make sure."

She exhaled, leaning back in her chair. "Could be a prank, but..." Her voice trailed off. She knew better than to keep on talking. The weight in Trevor's gaze told her he had already gone through every possible rational explanation. None of them set right with him. Which meant a phone call needed to be made ASAP. "I'll call the prison now. We need to know what we're dealing with."

She dialed the number, identified herself, and asked to speak to the warden.

"Warden Mills."

"Sheriff Callahan from Misty Hollow. I'm calling regarding an inmate by the name of Troy Bolton."

"That inmate was moved to a maximum-security psychiatric hospital a month ago for shanking a fellow inmate over a game of cards."

She narrowed her eyes at Trevor. "Why wasn't his brother, Deputy Bolton, notified of this?"

"The hospital should've done that."

"Deputy Bolton checked on his brother a week ago. Are you telling me he'd already been transferred and no one thought to let him know?" She heard the ice in her voice.

"I'm sorry. We're behind in updating our reports." He gave her the phone number to the hospital.

"What?" Trevor asked the moment she hung up.

"Troy was transferred a month ago." She dialed the new number and once again identified herself. Few things bothered her as much as incompetence.

News from the hospital was far worse than Trevor not being told. "Inmate Bolton escaped earlier this week en route to medical," the doctor stated. "We believe he had outside help."

Shea's heart plummeted. "Say that again?"

"Troy Bolton escaped our facility. We've been working feverishly to locate him. I fear he may be headed back to Arkansas."

"He's already here." She slammed the phone down and took a deep breath. "Your brother escaped earlier this week."

Trevor's face darkened. "No one thought to inform me or this department? It doesn't take a genius to know he's headed back here. No, he's already here. That explains the knife."

Troy had had plenty of time to retrieve the weapon and locate Trevor. His brother had been on his porch. Watched him for days. He'd returned to finish what he'd started.

Clearing her throat, Shea stared at the knife. "You aren't safe staying alone." This time it wasn't her life in danger but his. "You'll stay in my guest room." She moved her gaze back to his. "We'll find him, Trevor. I promise."

"What a way to welcome you home." He gave a wry smile.

"Fill me in on what else happened while I was gone." She listened as he listed everyday things like car accidents and vandalism, then straightened when he mentioned one of the elementary teachers being stalked.

"The man and his wife are both locked up now. No one died, and Deputy Harris has fully recovered."

"You did a good job as acting sheriff, Trevor." She couldn't have left things in better hands. "And thank you for watching Heidi."

"She provided company, but she missed you a lot." His smile widened. "I'm great and all, but I'm not you."

She slid the evidence bag across her desk. "Send that to forensics. See what they can pull from it, then lock it up once we have it back. I'll put out an APB on your brother and post his photo everywhere. Someone will see him."

"If they do, he'll kill them. My brother has no

regard for life." Trevor marched from the room.

Shea booted up her computer and located the police report on Trevor's attack. The young boy hadn't been expected to survive the attack, but he did. They'd found Troy hiding in a neighbor's barn among dead livestock. How could one brother turn out so good and the other so evil? Same blood, same parents, same upbringing…twins.

She stared at Troy's mug shot. A handsome young man with dead eyes. Not an identical twin. No one would even mistake the evil Bolton son with his brother.

Six people, all under the age of eighteen, had died at the hands of Troy Bolton. All were stabbed seven times. What significance did the number seven have?

"He claimed it was his lucky number," Trevor said from the doorway.

She hadn't realized she'd asked the question out loud. "He only stabbed you five times."

"I fought back. Hit him in the head with a rock. A hunter heard the commotion and fired a warning shot in the air. Troy disappeared in the forest and wasn't seen again until they found him a week later hiding in a barn."

"So, he wants to finish the stabbing he hadn't been able to finish on you."

Trevor shrugged. "I doubt he'll be satisfied with two stabs unless he goes for the heart. Otherwise, he'll start over and try for seven again."

"Six people before you. You were to be his last."

"I doubt he would've stopped." He sat across from her again. "You didn't see the look in his eyes. He enjoyed the killing."

And now he was in Misty Hollow. Evil had returned.

www.cynthiahickey.com
Cynthia Hickey is a multi-published and best-selling author of cozy mysteries and romantic suspense. She has taught writing at many conferences and small writing retreats. She and her husband run the publishing press, Winged Publications. They live in Arizona and Arkansas, becoming snowbirds with three dogs. They have ten grandchildren who keep them busy and tell everyone they know that "Nana is a writer."

Connect with me on FaceBook
Twitter
Sign up for my newsletter and receive a free short story

www.cynthiahickey.com

Follow me on Amazon
And Bookbub
Shop my bookstore on shopify. For better price and autographed books. You can also subscribe to *Mysterious Delivery*, a mystery and suspense monthly book subscription with a book and several surprise goodies to pamper the reader.

Enjoy other books by Cynthia Hickey

Cowboys of Misty Hollow
Cowboy Jeopardy

<u>Cowboy Peril</u>
<u>Cowboy Hazard</u>
<u>Cowgirl Blaze</u>
<u>Cowboy Uncertainty</u>
<u>Cowboy Christmas Crisis</u>
<u>Cowboy Pitfall</u>

<u>Girls' Weekend Survival</u>

Misty Hollow
<u>Secrets of Misty Hollow</u>
<u>Deceptive Peace</u>
<u>Calm Surface</u>
<u>Lightning Never Strikes Twice</u>
<u>Lethal Inheritance</u>
<u>Bitter Isolation</u>
<u>Say I Don't</u>
<u>Christmas Stalker</u>
<u>Bridge to Safety</u>
<u>When Night Falls</u>
<u>A Place to Hide</u>
<u>Mountain Refuge</u>

Stay in Misty Hollow for a while. Get the entire series <u>here</u>!

The Seven Deadly Sins series
<u>Deadly Pride</u>
<u>Deadly Covet</u>
<u>Deadly Lust</u>
<u>Deadly Glutton</u>
<u>Deadly Envy</u>

Deadly Sloth
Deadly Anger

The Tail Waggin' Mysteries
Cat-Eyed Witness
The Dog Who Found a Body
Troublesome Twosome
Four-Legged Suspect
Unwanted Christmas Guest
Wedding Day Cat Burglar

Brothers Steele
Sharp as Steele
Carved in Steele
Forged in Steele
Brothers Steele (All three in one)

The Brothers of Copper Pass
Wyatt's Warrant
Dirk's Defense
Stetson's Secret
Houston's Hope
Dallas's Dare
Seth's Sacrifice
Malcolm's Misunderstanding
The Brothers of Copper Pass Boxed Set

Time Travel
The Portal

Tiny House Mysteries

No Small Caper
Caper Goes Missing
Caper Finds a Clue
Caper's Dark Adventure
A Strange Game for Caper
Caper Steals Christmas
Caper Finds a Treasure
Tiny House Mysteries boxed set

Wife for Hire – Private Investigators
Saving Sarah
Lesson for Lacey
Mission for Meghan
Long Way for Lainie
Aimed at Amy
Wife for Hire (all five in one)

A Hollywood Murder
Killer Pose, book 1
Killer Snapshot, book 2
Shoot to Kill, book 3
Kodak Kill Shot, book 4
To Snap a Killer
Hollywood Murder Mysteries

Shady Acres Mysteries
Beware the Orchids, book 1
Path to Nowhere
Poison Foliage
Poinsettia Madness
Deadly Greenhouse Gases
Vine Entrapment

<u>Shady Acres Boxed Set</u>

CLEAN BUT GRITTY Romantic Suspense

Highland Springs

<u>Murder Live</u>
<u>Say Bye to Mommy</u>
<u>To Breathe Again</u>
<u>Highland Springs Murders</u> (all 3 in one)

Colors of Evil Series

<u>Shades of Crimson</u>
<u>Coral Shadows</u>

The Pretty Must Die Series

<u>Ripped in Red, book 1</u>
<u>Pierced in Pink, book 2</u>
<u>Wounded in White, book 3</u>
<u>Worthy, The Complete Story</u>

<u>Lisa Paxton Mystery Series</u>

<u>Eenie Meenie Miny Mo</u>
<u>Jack Be Nimble</u>
<u>Hickory Dickory Dock</u>
<u>Boxed Set</u>

Hearts of Courage
<u>A Heart of Valor</u>

<u>The Game</u>
<u>Suspicious Minds</u>
<u>After the Storm</u>
<u>Local Betrayal</u>
<u>Hearts of Courage Boxed Set</u>

Overcoming Evil series
<u>Mistaken Assassin</u>
<u>Captured Innocence</u>
<u>Mountain of Fear</u>
<u>Exposure at Sea</u>
<u>A Secret to Die for</u>
<u>Collision Course</u>
<u>Romantic Suspense of 5 books in 1</u>

INSPIRATIONAL

Nosy Neighbor Series
<u>Anything For A Mystery</u>, Book 1
<u>A Killer Plot</u>, Book 2
<u>Skin Care Can Be Murder</u>, Book 3
<u>Death By Baking</u>, Book 4
<u>Jogging Is Bad For Your Health</u>, Book 5
<u>Poison Bubbles</u>, Book 6
<u>A Good Party Can Kill You</u>, Book 7
<u>Nosy Neighbor collection</u>

<u>Christmas with Stormi Nelson</u>

The Summer Meadows Series
<u>Fudge-Laced Felonies</u>, Book 1

<u>Candy-Coated Secrets</u>, Book 2
<u>Chocolate-Covered Crime</u>, Book 3
<u>Maui Macadamia Madness</u>, Book 4
<u>All four novels in one collection</u>

The River Valley Mystery Series
<u>Deadly Neighbors</u>, Book 1
<u>Advance Notice</u>, Book 2
<u>The Librarian's Last Chapter</u>, Book 3
<u>All three novels in one collection</u>